FINDING LOVE AT ROSEFORD BLOOMS

FAY KEENAN

Boldwood

First published in Great Britain in 2023 by Boldwood Books Ltd.

Copyright © Fay Keenan, 2023

Cover Design by Alice Moore Design

Cover Photography: Shutterstock and iStock

The moral right of Fay Keenan to be identified as the author of this work has been asserted in accordance with the Copyright, Designs and Patents Act 1988.

A CIP catalogue record for this book is available from the British Library.

Paperback ISBN 978-1-80280-571-0

Large Print ISBN 978-1-80280-572-7

Hardback ISBN 978-1-80280-570-3

Ebook ISBN 978-1-80280-573-4

Kindle ISBN 978-1-80280-574-1

Audio CD ISBN 978-1-80280-565-9

MP3 CD ISBN 978-1-80280-566-6

Digital audio download ISBN 978-1-80280-567-3

Boldwood Books Ltd
23 Bowerdean Street
London SW6 3TN
www.boldwoodbooks.com

To all the girls, everywhere: you are enough.

1

'Which part of "I never want to see you again" do you not understand?'
Lizzie Warner wished she were speaking on a landline instead of her
mobile, just so she could have the satisfaction of slamming down the
receiver. Somehow, ending the call with a voice command didn't seem to
cut it. She gazed gloomily at the traffic ahead of her, wishing for the thousandth time that she'd elected to have this meeting on Zoom instead. But
she'd needed to get out of the office, away from Paul and the inevitable
conflicts that working with and loving the same person had created, ever
since he'd decided to pull the rug so spectacularly out from under her feet.

That was the third call since she'd left, she realised wearily. And there
had been plenty of 'discussions' before then. But it was no good. The
writing had been on the wall long before Paul had decided that he wanted
not only to sign over the business they'd set up together to a larger firm, but
also to spend several nights with the gorgeous lawyer whom he'd engaged
to negotiate the contract. The marketing firm that had been their dream
was effectively over. Not to mention their relationship. Although he
couldn't proceed with the sale of the business without her say-so, in the
end, it had just been easier to agree. After all, they'd both walk away with a
lot of money in the bank, and, in theory, they could both start afresh. But
that didn't mean it didn't hurt.

Seven years of their life together had been spent building the business, forming a client base and becoming one of the most talked about marketing businesses in the country. Warner-Basset had been all over social media, with a client list that many larger firms had envied. In tandem with their commercial success, Lizzie and Paul had discussed marriage, but it had always been an 'in the future' kind of decision. Now, both marriage and the business were off the table, and, despite the boost to her bank balance that selling her half of the partnership would net her, Lizzie had never felt more insecure.

As the traffic picked up, Lizzie glanced at the screen of her phone to double-check her route. Her final client before she signed on the dotted line was based in Hindhead, a fair drive from the offices in London, and she'd never been completely comfortable with driving the route from memory. The sudden onslaught of a summer rainstorm added to her anxiety, and she scrabbled to switch on the wipers and de-mist her windscreen. The dust that seemed to habitually cover her car in the summer obscured her vision even further for a long moment, until the road ahead became clear again. She swore when she realised she'd missed the turning she needed. The ETA on Google Maps already told her she was going to be ten minutes late, and now she had to make an unexpected detour.

As Google's soothing map voice told her to take the next left, she drew in a deep breath. It didn't really matter, she thought. This was a handover, not a pitch. It was just that the client had been one of their first, and Lizzie had always been the main contact for them. She felt she owed them a final face-to-face meeting. However, as the rain got heavier, she felt herself beginning to regret that decision.

Proceeding cautiously down a dark tunnel of trees, Lizzie tried to bring her mind back to the imminent meeting. The stuff with Paul could wait. Everything else could wait. She used to laugh when her sister, Georgina, had told her to live in the moment more. Now, the moment seemed the safest place to be. The past was too painful, and the future too uncertain for her to feel at home in either.

At least the heavy tree cover was keeping the rain off. It hadn't rained for weeks, and Lizzie could feel the tyres of her Ford Kuga gripping the slippery surface of a road covered with weeks of dust and oily emissions. The rain was making the surface treacherous, and Lizzie slowed her speed a little, nervously aware that she wasn't a terrific driver at the best of times, and these conditions weren't making her any more confident.

She pulled closely into the hedge as a huge Range Rover Sport came hurtling in the opposite direction, so close to her own car that it set off the proximity sensors. Just in time, the Range Rover slowed, narrowly avoiding taking her wing mirror off.

'Calm down,' she muttered to herself. With a bit of luck, she'd be off this lane soon and back out onto the main road.

As she emerged from the tree-lined tunnel, to her relief, the next turn put her on a wider road. Glancing at the clock on her dashboard, she pushed her foot down harder on the accelerator. Hopefully, if she got a move on, she'd only be a few minutes late. The rainstorm had abated and the sun had re-emerged from the bruised purple-black clouds above her, bathing the road in a mirror-like sheen. If she'd been in a better mood, she'd have taken in the quaint, chocolate-box prettiness of the village she was driving through, its red-brick houses and green spaces all beautifully representative of the charming Hampshire landscape, but she was too concerned about making this last appointment on time.

As she accelerated on reaching the faster speed limit sign on the outer edge of the village, the phone rang again. Glancing down at it, she reached to block the call, but as she looked back up she saw a large roe stag haring across the carriageway not twenty metres ahead. In a blind panic, Lizzie slammed on her brakes, forgetting that the surface of the road was like turkey fat in a roasting tin as a result of the rain. As her back wheels spun out towards the white line, and the front end of the car hurtled towards the chevrons marking a harsh bend, Lizzie screamed. The car, lacking purchase on the slippery surface, turned over and hit the bank at the side of the road, which caused the airbags to detonate. The last thing she saw before she blacked out was the stag, jumping over the green bank that eventually stopped the progress of her spinning car.

2

When she regained consciousness, the first thing Lizzie noticed was that her phone was ringing. And that the world was the wrong way up. *I must stop that phone*, she thought irrationally. But as she reached out to silence it, an excruciating pain in her left clavicle stopped her. As she yelled out in response, Lizzie's breathing started to get shallower, and she felt the panic rising. What if she was stuck here for hours? What if she already had been and just didn't know it? What if the car was going to explode with her in it? All of the most terrible scenarios from the worst car crashes in the direst films and TV shows she'd ever seen vied for dominance in her confused mind until she was shaking all over, not just from pain but from sheer, blind fear.

Lizzie could hear her engine ticking over still and forced her mind to slow down. Even if she couldn't get out, surely if she could switch the ignition off, that would minimise the risk of a fire? Reaching out her right hand, which, thankfully, didn't cause any additional pain, she burrowed under the hanging remnants of the deployed airbag and found the ignition key, remembering, eventually, that, because she was inverted, she'd better not drop the keys. With a shudder, the engine cut out and Lizzie breathed a trembling sigh of relief. One less thing to worry about.

She was starting to get a headache from hanging upside down in the car, and her left shoulder was throbbing. Raising a hand to her face, she could also feel the beginnings of a nasty bruise on her cheekbone, presumably from the force of the airbag. Then the phone cut into her consciousness again.

'Just fuck off!' she screamed at it, the tears starting to drip, irritatingly, into her hair.

'Can you hear me, love?' A voice came from the passenger's side of the car. 'Are you awake in there?'

Lizzie's head shot to the left, and through the glass on the passenger's side of the car she could see a concerned face peering in at her.

'I'm awake,' she said quickly, relieved beyond measure to see another human being.

'I've called 999 and they're sending someone out. Shouldn't be too long.' As Lizzie focused on the face, she could see it was that of a kindly looking white-haired older man, old enough to be her grandfather. She thought she could hear the creak of his knees as he adjusted his position so she could see him better from where she was hanging in the upside-down car.

'Thank you,' she stammered. 'I saw a deer and just panicked.'

'They're responsible for a lot of accidents on this bend,' the old man replied. 'A law unto themselves, they are.' His voice was steady, reassuring, and Lizzie realised that he must be trying to keep her calm, too.

'Should I try to get out?' she asked him.

The old man furrowed his brow. 'Have you been through a check on yourself?' he asked.

'What do you mean?'

'Have you checked to see if you've got any obvious injuries?'

Lizzie ran through a quick mental head-to-foot check. Having someone there with her, even a stranger, was helping her to keep focused. Her head hurt, and her cheek, and one side of her collarbone was excruciating, but her back felt fairly normal, even though her neck hurt from the impact.

'I think I'm OK, apart from my collarbone,' Lizzie concluded.

The old man looked kindly at her. 'I used to be the local copper around these parts. I've seen a few of these in my time.'

Lizzie nodded, then winced as the movement sent a bolt of pain through her shoulders. The headache was getting worse, too, and she hoped the emergency services wouldn't be long.

'Can you unclip your seat belt?'

'I think so.'

'Brace your good arm on the roof so you don't fall when you do,' the man said.

Doing as she was told, Lizzie carefully undid the belt, and felt her body slacken towards the roof of the car as she did so. Biting back a moan of pain as she changed position, she took several deep breaths.

'Now, can you get out of your side of the car?' the man asked.

'I don't know.' Lizzie's voice trembled. 'I don't think there's enough room between the car and the bank to open the door.'

'All right,' he replied. Then he paused as the distant wail of sirens reached them. 'I think you're about to get some real help, anyway.'

'Don't go!' Lizzie called out as the man began to move away from the window.

'I'll just let them know you're awake, and what you've told me about your injuries,' he replied. His face appeared briefly at the window once more. 'Sit tight. Help's nearly here.'

'Thank you,' Lizzie called out faintly. She was still upside down, and stars were filling her vision again. As she closed her eyes, she relaxed in relief as she heard the sirens stop and the crunch of large tyres on asphalt.

The next thing Lizzie saw was a pair of green-trousered legs at the upside-down window, shortly followed by another calm face.

'Hi.' The paramedic peered in. 'Let's see if we can get you out of here, shall we?'

After confirming the engine was off, and a couple of details about her suspected injuries, the paramedics helped Lizzie through the window of the car, and then put her carefully on a stretcher to the back of the ambulance. The situation now had a distinct sense of unreality to it, but as she glanced back, the sight of her beloved Kuga, looking as battered as she was and still on its roof, made her burst into tears.

'Don't worry, we'll have you sorted out soon,' the paramedic who was travelling in the back of the ambulance soothed. The rumble of the engine made the ambulance shudder as they set off.

Lizzie tried to relax as the ambulance made its way to the Royal Surrey County Hospital. The painkillers she'd been given for her injuries were taking effect, and she was feeling quite woozy anyway. She was grateful to the old man for speaking to her in such a reassuring way, and for calling the emergency services. At the memory of his kindness to her, the tears started again.

The paramedic reached out and gave her good hand a squeeze. 'Is there anyone you'd like us to call?' she said gently.

Lizzie shook her head. 'Not at the moment.' After all, she'd told Paul to get lost, and the last people she wanted to see were her parents. They'd only, after their initial shock, settle into the head-shaking routine they'd been employing ever since she and Paul had split, and the company had been sold and she really couldn't handle that right now. She needed time for everything to sink in. Then she thought about her sister, Georgina. Should she ask the paramedic to call her? But she dismissed that thought, too. Georgina hadn't ever been there for her: why should crashing a car change that?

3

In the end, Lizzie's face had taken the brunt of the collision with the airbag, and her collarbone would mend over time, but she'd have to keep it immobilised by wearing a sling for a couple of weeks. Under gentle pressure from the hospital to provide some details, she'd given her parents' names as next of kin, and so she was unsurprised, when she came to after long sleep induced by painkillers, to see her mother hovering, a look of concerned disappointment on her face.

'You're awake,' Cordelia Warner said. Then, after a pause, 'How are you feeling?'

Lizzie leaned deeper into the pillows, wishing she could just close her eyes and go back to sleep. 'OK, I suppose.'

'Well, the car's a total write-off,' Cordelia said briskly. 'It's in the hands of the claims investigators now, but they were pretty clear when they phoned Paul that it was unsalvageable.'

The waves of disapprobation seemed to be coming off her mother, and Lizzie could feel them washing over her. Her mother had never been one for pleasantries, or unnecessary affection, and even now she was lying in a hospital bed, Lizzie clearly hadn't cut herself any slack in that department.

'Why you had to arrange that meeting, I don't know. A phone call would have been just as good.'

'I wanted to see Emma and Seb one more time,' Lizzie muttered. 'I felt I owed it to them. That Warner-Basset owed it to them.'

'They're going to be far better off with the resources the new company has,' Cordelia replied. 'You didn't owe them anything.'

Lizzie let a sigh escape her lips. 'Well, thanks for hammering it home, Mum. Was there anything else you'd like to have a go at me for while I'm lying here unable to escape?'

Cordelia's face softened a fraction, as far as the Botox would allow. 'I was going to suggest that you came home with me, as soon as you're discharged. Under the circumstances, and with Paul moving out, it might be easier for you if you had someone to keep an eye on you.'

Lizzie's heart sank. She hadn't lived with her parents for fifteen years, and the last thing she wanted to do was move back in with them now, however temporarily. The thought of being under their roof filled her with a kind of anxious despair.

'Thanks for the offer, but I'm sure I'll be fine,' Lizzie replied. 'I mean, I'll have to learn to cope sometime, won't I?'

'And in the meantime?' Cordelia said, and for a moment Lizzie saw genuine concern in her eyes. It knocked her off balance a bit, especially in her medicated state.

'I'll be fine, Mum, honestly,' Lizzie said softly. 'I live in London, remember? I don't have to drive anywhere if I don't want to.'

'Thank goodness for that,' Cordelia said. 'After all, it was driving that got you into this mess in the first place!'

Lizzie suddenly felt like the twenty-year-old who couldn't pass her driving test, even after six attempts and hundreds of hours of lessons. That sense of failure still stung, especially because Georgina had, naturally, passed first time. 'Perfect' Georgina, who'd made such a success of everything. Lizzie winced as she gritted her teeth, and tried hard to relax again.

'Well, I don't think I'll be getting back behind the wheel any time soon.' Lizzie gazed down at the substantial cuff that led to a foam loop around her neck. She couldn't feel the pain now, but she knew it would be a different matter once the painkillers wore off.

'Six weeks, the doctor said,' Cordelia replied. 'But if you're a good girl, they'll let you out of here tomorrow.'

Lizzie was relieved. She hated being inactive, and the thought of staying in hospital any longer than she had to was filling her with a great deal of anxiety. Although what she intended to do when she escaped the Royal Surrey, she honestly had no idea. The idea of an empty flat, from which Paul had effectively removed any trace of his existence, filled her with a mixture of sadness and anger. In one fell swoop, their decision to split had taken away her career and relationship. And although she'd had months to come to terms with both, in her vulnerable state, the emotional wounds had burst open again.

To her mother, she simply replied, 'That's great.' But inside, she was starting to quake. She didn't want to go back to her parents' place in Surrey, but she didn't want to be alone either. At the moment, though, these seemed to be her only escape routes from the hospital. Her father and mother had always tried to micro-manage her life, under the guise of guiding her in the 'right' direction: a 'good' school, a 'good' university and even an influence on where she got her first job. At the time, Lizzie had been grateful, but as she'd got older she had found their interference more and more restrictive. With the Warner family, there had been one way: their way. If you expressed an interest in doing things differently, you were quietly and studiously ignored.

'Well, I'll leave you to rest,' Cordelia said after a slight pause. 'Text me if you need anything.'

'I don't have my phone,' Lizzie said. As she realised this, her anxiety ratcheted up a notch. 'Did anyone tell Emma and Seb what happened? I'd hate them to think that I stood them up.'

'Oh, will you stop worrying about your stupid clients?' For the first time, Cordelia seemed to lose her careful composure, and Lizzie couldn't help feeling surprised. It was so unlike her mother. 'Paul phoned and told them. You don't need to worry.'

At least that was something, Lizzie thought. She barely even registered her mother also saying that her phone was in the bedside locker. The paramedics had collected it, and her laptop bag, from the car when they'd got her out.

Cordelia leaned over and kissed Lizzie's forehead. Her lips felt cool, although that could have been just Lizzie's perception. A fleeting thought that, if it had been Georgina in the hospital bed, her mother would have been far more effusive flitted across Lizzie's mind before she could stop it. It was *far* too late to open that can of worms again. And pointless.

'Can I think about coming back with you?' Lizzie said.

'Of course,' Cordelia replied. Rather stiffly, she took Lizzie's uninjured hand. 'I know you've had a horrible time lately, darling, but things will get better.' Then, seemingly embarrassed that she'd allowed herself a moment of unguarded emotion, she dropped Lizzie's hand again.

'Bye, Mum,' Lizzie said. 'And thanks for being here for me.'

Cordelia nodded. 'See you soon.'

As she watched her mother leave the small private room, Lizzie turned her head to one side to look out of the window, which had a rather unedifying view across the car park. She couldn't wait to get out of here, but she still didn't know where to go. Leaning over, rather precariously, to retrieve her phone from the locker by her bed, she saw that the vase of flowers on top had a card that hadn't been opened. She'd just assumed they were from her parents, but, on reflection, they seemed a little too wild an arrangement to be her mother's choice of blooms, being a mix of fragrant freesias, love-in-the-mist and sweet peas. Risking a fall, she grabbed the card and, somehow, managed to rip open the small envelope by jamming it under the cuff of her sling.

Inside was a small card, with an expression of sympathy and a sweet message from the last person she'd expected to hear from. And in that moment, Lizzie wondered if she had a third alternative to her unwelcoming flat or her parents' house. The card simply said:

Sorry about your accident. Would love to see you soon. Bee.

Next to the name was a small, perfectly formed doodle of a bumblebee. And as Lizzie gazed at the card, she felt her spirits lift a fraction, despite the situation she found herself in. Then she remembered exactly why she hadn't seen Bee in such a long time, and her heart sank through the floor once again.

4

The next morning, after being given the all-clear from the consultant and the medical team, Lizzie prepared to leave hospital. Her mother had travelled up to Lizzie's flat and gathered up some bits and pieces for her, so at least Lizzie didn't have to leave the Royal Surrey in the clothes she'd come in with. Dressing herself proved to be a bit of a challenge, but thankfully a nurse was on hand to help with the top button of her jeans and to sling the dark blue hoodie around her shoulders. A baggy vest top underneath covered the essentials but was the most sensible thing to wear with a collar and cuff sling in the equation. Tying her trainers was going to be an ongoing challenge, though, and Lizzie made a mental note to sort out ballet flats for the next few weeks.

The car journey back to her flat was just about bearable, and after her mother had made them both a cup of tea, the inevitable discussion, begun yesterday, continued, much to Lizzie's annoyance.

'I'll be fine now I'm home, Mum, honestly. And you don't need to stay with me. I know how you hate being away from Dad. I've got everything I need here.'

'But I don't like the idea of you being lonely here all by yourself,' Cordelia replied.

Lizzie only just stopped herself from snapping back that she'd be just as lonely stuck in her parents' house in the back end of Surrey, far away from everything and everyone she knew, but she knew it wouldn't go down well. Her mother, in her own way, was trying to help, and, despite herself, she was grateful.

'Just promise me you'll call if you need anything,' Cordelia said as Lizzie saw her to the door of the flat.

'I will,' Lizzie said, and forced a smile. But even as she received a slightly awkward hug from her departing mother, she knew she wouldn't. She'd kept her parents at arm's length for years, now, and a car accident wasn't going to change that. Apart from the obligatory Christmas and Easter visits, and a duty phone call once a week, she limited how often she saw them. One of the few things she could thank Paul for was that he'd never tried to pressure her into seeing them more often. It wasn't as though they were terrible people, but, after a lifetime of doing everything that had been 'expected' of her, in her mid-thirties she'd needed some distance. Unlike her sister, Georgina, of course, who even now lived only half a mile from their parents' place with her husband and two children. But that was Georgina. Dutiful. Compliant. She couldn't compete with that. She knew. She'd tried.

As she closed the door to the flat, Lizzie realised, for the first time, just how empty the place felt without Paul and his stuff there. He'd been slowly moving out for a couple of months, and hadn't actually lived there for about the same amount of time, but, in her vulnerable state, all of the emotions she'd kept bottled up after their relationship had ended threatened to bubble to the surface. She tried valiantly to feel grateful that, in selling her half of Warner-Basset Marketing Solutions, she had a very healthy bank balance, which would be a decent cushion and give her the time to think carefully about what she wanted to do next, but the shock of the events of the last couple of days suddenly hit her like a thunderbolt now she was back home, and alone.

Staggering to the sofa in the small living room of the flat, she felt the panic rising. She needed to get a grip. She couldn't spend the next few weeks sitting alone in here, with nothing to do except wait for her arm to mend. She had to get out. But where?

Suddenly, Bee's message on the card that came with the flowers came back to her. Could that be a possibility? Thinking about the last time she'd been at Bee's house caused a whole raft of new emotions to rise to the surface; feelings that, in her weakened state, she really didn't want to add to the mix. But given the choice between her own flat, upon which the lease would be up in a few months anyway, going to live with her parents and going to see Bee, even the past felt like a preferable option.

Scrabbling around in her bag for the card, Lizzie turned it over and looked at the phone number that had been written on the back of it. Could she impose on Bee, after all these years? Or was that just hope born of desperation? There was only one way to find out.

Grabbing her mobile, she dialled the number and waited. She was almost relieved when, eventually, it cut to voicemail.

'Aunt Bee? It's Lizzie.' Lizzie swallowed hard. The sound of Bee's voice on the automated system had caused a rush in her head that she hadn't been prepared for.

'Thank you so much for the lovely flowers. I was wondering if I might come and see you for a bit, but not to worry if it's inconvenient.' She paused again. 'Well. Hope to speak soon. Bye.' Clicking the 'end call' button, Lizzie carefully put the phone down on the seat beside her.

The minute she did so, she started second-guessing herself. What was she thinking? Going to see Bee was not the answer. More likely, it would stir up a whole new soup of discord that she didn't have the physical or mental strength to deal with. So why on earth had she been compelled to make the call? Was it just because Lizzie was touched that Bee, despite not having been in regular contact for a few years, had been thinking of her enough to send those flowers? Or was it that Lizzie needed to force some kind of closure on what had happened to make her stay away from Roseford in the first place? One thing was for certain, she needed to make some decisions one way or the other, and sitting in a flat that very soon wasn't going to be hers anyway wasn't the way to go about it.

She was trying to decide what to get delivered for her dinner that night, cooking anything one-handed being out of the question, when her phone rang. Grabbing it, she felt a flutter of pointless hope that it could be Paul, and all of this was just some bad dream. But no. Looking at the name and number, it was immediately clear it wasn't. She couldn't handle Georgina right now. She needed time to think. Her sister, for all of her 'good' intentions, could wait. She declined the call and slumped back on the sofa. What did it matter, anyway? Georgina couldn't offer any comfort, or answers, from where she was. This was something Lizzie had to work out for herself.

But, before she could muse on this any longer, the phone rang again. This time, it was Bee, returning her call.

'Lizzie!' she exclaimed down the line. 'How wonderful to hear from you. How are you? Did you enjoy the flowers?'

Lizzie, despite her mood, smiled slightly at the enthusiasm and genuine interest in her aunt's voice. How different things could have been if Bee had been her mother, she thought, not for the first time.

'I'm OK, Aunt Bee,' she began. But the enormity of that lie suddenly smacked her in the face. She most certainly was not OK. On any level.

'You've had such a horrible time, my love. What can I do to help?' Bee's voice was so gentle that Lizzie's tears had no choice but to fall.

'Can I come and stay with you?' Lizzie's voice trembled.

There was a slight pause on the line before Bee replied. 'Of course. When would you like to come?'

'As soon as I can?' Lizzie said. 'If it's convenient?'

'I'll make up the spare room downstairs,' Bee said. 'Come as soon as you like.'

'Thank you, Aunt Bee,' Lizzie replied. 'Mum's offered to have me while I recover, but...'

'Say no more,' Bee said, a note of amusement in her voice. 'Let me know when you're getting here, and I'll get everything ready.'

After Lizzie had ended the call, she rang the private hire taxi firm that Warner-Basset had always used and told them the details of her journey. That confirmed, she began the slow process of packing her things.

5

As the taxi wended its weary way towards the village of Roseford, Lizzie's spirits plummeted in parallel with the darkening skies. A night's perspective had given her an altogether different view of the decision she'd made. Much as she'd adored Aunt Bee when she was younger, Roseford was a place she'd hoped never to see again, despite the fact that it was one of the most picturesque villages in the south-west of England. For Lizzie, the sight of the baked-shortbread-coloured buildings, the vibrant and colourful hanging baskets that adorned every shopfront, and the many tourists buzzing about the place like so many nectar-drunk bumblebees filled her with trepidation, which was completely at odds with the cheerful scenes around her. She knew, by being here, that she was going to end up thinking about things she'd not given herself permission to for twenty years and she suddenly began to wonder if she'd made the right decision in coming back here. *Too late now*, she thought.

Lizzie and Georgina had stayed with Bee a few times during their holidays from the boarding school they'd both attended. The distance between the school and Roseford was roughly the same as between school and their family home, so Bee had opened her house to them from time to time, encouraging them to come and visit. Bee had no children of her own, and had seemed to enjoy having the girls to stay.

Lizzie *had* enjoyed the time she'd spent in Roseford, until one awful weekend had changed all that. She hadn't been back since, and was now wondering if she'd really made the right decision to return. But where else could she go? It wasn't as if she had an army of friends who were willing to help her out. Most of her school and university mates were spread across the country now, and since the vast majority of her work friends from before she and Paul had founded Warner-Basset had spent the past year working from home, the friendships she had forged with them had assumed a kind of nebulous distance. Most people had decided to move out of London and either into the suburbs or further afield, leaving Lizzie one of the very few people living in the centre of town. But with the lease on the flat running out and the business sold, for the first time since she graduated, Lizzie felt rootless, alone and not just a little bit afraid. Was coming back to Roseford really the right decision?

These thoughts were mercifully cut short as the taxi drove carefully through the centre of the village and then turned a slow sloping right to ascend one of the side streets. Lizzie remembered, with a combination of trepidation and nostalgia, that Bee's small cottage was on the eastern side of Roseford, about half a mile from the centre of the village. The gentle incline of the road as it began its ascent out of the village was lined with trees and as the taxi driver's satnav chirped to make a right turn, Lizzie's stomach again did a little flip. There was no disputing the beauty of where Bee lived. Lizzie just wished she weren't visiting it under such strange and stressful circumstances.

The last time she'd been in Roseford, she'd begun her visit full of hope and excitement and it had ended with a night of trauma and despair. There was some irony in the fact that she was beginning her stay in the state she'd left twenty years earlier, she considered grimly, but the prospect of hope and excitement being her endpoint seemed completely out of the question.

Lizzie felt the jolt in her body as the taxi came to a stop outside a charming whitewashed cottage with the most incredible kitchen garden at the front of it. Bee's passion for plants and flowers had driven her entire life, and this was no more so on display than in the garden of her own home. As a child, Lizzie had loved meandering up and down the channels that Bee had created in the gardens, seeking out the highly scented blooms and the unusual flowers but always remembering to ask permission before she picked any.

'Can you manage, love?' the taxi driver asked as Lizzie opened the car door.

'I'm fine,' she said quietly.

The driver, clearly realising that Lizzie had not been in the mood for conversation during their long trip from London, had left her to her own devices, only interjecting when they'd pulled over at a service station about an hour ago. Lizzie was grateful. If she'd been in a better mood, she would've worried that she had seemed rude, and as she finally exited the car she gave the driver the best smile she could muster and thanked him for bringing her safely to Roseford.

'I'm sorry I've not been a big talker on this trip,' she said.

'I've had worse.' The driver smiled back. 'And given the state of your arm, I think I can let you off.'

He got out of the car himself and strode round to the boot, stretching his legs out in front of him as he walked. In no time at all, he pulled out her suitcase and the holdall she'd packed for her stay. 'Would you like me to take this to the door for you?' he said.

Lizzie nodded. 'Thank you. That would be great.' She trailed in his wake, having managed to close the car door by leaning back on it. As she navigated the slightly uneven path to Bee's crimson-painted wooden front door, she took a deep breath and the scents of the vibrant array of flowers on either side of the path hit her like the perfume counter of some high-end department store. All of a sudden she was transported back to her teens, breathing in the air that had been such a contrast to the starchy, disinfected odour of the boarding school that she'd come from to spend the weekend in Roseford.

The memory was almost too much. Lizzie stumbled on the path and only just caught herself from falling flat on her face and doing herself more damage. The taxi driver, having dumped her bags on the small open porch by the front door, hurried to her side.

'Are you all right, love?' he said. He didn't touch her, for which Lizzie was grateful, but she did meet his concerned gaze with another smile.

'I'm fine,' she said. Then, making a conscious decision to pull herself together as she had on so many other occasions, she raised her head. 'Thank you again,' she said. 'I can take it from here.'

The driver was clearly about to suggest he waited until whoever owned the cottage opened the door, but there was something in Lizzie's tone that deterred him. Bidding her farewell, he strode back down the path, got into his car and drove away.

Lizzie, left on the doorstep, tried to take another deep, steadying breath. Before she could contemplate her situation any further, though, the cottage door opened and on the other side stood the kindly, still beautiful, calm and wise Aunt Bee.

Lizzie, who until this point hadn't realised how tightly wound she actually was, took one look at her aunt and burst into tears.

6

Having been ushered through a small, dark hallway into Aunt Bee's charming and very cosy living room, Lizzie collapsed onto the brightly coloured patchwork-patterned sofa that was situated on the far wall. She was shaking so badly that for a moment she couldn't get a grip on the bunch of tissues that Bee passed her from the box on the coffee table beside the sofa. Suddenly, all the trauma of the past few weeks had hit her again, and in one fell swoop she'd become a messy, blubbering blancmange.

'I'm so sorry.' She shuddered, before blowing her nose loudly and unceremoniously. 'I don't know what's come over me.'

Bee, who up until this point had remained quiet, just put an arm around her and gave a supportive smile. Lizzie was grateful that Bee was obviously mindful of the cuff and sling that supported her arm and the fact that the slow careful way she'd moved through the hallway had shown Bee just how achy and tired she really was.

'There's nothing to apologise for,' Bee said gently as Lizzie tried to get a grip. 'You've really been through it, these past few weeks, haven't you, darling?'

The gentleness in Bee's tone only served to make another ugly sob rise up in Lizzie's throat. It felt simultaneously like a release and a terrible admission. After a few moments, however, Lizzie's internal voice grew too strong just to sit and cry.

It had been a long journey from London and, as Bee had observed, a long few weeks, but now she was in Roseford she should try to make the best of it. It was better than being alone in her flat, after all.

'Tea?' Bee asked, once Lizzie had blown her nose again.

Lizzie nodded, still not trusting herself to speak.

Once Bee had returned with two steaming, flower-patterned mugs of tea, Lizzie felt strong enough to recount the whole sorry story. As she finished, Bee cocked her head to one side and regarded her niece levelly.

'Well,' she said, 'that is all rather unfortunate. But I'm sure your dear mother and father have already commiserated and come up with at least fifteen alternatives for you to consider about how you spend the rest of your life. So you'll forgive me if I don't offer any immediate solutions to your problems.'

Lizzie suppressed a smile. Bee's full name was Verbena, although Lizzie had always known her just as Bee. The flower she was named after was said to have balm-like properties, and her calm, pragmatic approach to Lizzie's current predicament definitely felt that way too. Her gentian-blue eyes regarded Lizzie with sympathy, but belied the determination she'd shown over the years to live her life on her own terms. While Bee and her sister, Lizzie's mother, Cordelia, had shared many things in common as children, the two women had grown apart over the years as their lives had moved in different directions. The echoes of that in her own sibling relationship with Georgina were not lost on Lizzie.

'It's lovely enough that you've given me somewhere to recuperate for the next few weeks,' Lizzie said, her voice still bearing the tremors of her recent crying fit. 'I know I haven't kept in touch as much as I should've over the years, but I do really appreciate it.'

'It was the least I could do,' Bee replied. She paused for a moment as if considering her next sentence carefully. 'After all, I'm sure the last place you'd really want to be is recuperating at home with your parents. Well intentioned as they may be, I hardly see that house as an inducement to getting better, somehow.'

Lizzie gave a wry smile. 'Believe it or not, Mum did offer, but I wasn't sure if staying there would do me more harm than good.' Then, remembering that Bee was Cordelia's sister, she tried to back-pedal a little. 'I know they mean well, but even so it just didn't feel like the right thing to do.'

Bee looked at her shrewdly. Then, clearly deciding that it was better to change the subject than dwell on what potentially could be painful or at the very least frustrating family memories, she moved on.

'I've made up the guest room on the ground floor for you,' Bee said. 'I wasn't sure how you'd be, navigating the steep stairs to the first floor, but of course if you'd rather have the bedroom you stayed in when you were a teenager...'

'No, thank you, the downstairs room will be lovely,' Lizzie interjected hurriedly. She already felt pretty helpless having to wear the sling, and with a body covered in bruises. She didn't really need to be reminded of the lanky, gangling teenager she used to be when she had stayed here with her sister in the holidays. Back then, she and Georgina had shared a room, giggling long into the night, even when Bee had come in to remind them that they had to get some sleep. But the last time she'd visited had been different. And painful...

Lizzie took another sip of her tea, which had gradually cooled. Looking around the living room, she felt immediately reassured to see that, bar updating a few pieces of technology, it felt and looked very much the same as it had the last time she'd visited. She was tickled to see an Amazon Alexa tucked away on the corner of the mantelshelf above the fireplace, and a medium-sized flat-screen television in one corner. Also on the mantel were various framed photographs, including, Lizzie realised with a pang of pain-infused nostalgia, one of herself and her sister, aged about sixteen, smiling broadly into the camera. She remembered it had been taken the afternoon before the night that, for her at least, had changed everything. That had shifted the balance in her relationship with Georgina and altered it irreparably.

'I noticed that the flower shop has changed its signs and logos from the last time I was here,' she said, turning her attention back to Bee, desperate to backtrack from a potential path of introspection she wasn't quite ready to go down yet.

'Well, it has been quite a while since you visited,' Bee replied. 'I might be approaching my dotage but there's still life in the old dog, and shop, yet!'

Lizzie, with her keen eye for marketing, voiced her approval of the new colour scheme.

'Have you thought about going online yet?' she asked her aunt. Although marketing was the last thing she wanted to think about, having made her exit from that world so recently, she couldn't help herself. She'd immersed herself in the finer points of how to market and promote businesses for more than a decade. It wasn't something she could easily just switch off.

'Oh, I think that's for the person after me to think about,' Bee replied. 'I get kept busy enough with local orders, especially in the summer.'

'Even so, it couldn't hurt to at least set up a website,' Lizzie said. Then, abruptly, she paused and laughed nervously. 'Sorry,' she continued. 'Just can't seem to stop thinking about work, can I?'

'Well, you're going to have to learn, at least for a few weeks.' Bee laughed too. 'And there are worse places to do that than Roseford, aren't there?' With a creak of bones, she got back up from the sofa. 'Now, shall we see about another cup of tea? I've got some lavender cupcakes from Roseford Café to bridge the gap between now and dinner time, if you'd like one?'

'Thanks, Aunt Bee,' Lizzie replied. 'That would be lovely.'

As Bee walked out of the living room and headed towards the kitchen, Lizzie felt a flutter of nerves. Bee, for all her positivity and cheer, couldn't have been more wrong about Roseford. Even though the thought of convalescing with her parents was immeasurably worse, Roseford held its own secrets; secrets Lizzie wasn't sure that she was strong enough to confront.

7

After a night's sleep born more of exhaustion than relaxation, Lizzie awoke in the quiet back bedroom on the ground floor that Bee had prepared for her, feeling a whole lot better than she'd thought she would. Despite Bee's raised eyebrow, she'd left the sash window open, and a slight breeze was ruffling the flower-patterned curtains, letting in slivers of warm sunlight as it did. The scent of the honeysuckle growing adjacent to the window and the lavender below it reached Lizzie as she tried to roll over on her left side, before the cuff on her arm reminded her.

Every. Single. Time.

Sighing in exasperation, she rolled to the right and got out of bed. The varnished floorboards felt warm under her feet, and she mooched over to look out of the window. Drawing back the curtains, she smiled to see the beauty of Bee's back garden, which was just as well kept as the front. Although she got most of her flowers from larger suppliers, Bee liked to bundle the lavender, which was abundant, and other seasonal blooms from her own garden for those who wanted to keep their shopping a little more local.

Lizzie's peaceful contemplation of Bee's garden was interrupted by the abrupt buzzing of a large bumblebee past her face and into the room. Lizzie jumped back reflexively, and then berated herself for having taken fright at a creature that had obviously just lost its way. She watched the bumblebee's leisurely progress around the room before, obviously realising it had taken a wrong turn on its quest for sweetness, it continued its languorous flight back out of the sash window and the buzz faded away once again.

The day was going to be warm; that much was already obvious. Lizzie slid her feet into her slippers and then decided that coffee was in order. In her 'normal' life, she couldn't function before she'd had a measure of double espresso from the machine in the corner of her modern kitchen. She hadn't spotted a coffee machine in Bee's kitchen when she'd gone to grab a glass of water before bed the night before, but she hoped she could find some ground coffee or, at a push, some instant to see her through until she could find another source. Paul had always known better than to talk to her before she'd had her first coffee of the day. She felt a pang of loneliness as she thought back to the times he'd gently teased her for her muddle-headedness in the mornings, and then brought her the first, perfectly brewed cup while she was still in bed. Despite everything, she missed little gestures like that. She didn't regret the break-up, but she missed the little things.

When she got to the kitchen, she saw that Bee had left a note for her, propped up against a small posy of wildflowers, presumably also from the garden that she'd just been admiring.

Dear Lizzie,

I hope you slept well. I'm expecting an early delivery so I'm off to open up the shop. Help yourself to what you want for breakfast but most importantly... RELAX!!

See you later,

Bee

Lizzie smiled when she saw that Bee had added that same doodle of a bumblebee after her name, as she always had when she'd signed birthday cards to Lizzie and her sister when they were kids. And, most recently of course, the card with the flowers she'd sent.

When the quest for coffee, even a jar of instant, came up fruitless, Lizzie decided to get dressed and go on the hunt for it elsewhere. As the taxi had travelled up Roseford's main street yesterday, Lizzie had noticed a café that hadn't been there the last time she'd visited. Although she couldn't recall the sign over the door, she assumed it was the Roseford Café that Bee had bought those delicious lavender cupcakes from. She figured that it was as good a place to start her hunt for decent coffee as any. Taking a careful shower, happy to remove the collar and cuff for a few minutes, she managed to get a strappy top and a pair of skinny jeans on, before pulling the sleeve of her hoodie over her good arm and wriggling until the other side was draped over her shoulder. Tying her hair back proved rather more difficult, so she just brushed it and left it loose. It was a contrast to her usual style, which was to tie the wavy, dark, shoulder-length mass back as often as possible, but for the moment it couldn't be helped. It felt weird to have it loose; she far preferred it out of her face, but, she figured, at least she could hide behind it if she saw anyone she didn't want to talk to.

Not that she imagined that that was really a possibility. Two decades was a long time to stay away, after all. Trying to put the past out of her mind and concentrate on the present, Lizzie strolled down the hill towards the village centre. She was pleased to see that, with the arrival of the British Heritage Fund, the village was looking more prosperous. Freshly painted cottages butted up against those who'd clearly had their local stone cleaned up, and most gardens were a riot of tubs, hanging baskets and shrubs. Overhead, magpies chattered in the oak trees and blackbirds swooped down, busily searching for food to take back to nearby nests. The tang of meadow grass was in the air, and the musky scent of lime hedges, interspersed with buddleia and the sweet, almost cloying scent of philadelphus. She remembered Roseford for its scents, and was assailed by them as she passed the well-kept gardens of the parish.

Walking up the main street, she noticed that, even at ten o'clock on a weekday, the place was doing brisk trade. The tourist season was well under way, and Roseford's popularity had clearly increased over the years. Lizzie hoped that Bee's flower shop had seen a similar uptick in trade. Perhaps her aunt was right when she said she had no need of a website just yet. Although Lizzie wondered what happened in the winter months, when most of the tourists stayed away. She'd pop in after she'd had a coffee and see how trade was.

Soon enough, she was walking through the door of Roseford Café, and was relieved to see a large, serious-looking chrome coffee machine behind the counter. A pretty blonde woman was chatting to a customer while she put their order together, and Lizzie waited, next in line, appreciating the scent of what smelled like perfectly percolated coffee. While the previous customer paid, Lizzie took in the array of freshly baked cakes and scones under glass cloches on the counter, wondering if it would be too decadent to have a slice of carrot and walnut cake, complete with mascarpone icing, for breakfast. As her stomach gave an almighty rumble, she decided that it was *exactly* what she needed.

'Hi.' The woman behind the counter beamed as Lizzie's turn came. Lizzie noticed that she had the name 'Lucy' embroidered on her apron, just above and to the left of the café's name. 'Welcome to Roseford Café. What can I get you?' Her eyes flickered to the sling, but she didn't ask. Lizzie was relieved; she didn't want to go over it again, and not with a total stranger.

'Can I have a latte with a double shot of espresso, and a slice of that carrot cake, please?' Lizzie asked. She was amused that just saying the name of the cake made her salivate. She hadn't had much of an appetite since she'd come out of hospital, so she took this as a good sign.

'Of course,' Lucy replied. 'Why don't you take a seat and I'll bring them over to you?'

'Thanks,' Lizzie replied, presenting her bank card to pay. She managed to pour herself a glass of water from the jug on the counter, and took it to the table in the front corner of the café. Sitting so that she could look out of the window and see who was coming through the door, she spent a few minutes just watching the world go by, until Lucy came over with her cake and coffee.

'Here you go,' Lucy said, carefully setting the plate and the mug down in front of Lizzie. 'Can I get you anything else?'

'No, thank you,' Lizzie replied. 'That looks fabulous.'

'Freshly baked yesterday, and iced this morning,' Lucy replied. 'It's based on the Treloar family's recipe from the late nineteenth century, with a few modern, more indulgent additions, of course!'

Lizzie, who already had the first forkful halfway to her mouth, tried to swallow down the tumult that Lucy's innocent titbit of history had created in her mind. Treloar was a name she didn't want to dwell on. But, she figured, it was inevitable that she was going to hear it a great deal for as long as she stayed here in Roseford; it had been their village, after all, for over four hundred years. They had a lot more history than the few moments she'd had in their company. Steeling herself, she tasted the cake, and, thankfully, it was exactly as delicious as it looked. That was some compensation.

'It's absolutely lovely,' she said, once she'd swallowed the mouthful.

The café wasn't overly busy, in the lull between breakfast and lunch, and Lucy seemed in no hurry to get back behind the counter.

'So, what brings you to Roseford?' she asked as Lizzie took a sip of her coffee, which was as delicious as the scent that had preceded it.

Lizzie paused, not wanting to get into a discussion about her injuries. She knew if she said *convalescence*, she'd certainly have to elaborate, so instead she just replied, 'Visiting my aunt. She runs the flower shop.'

'Oh, yes.' Lucy smiled happily. 'Bee's so lovely, and she's been so helpful with the wedding preparations. What she doesn't know about flowers isn't worth knowing!'

Noting the large diamond solitaire on the third finger of Lucy's left hand, Lizzie congratulated her.

'Oh, no.' Lucy laughed, seeing where Lizzie's eyes had gone. 'Despite the engagement ring, I'm not planning a wedding just yet! It's my best friend, Serena, who's getting married, and Bee's sourcing all kinds of amazing flowers for the bouquets and the church. She told Serena that it's the biggest order she's had in a while, but she's been absolutely amazing. I can't wait to see what they look like on the day.'

'Well, I'm glad she's been able to help,' Lizzie replied. It was nice to know that Bee was so well regarded in the village. She'd cherished her view of Bee as a slightly eccentric, rather hokey flower seller for so many years that hearing about her expertise from someone else was lovely as much as it was surprising.

'I'll leave you to your cake and coffee,' Lucy said. 'But let me know if you need anything else.'

'Thanks,' Lizzie said. 'I will.' She turned back to the window as Lucy headed back to the counter to serve a customer who'd just walked through the door. Glancing idly upwards, Lizzie noticed the customer was tall, broad-backed and had darkish blond hair. As Lucy greeted him with a wide smile, clearly pleased to see him, Lizzie wondered if this was the fiancé who'd given her the hefty diamond ring. She couldn't help eavesdropping as they made cheerful conversation.

'Just a latte to go, please, Lucy,' the man said. 'I've got to get back to the office. The wedding of the year's hit a couple of bumps in the road that the British Heritage Fund has asked me to sort out by the end of the day.'

'Nothing serious, I hope,' Lucy said. 'I'm not sure Serena could cope with any more hiccups. The thing's had to be rearranged three times already.'

'Oh, nothing I can't work out, I'm sure,' the man replied.

There was something so familiar about his voice, Lucy thought. Then, as he turned, she nearly dropped her fork. Twenty years might have passed, but she was stunned she hadn't realised the moment he'd spoken. There he was. Simon Treloar in the flesh. Suddenly feeling short of breath, she needed to get out of the café, and quickly. Leaving half of her carrot cake untouched, and gulping back the last third of her latte, wincing as it scalded the back of her throat, she heaved herself up out of the chair and made for the door.

'Thank you,' the rather surprised voice of Lucy drifted after her, but Lizzie couldn't stop to respond. She had to get out of there. The rush of memory was just too much, even after all this time. Hurrying away from the café, she saw the welcoming signs of Bee's flower shop a few doors down, and felt as though she were seeking sanctuary from memories, like a swarm of wasps, chasing her. Maybe coming back to Roseford hadn't been such a good idea after all.

8

'Was it something I said?' Lucy looked quizzically at Simon Treloar, who'd turned, just too late, to see the departing back of the customer who'd left so hurriedly.

'You know what some people are like,' Simon replied. 'Especially tourists. They tend to forget their manners when they're on holiday.'

'She seemed perfectly fine before you walked in,' Lucy teased. 'Did you forget your deodorant this morning?'

'Bloody cheek,' Simon said. 'I can still get you turned out of here, you know. I'm sure I've still got some ancestral rights over the building!'

'Not when I pay the mortgage!' Lucy laughed. 'But nice try.' She shook her head. 'So, what are you going to do about this, er, *hiccup* with the wedding?'

'Oh, I don't know.' Simon sighed. 'Just when I thought I'd dotted the i's and crossed every last possible t, the BHF throws another spanner in the works and I have to rewrite the rule book. If that's not too mixed a bag of metaphors.'

'What's the problem?' Lucy asked. 'I mean, you had a whole bloody film crew swarming over Roseford Hall and the grounds two Christmases ago. How much more demanding could a wedding be?'

Roseford had been the location for FilmFlix's smash-hit Christmas movie, *A Countess for Christmas*, which had caused as much upheaval as it had fun for the residents of Roseford. Lucy had fallen in love with one of the lead actors, ex-teen-star Finn Sanderson, and Lucy's best friend, Serena, had fallen just as hard for Finn's glamorous co-star, Montana de Santo.

'The chapel wasn't open then,' Simon said. 'Now it's been restored, there's a whole bunch of red tape to cut through. It's got more preservation orders on it than any other part of the estate, and they're only prepared to sign off on the wedding if they can have a rep from Head Office overseeing every last moment of the ceremony.'

'So why haven't they mentioned this before?' Lucy asked. 'I mean, this wedding's been booked for nearly a year.'

'Rule changes, instituted by government pressure from the Department for Digital, Culture, Media and Sport,' Simon said. 'So, even though this was in the diary long before the most recent legislation, we still have to abide by it. Some suited nob from BHF headquarters wants to be on hand for compliance on the day, and wants every single flower, decoration and order of service documented, so they can be sure there'll be no damage to the building.'

'Confetti's off, then?' Lucy said in amusement. Simon knew she was enjoying teasing him, but the thought of thousands of paper petals, no matter how biodegradable, put the deodorant he'd definitely applied that morning to the test.

'We'll be lucky if we can have it on the estate at all, let alone outside the chapel.' Simon sighed. 'Do you think Serena will be OK with that?'

'It's not Serena you should be worrying about,' Lucy said, smiling. 'She's not the demanding one of the partnership, remember?'

Simon shook his head. 'Well, I'll leave it to the actual wedding planner to break that news. I'm just the intermediary, thank goodness.' He took the latte that Lucy had prepared and said goodbye, smiling as Lucy wished him luck. It was a real coup, having such a high-profile wedding as the first one at the Roseford Hall chapel, but it hadn't come without its headaches. Much as he loved still being involved in the running of what had once been his family's estate, the whole property having been taken on by the British Heritage Fund several years ago, there were times when he wished he'd just walked away from it all, bought a house with his share of the proceeds from the sale and started a whole new life. But, he'd conceded at the time, as the tenth Lord of Roseford, walking away from Roseford Hall would've been tantamount to burning it down. He just didn't have it in him to rise from the ashes of four hundred years of history and ignore the metaphorically disapproving gaze of the portraits of the ancestors on the walls of the Great Hall.

Heading back out onto Roseford's main street, he could see ahead of him the woman who had scuttled out of Lucy's café. She didn't appear to be in such a hurry now, and as she turned left and through the door of Roseford Blooms, the local flower shop that was handling the decorations and bouquets for Serena's wedding, his curiosity was piqued. Deciding to pop in and see Bee, who had been so incredibly helpful with this wedding, Simon wondered if she might be able to come up with an alternative for the confetti that the British Heritage Fund had so effectively vetoed. He'd heard of rose petals being used instead, but wondered if the cost would be too prohibitive. Then again, it wasn't as though any expense was being spared for Serena and Montana's wedding, so he figured it was worth asking. At least then, if Serena came back in screaming hysterics or, indeed, Montana did, he would have an alternative plan that might well just go some way to placate them.

The brass bell above the door of the florist's jangled merrily as Simon stepped into the shop. It was a tiny place really, he reflected, and felt like a throwback to a far earlier time. Bee had placed a couple of buckets of flowers outside the front door, but had saved her best blooms for the stepped shelves inside the shop, painted green and rising like a miniature Quantocks to the ceiling. Despite the lack of floor space, Bee managed to make the place feel airy and welcoming, and that irresistible combination of freshly cut flowers and their scents and earthy, ozony compost where the rooted blooms sat in various pots, made the whole experience seem like stepping into a summer meadow.

'Simon!' Bee's voice called from the counter as she caught sight of him. 'How are you today?'

'I'm well, thanks,' Simon replied. He paused to bury his nose in a nearby bunch of strong-smelling pink roses, and wondered if his mother would like a bunch of them for her hall table. Deciding that they could wait, he headed up to the counter.

'How are the preparations for the wedding of the year going?' Bee asked. She was pruning the stems of a deep red bundle of roses, stacked up on the counter, and her fingers worked with cool efficiency, stripping the bottom two inches of each stem and removing any inconvenient leaves or thorns, before they went out on display in the shop. She was so practised at this that she barely needed to look, working by touch alone. Seeing Simon's admiring glance at the blooms, she added, 'These came over from your head gardener this morning – Phoenix Rosa, he called them.' She paused. 'Supposed to symbolise the estate rising from the ashes, apparently.'

Simon smiled, remembering his own thought processes of a few minutes ago. 'Yes, the British Heritage Fund commissioned Henry to create some new hybrids for the garden. Glad the first one's come out so well.' Although, he thought, if the Roseford Hall estate was rising from the ashes, he himself sometimes felt mired in the bog of history and tradition.

Briefly, he filled Bee in on the confetti conundrum. As he was recounting the story, she nodded, still paring the roses as he talked.

'Well, it's not the end of the world,' she said. 'Even if bird-friendly or biodegradable confetti's off the cards, I'm sure the BHF can't object to dried rose petals. Most of them'll be gone on the summer breeze in a day or two, anyway.'

'That's what I was hoping you'd say,' Simon replied, feeling relieved. 'And can you get hold of some?'

'Shouldn't be a problem. Have you discussed this with the wedding planner and the happy couple, or shall I hang fire until you have?'

'Better make sure it's all OK with them,' Simon said. 'Just to be on the safe side.' How had it come to this? he thought. He wasn't much more than a messenger boy for the BHF these days. A go-between. A middleman.

'Are you all right, dear?' Bee asked gently. She'd obviously noticed the look on his face.

Forcing a smile, he replied, 'I'm fine,' a little too quickly. What else could he expect, these days, after all? A lord without a manor was about as much use as...

'Oh, Lizzie, darling, thank you so much.' Bee's voice brought him back from another melancholy thought, as did the smell of coffee that gradually overlaid the sweet scents of the blooms in the flower shop.

Simon glanced up from the Phoenix Rosa that Bee had nearly finished paring, and noticed, with some surprise, that the other woman behind the counter appeared to be the tourist who'd exited Lucy's café so summarily.

'Simon, this is my niece Lizzie Warner,' Bee said brightly. 'She's come to stay with me until her blessed arm gets better.' She turned Simon's way. 'Lizzie, this is Simon Treloar, Tenth Lord of Roseford and resident of Roseford Hall. I'm not sure if the two of you ever met when Lizzie and her sister, Georgina, used to come to stay with me.'

'And wedding planner's assistant at the moment,' Simon said, still not quite able to keep the trace of irony from his tone. He regarded the other woman behind the counter, and found himself smiling. The bruising on her face didn't detract from her direct green eyes, her long, thick almost black hair that fell to just below her shoulders and her statuesque, straight-backed figure.

Bee turned from Simon to Lizzie, smiling. 'The pair of them used to come over during the school holidays, so it was quite a while ago!'

Lizzie did look rather familiar, Simon reflected. Perhaps their paths had crossed when she'd stayed with Bee before? But then he'd been preoccupied during the holidays helping out on the Roseford estate, and hadn't really taken much notice of what other people were doing.

'It's nice to meet you, Lizzie,' he added quickly, realising that she might misconstrue his staring. 'I hope your arm feels better soon.'

Lizzie, he observed, must have been on some pretty strong painkillers, since she barely seemed to register what either he or Bee had said. Eventually, she seemed to zone back into the moment.

'Th-thank you,' she stammered. 'It's, er, nice to meet you, too.'

She turned back to Bee. 'I think I might go back to the cottage for a bit, if you don't mind, Aunt Bee. I'm not feeling so great.'

'Of course, darling,' Bee said. 'Did you want me to run you back up the hill in the van? You look a little pale.'

'No, I'll be fine,' Lizzie replied. 'I'll see you later.'

'All right, then. See you later.'

Simon noticed Bee's gaze, writ large with worry, lingering on the departing back of her niece as Lizzie exited the flower shop. She'd left her own mug of coffee untouched on the counter, too, he observed.

'Is everything all right?' Simon asked.

'Oh, don't worry,' Bee said quickly. 'She's not really herself at the moment. The broken collarbone doesn't help, but she's really rather down in general. I hope a few weeks here in Roseford, away from it all, will help.'

'Well, if anyone can help, you can,' Simon said. He glanced at his watch. 'I'll keep you updated about the confetti.'

'Please do,' Bee replied. She passed him a couple of the Phoenix Rosas. 'Give these to your mother, with my regards.'

'Thank you,' Simon said, touched. Bee and his mother had been close when they'd been younger, and still met for the occasional cup of coffee from time to time. 'She'll love them.'

As he left the shop, he glanced up the main street towards Bee's house, hoping to catch another glimpse of Lizzie, but she'd already gone. He felt the strangest sense of protectiveness towards her, even from that brief meeting. But there was something else, too, nagging at his brain. He wondered if he *had* met her before when she'd come to stay with Bee in the past, although he couldn't place exactly when, or where. And he couldn't help thinking that it wasn't only her injuries that had made him feel as though he wanted to protect her. Something else was making him feel that way, some event long ago, lost to the mists of time and his own vague memory. He just couldn't quite put his finger on what that might be.

9

Lizzie's heart raced as though she were back in school doing the hundred-metre sprint as she hurried up the hill and back to the sanctuary of Bee's cottage. She ignored the thud of her wrist in the cuff against her chest as she picked up the pace, consumed instead by the memories that seeing Simon up close had evoked.

She hadn't expected to come face to face with Simon Treloar so soon, and twice in one morning, to boot. Of course, she'd known she'd have to face him some time, but she'd hoped she'd be able to stay out of the way and convalesce a little while longer first. She felt stripped back, vulnerable. As if all the years between now and the last time she'd seen them had vanished, and she were that girl again. The joke.

No. That girl's gone.

But she hadn't; not really. She was still there, underneath the better clothes, the contact lenses and the straighter hair. She still lurked in all of her awkwardness, peering out from Lizzie's eyes as if no time had passed at all.

As she let herself into the cottage, closing the door firmly behind her, she let out a shaky breath. What was she still so afraid of? Simon clearly hadn't recognised her. And she had nothing to feel ashamed about, after all. What she was remembering had happened many, many years ago. It wasn't who she was now. All the same, she couldn't shake her sense of growing disquiet. That night, in some senses, had changed everything. That night had been the catalyst that had impacted so many things; had changed the relationship with her sister irrevocably. Simon Treloar, whether he remembered or not, had been part of that.

Unwilling to confront the memories that had lain buried for so long, Lizzie decided to make herself useful, as much as she could. Bee would appreciate some lunch, she was sure, so she thought she'd make a picnic to take back to the flower shop a bit later, when surely she wouldn't be unlucky enough to bump into Simon a third time.

This proved more difficult than she'd anticipated, with only one hand, but eventually she'd sorted out some sandwiches and packed them up with the punnet of strawberries she'd found in the fridge. Then, to rest up a little before heading back to the flower shop, she went to her room, where she'd left her phone, to check her messages.

As she'd anticipated, there were a couple of texts from her mother, wishing her a lovely stay with Bee, one from Paul, asking her to call him, and a voicemail from Georgina. She'd not spoken to her sister yet, so perhaps this was a good opportunity to put that right. She pressed play on the voicemail, and Georgina's slightly breathy voice filled the air.

'Hi, Lizzie-bobs! I hope you got to Aunt Bee's all right. Call me when you have a minute, and we'll arrange a proper catch-up. I have so much to tell you! You'll never believe what's been happening. I hope you're feeling better. Speak soon, bye!'

Lizzie tried not to wince. It was typical of Georgina to send her good wishes as an afterthought. She'd always been the same. Why would her sister having a car accident mean she behaved any differently? Then Lizzie chided herself. Georgina had her own busy life, after all. It wasn't entirely Georgina's fault that the two of them had become less close as adults than they'd been as teenagers. Lizzie had to take some responsibility for that. All the same, she was discombobulated enough at being back in Roseford without arranging a 'proper catch-up' with Georgina. She was feeling too battered to add that to the mix.

Mooching about in her room, Lizzie noticed the top of the built-in unit of cupboards in the corner was open slightly. She assumed Bee had grabbed the bedding out of it in a hurry, and forgotten to shut it back up, and so, more for the want of something to do than anything else, she figured she should close it. Bee was quite short, and would have to get up on a step stool to do it, whereas Lizzie was tall enough to do it if she reached, even with a broken collarbone.

As she pulled open the cupboard to make sure there was nothing getting in the way of it, she saw a plastic carrier bag obstructing the brass arm mechanism that lifted and closed the cupboard. Straining slightly, mindful of the sling on her arm, Lizzie pulled the carrier bag towards her. She intended only to move it out of the way, but the retro logo of some long-defunct high-street chain store made her smile. Trust Bee to cling onto even the daftest of items. Bee's house was neat and tidy, but only because she kept the clutter out of sight in the cupboards that adorned every room. From the weight of the bag, Lizzie guessed it contained old fabrics, probably clothes that Bee hadn't the heart to get rid of.

Lizzie knew she should just shove it back in the cupboard, but she was overwhelmed with curiosity. She'd seen pictures of Bee and Cordelia from back when they were younger and wondered if Bee still had some of the fabulous outfits she'd worn in the seventies and early eighties. Where her mother had been more sensible with her clothing choices, Bee loved vibrant colours and styles, and Lizzie had enjoyed going into her dressing-up box whenever she and Georgina had come to stay. Georgina had had more of an eye for fashion, but back when the sisters were each other's best friend, Lizzie had joined in, giggling at the bright geometric patterns on the fabrics of the dresses and tops, and trying on as many as they could get away with.

Bee might be older now, but her love of colour still persisted, and was expressed in her flower arrangements as well as her clothes. Lizzie was curious to see what she'd shoved in this old shopping bag, at the back of the cupboard.

Pulling out the first couple of items, which were the kind of colourful summer dresses Lizzie could imagine her aunt wearing, Lizzie held one of them up to herself and approached the mirror on the back of the bedroom door. She'd never been one for too much pattern or colour, but she could see the potential in the seventies summer maxi dress. Its ruched front would be easy to slip on while she still had the sling on her arm, too. She placed it carefully to one side and resolved to ask Bee if she could help her to try it on later.

Delving back into the bag, she found another frock. This one wasn't in colours that she was particularly fond of though, so, after a cursory glance, she popped it on the bed.

The final item was scrunched up tightly, and as Lizzie's fingers touched it, a shock of remembrance ran through her. The texture of the lambswool brought back a powerful memory, one that she'd managed to bury away for the past twenty or so years.

Gingerly, after taking a deep breath, she reached in again and carefully pulled the item out of the carrier bag. As it unfurled, her hand clenched reflexively. Why had Bee kept it? Why hadn't she just chucked it out? It smelled musty, having been at the bottom of a bag in a cupboard for so long, but it was completely unmistakeable. It was out of shape, and there was a pull on one sleeve that Lizzie remembered worrying at with agitated fingers. As she turned it over and examined the left arm, she found two small holes at the elbow. Almost without realising what she was doing, she brought it to her face and breathed deeply, but there was no longer any trace of the scent it had once. It just smelled of a long time in storage.

Bringing it down to the bed, she carefully smoothed it out, recalling the way it had felt, and the night that had led to it being in her possession. She still couldn't quite believe, after all the years that had passed, that she was looking at Simon Treloar's old, black, worn-out woollen jumper.

10

'Lizzie! Are you here?'

Bee's voice snapped Lizzie out of her reverie, and, feeling guilty for snooping, she hastily shoved Simon's jumper and the two dresses into the carrier bag, and threw it to the back of the cupboard. She knew she hadn't done anything wrong, really, but she still felt as though she had.

'I'm here,' she called back. Hurrying out of her room, she headed to the kitchen, where Bee already had the kettle on.

'I don't usually shut up shop for lunch, but I was worried about you when you left this morning,' Bee said as she turned briefly to smile in Lizzie's direction. 'Is your arm hurting still?'

Lizzie shook her head. 'No, it's the same old aches and pains.' She paused. Should she tell Bee why she'd left Roseford Blooms so summarily, after Simon Treloar had come in? Having discovered Simon's jumper, she felt even more confused.

'Oh, I see you've made some sandwiches already,' Bee said as she opened the fridge to get the milk for the tea. She pulled out the two cling-filmed packages and put them on the counter.

'I was going to bring them down to the shop,' Lizzie said, 'but I must've, er, lost track of time.'

Bee brought the sandwiches to the kitchen table and then poured two steaming mugs of tea.

'Right,' Bee said. 'Now, it goes without saying that you don't have to tell me anything you don't want to, but I'm pretty sure I know there's something on your mind, Elizabeth. So, if you want to talk about it, I'm here.'

Lizzie allowed herself a small smile. Bee had never beaten about the bush, but she'd also never aggressively pried into the lives of her nieces. She had that perfect balance of diplomacy and care that made Lizzie instinctively want to open up to her. But it was all too overwhelming at the moment; she couldn't be sure, in telling Bee what was on her mind, that she wasn't going to open an emotional can of worms.

'I appreciate that, Aunt Bee, I really do,' Lizzie began. 'Just being here is really helping, honestly.'

'Well, I'm glad about that,' Bee replied. 'But you can't hide down here forever. You're going to have to work out what to do next with your life.'

The sense of relief Lizzie felt at that moment almost floored her. Bee clearly hadn't picked up on her strange reaction to Simon Treloar, and obviously thought, not unreasonably, that her current malaise was down to the car accident and her change in professional and personal circumstances. These were the major issues in her life, after all, she thought, with a sudden, clearer sense of perspective. What did it matter about an old jumper and a bad night twenty-odd years ago?

'I've only been here two days, Aunt Bee.' Lizzie smiled more broadly. 'Are you trying to get rid of me already?'

'Of course not!' Bee exclaimed. 'You know you can stay here as long as you want to. I'm just worried about you, darling. I know things between you and your mother aren't always... *easy*... and I'm guessing you probably haven't really spoken to anyone about what's been happening to you.' She took a bite of her sandwich. 'This is marvellous, by the way.'

'Thank you,' Lizzie said. She took a nibble at her own, which, considering she'd prepared it with one hand, wasn't half bad. 'I've never been one to confide in people, you know that.'

'Unlike your sister.' Bee raised an eyebrow. Georgina, for all of her warmth and gregariousness, had some serious Ancient Mariner tendencies when it came to the drama in her own life, which had left little room for

Lizzie's problems. She'd improved with age, but Lizzie had learned, early on, to keep things to herself.

'Georgina was always better at talking things through,' Lizzie replied diplomatically.

'Your sister is an open book,' Bee said, and Lizzie saw the twinkle of amusement in her eyes as she took another sip of her tea. 'Unlike you.'

'I've never been the confiding type,' Lizzie said. Although it was strange, she reflected. Her marketing job had meant that she was always talking, nineteen to the dozen, about the products and services that Warner-Basset offered. But that was easy; those were her areas of expertise, built up from years of hard work and dedication. Talking about herself, her own emotions, was a totally different matter.

'Maybe it's time you learned,' Bee said. 'You've been through a great deal in these past few weeks. You can't pretend that it hasn't affected you. Talking about it will help you to move on.'

Lizzie shook her head. 'I don't know how,' she said quietly. 'I've always just sucked it up and got on with it. It's something Mum taught me to do, and it's a difficult habit to unlearn.'

'I can completely see that,' Bee replied. 'And it's all very well, but what *are* you going to do when your arm's fixed?'

'Honestly?' Lizzie gave a hollow laugh. 'I've got no idea. The sale of the business means I've got a lot of options, but I don't know if starting up on my own again is what I want. I've spent my whole career working in marketing. The problem is, I don't know what else I'm good for.'

Bee regarded her carefully. 'And the rest of it?'

'What do you mean?'

'Oh, Lizzie, you can't hide away from how you feel forever. You and Paul split up months ago. Don't you want to talk about it?'

Lizzie's temper flared. She knew it was irrational to be angry at Bee, but she really didn't want to face it now.

'I don't need to talk about it!' Lizzie retorted. 'What's done is done. There's no point brooding on it – on any of it.'

'That's what your uncle used to say,' Bee replied. 'And I don't think it's any coincidence that he dropped dead at forty-seven. You can't let things eat away at you, you know.'

'I'm sorry.' Lizzie knew how much Bee still missed her uncle Matthew, eighteen years after his passing. But she couldn't face another post-mortem of her own disrupted life. 'It's just that… if I talk about it, I'm worried I'll discover I haven't really moved on after all. I don't want it to hurt any more than it already does.'

Bee reached over and squeezed Lizzie's good hand. 'I know it doesn't feel that way right now, but you will heal. You've had a rough ride, these past few months, but time will play its part. It always does.'

Lizzie nodded. Time was the best healer: Bee was right about that. After all, she'd come back to Roseford, which had been the scene of such a horrible event in her teens, and, as a fully grown adult, she was enjoying being here, despite the past. And there was no question that getting away from the flat she'd shared with Paul was doing her a lot of good, too. *One step at a time*, she thought. *That's the only way to do it.*

'Have you spoken to Paul since the accident?' Bee asked.

Lizzie nodded. 'He rang me before I left hospital, and we actually had a civilised chat!' She smiled. 'Maybe the crash gave me a bit more perspective on everything, but after we spoke I felt as though I was able to move on a little more with things. I want to keep hold of that feeling, rather than keep revisiting everything that's happened recently. I don't want to retread old ground.'

'Well, I'm here if you do decide you want to talk more,' Bee said. 'Any time.'

Lizzie smiled again. 'You've done so much already, allowing me to stay here and get better. Keeping me out of Mum and Dad's hair.'

Bee smiled back. 'It was the least I could do.' She continued eating her sandwich, and then, when they were both finished, she took the plates to the dishwasher. 'Why don't you take a little walk over to Roseford Hall this afternoon? The fresh air would do you good. You haven't seen it since the British Heritage Fund restored it, have you?'

Lizzie shook her head, trying to still the slight speeding up of her heart at Bee's innocent suggestion. 'No, I haven't.' She forced a smile. 'Maybe I will.'

'I'm sure it'll make you feel better.' Bee smiled. She glanced at the kitchen clock. 'Now, I'd better get back to the shop. Don't forget to take the spare keys with you if you do decide to go out.'

'I won't,' Lizzie replied. As she said goodbye to Bee, she shook her head. Roseford Hall wasn't a place she was going to rush back to in a hurry, despite her philosophical approach about recent events. She might be feeling better for being here at Aunt Bee's house, but she wasn't sure she was ready to test that theory any further yet. Seeing Simon Treloar, and then finding his old jumper, had been enough reminders for one day.

But she did feel as though she needed a little fresh air. Perhaps she should take herself off for a stroll? She didn't need to go near Roseford Hall, after all. She could just walk, and see where her feet took her. There were enough pretty places to visit in the village, and she was sure she'd be able to pass an hour or two exploring the place. It wouldn't do her any good to mope in Bee's cottage for the whole of her stay. And if she kept her distance from Roseford Hall, hopefully she wouldn't run the risk of bumping into Simon Treloar for the third time that day.

11

The post, Simon reflected, seemed to come later and later these days. It also didn't help that his personal mail was delivered in the same round as that for the British Heritage Fund. Often, the lovely but slightly overworked admin staff didn't get round to sorting it until late in the day, if at all, so he had taken to dropping by the office and picking up his post as and when he could.

That afternoon, as he rifled through the newest bundle of letters, most of which appeared to be either marketing shots or bills, he was brought up short by the name, logo and crest of a place that he'd thought he'd left behind years ago. Stopping halfway up the old servants' stairwell, which led to the offices at the rear of the building, he slid his thumb underneath the flap of the thick white envelope, drew a deep breath and pulled out the letter inside.

Over the years he'd received the odd missive, mainly requesting a donation, but as he unfolded the letter he noticed that there was a small cream card tucked into it this time. His hands started to shake as he took in the details on the card.

He'd sworn after he'd left that he'd never, ever, go back to that place. Just the thought of crossing the threshold once more was enough to send him into an anxiety spiral. But it had been over twenty years, for heaven's sake! Surely he should be over all this by now? Realising he was still frozen to the spot halfway up the staircase, he hurried back to his small office so that he could give this piece of correspondence his full attention. Closing his door firmly, he delayed the inevitable a little longer by pouring himself a mug of coffee from the flask on his desk. But then, the moment could be forestalled no longer.

He sat back down at his desk and looked at the details.

At first the invitation seemed benign enough:

Cross Dean Independent Boys' School requests the pleasure of your company at a reunion for old scholars. Black tie essential.
RSVP

He should ignore it. He didn't need the additional stress, with the first wedding in the Roseford Hall chapel at the start of August. And chances were, the school fund reps would try to do a number on him for a dona- tion to the coffers. The thought of that made him laugh out loud. As if he, the lord without a manor, had any extra cash to funnel to an institution he'd loathed nearly every minute of attending! But there was a part of him that was curious. It *had* been over twenty years, after all. Some little masochistic side of his psyche wanted to see if the place still had the power to hurt him, to make him afraid. Although, he reflected, that was hardly the most sensible reason to contemplate accepting the invitation, was it?

Simon shuddered as he remembered how, day after day, pretty much from the moment he'd unpacked his school trunk, that group of rowdy, self-confident boys had made his life a misery. How he used to have to sleep in his shoes so they didn't get pinched from under his bed at night in the lower-school dorm. How they'd laughed at his attempts to fight back, since he was never quick enough to gain the upper hand. And how, seven years later, he'd walked out of the school gates and never looked back.

Until now.

Over two decades on, things were different, weren't they?

'Hello-o-o...'

A voice broke into his reverie as he realised he'd been sitting, staring at the invitation in his hand, for a few minutes.

'Come in, Mum,' he said hurriedly, just at the moment that Margaret Treloar's head popped around the office door.

'Everything all right?' Margaret said. Her direct grey eyes missed very little, for better or worse, and despite the fact that they no longer lived under the same roof, Margaret having taken up residence in one of the cottages on the estate a few years back, she still prided herself on being attuned to her children's moods, and being a regular presence in their lives.

Simon quickly assumed what he hoped was a neutral expression. 'Fine,' he said, slipping the letter and the invitation under the notepad on his desk.

'I'm just checking to see if you had the updated guest list for the wedding,' Margaret replied. 'I need to send final numbers over to the caterer by the end of the day.' Because of the nature of the business some of the guests were in, although most of the RSVPs had been returned months ago, there were always going to be a few who couldn't confirm until the last minute. Margaret Treloar, with her keen eye for organisation, had volunteered to collate the late responses, and so far she'd proved a capable pair of hands.

'Um, yes, I think so.' Simon fumbled in a Manilla folder on his desk. 'Bear with me a sec.'

While Simon busied himself looking for the information, he could feel his mother's gaze upon him. 'Did you have any breakfast this morning?' she asked. 'You look a little peaky.'

'I'm fine, Ma,' Simon said hurriedly. The last person he wanted to discuss the invitation to Cross Dean with was his mother. She'd never found out just how miserable his school years had been, and he didn't see the point in enlightening her now, decades after the fact. And she'd only try to convince him to go. She was a lover of all things nostalgic, and viewed Cross Dean as the kind of place one *should* be nostalgic about. Simon, however, couldn't have felt more differently.

As Margaret chatted lightly about her grandchildren's latest exploits, Simon did what he usually did, and smiled and nodded. But he felt distinctly off balance. He should just chuck the invitation in the bin and have done with it. He didn't need to go back to Cross Dean. But there was that small voice inside his head wondering if by facing his demons, he might lay them to rest once and for all.

'Well, I can't stand here nattering all day,' Margaret Treloar said, forcing Simon to zone back into the conversation. 'Come over for dinner later in the week? I've got some fresh lamb from the local farm that needs cooking and it's far too much for just me.'

Simon smiled at his mother. She was forever trying to feed him up, even though he was nearly forty. 'Thanks. I'd like that. I'll ring you.'

As she said goodbye and left his office, Simon's smile faded. Deciding that a walk to clear his head was in order, he tucked the letter and invitation into his back pocket. He needed to check the chapel over again, anyway, to ensure that the information he'd sent the BHF about it was correct. The way they'd stuck their oar in over the wedding, it felt as if one inaccurate fact could jeopardise the event, or even cancel it altogether. He didn't want to be responsible for that; he knew Serena and Montana would be devastated. They'd waited so long to get married, he wanted to make everything as perfect for their big day as he could.

The sun was shining as he crossed the broad sweep of lawn at the front of Roseford Hall, taking the main route to the chapel at the southern end of the grounds. When the chapel was fully open to the public, this would be the acceptable way to get to it, although it could also be reached from one of the quieter streets in the village, where it lay beyond a large field. As he walked, Simon was pleased to see today's visitors enjoying a wonderful day out. He'd got used to seeing the crowds exploring his family home in the three years since Roseford Hall had been open to the public, and while, at times, he wished it were still his family's own private haven, it was in much better shape now than it had been when it had been in Treloar hands. And, most importantly, would remain so long after the last member of the family had shuffled off this mortal coil.

He began to approach the chapel, noting, as he walked, that some of the path needed mending. It wouldn't do to have tourists coming a cropper. Rounding the side of the chapel, making his way to the front door, he suddenly caught sight of a familiar-looking figure coming across the field from the village entrance to the chapel's grounds. She turned in his direction and he saw the arm in the sling, and the slight summer breeze lifting her dark hair away from her face as she crossed the grassy flat. She, too, seemed to be heading towards the chapel. Curious, he paused for a moment to watch her, and had a stronger feeling that he *had* met her before.

12

Lizzie was in no hurry as she ambled through the kissing gate that led, after a large sweep of field, to Roseford Chapel. She'd made her way down the village's main street, still uncertain as to whether she should cross the threshold of the hall again, but in the end deciding that, short of going back to Roseford Blooms and inflicting herself on Bee once again, or eating even more cake at Roseford Café, there weren't really that many other options. She wasn't in the mood for shopping, despite the many independent shops that seemed to have sprung up on the main street, and she really could do with the fresh air.

Funny, she thought, how things just came back to you. She could make out the impressive frontage of Roseford Hall in the distance behind the chapel, but she had to admit the whole village was looking smarter, its wild, abandoned beauty having been tamed by an army of employees and volunteers from the British Heritage Fund over the past few years into something a lot more manageable. The manicured hedges of the estate and closely cropped lawns, now populated by tourists. A civilised air. A sense that it was being preserved for the future, rather than falling into genteel decay. Lizzie was in no doubt that, should she venture into the house itself, she would find it completely different, too. But she wasn't quite ready to do that.

Today, a walk in the gardens and a quick peek at the chapel would be enough.

The sun was at full strength now, and Lizzie felt its warmth on her back. She wished she'd put on a T-shirt to stop her shoulders burning, instead of the strappy top, but she still had limited mobility when she raised her arms. Moving to the shade of the large oak trees that stood sentry along the edge of the field, she ambled along, catching glimpses of tourists in the Roseford Hall gardens playing with giant wooden versions of Connect 4, draughts and a rather large chessboard on the vast expanse of lawn. Off in the far corner, in the shadow of another gigantic oak tree, she could just make out a game of croquet being played. Roseford had _Bridgerton_ to thank for that, she thought.

She was so caught up in her observations, it was a few seconds before she recognised a familiar figure heading to the chapel from the lawns of the house. Simon Treloar. Was there no way to avoid the man? Immediately, her mood began to sink again. Surely this blessed estate was big enough that she shouldn't have to run into him everywhere she went? And, oh, Christ, he was heading straight for her.

'Hi,' he said as he approached. 'I, er, thought I recognised you.'

'What was your first clue?' Lizzie smiled briefly, and raised her arm slightly. The smile, though, vanished as quickly as it had appeared. She really wasn't in the mood for conversation, and especially not with Simon.

'How are you feeling?'

'I'm fine, thanks. You?' Lizzie's reply sounded perfunctory, even to her own ears.

'I, er, was just on my way to check out the chapel,' Simon said. 'Pre-wedding stuff, you know.'

'Oh, yes.' Lizzie regarded him curiously. 'Are you prepared for the paparazzi invasion that this place is bound to get, with that particular couple and their guest list?'

Simon laughed. 'There'll be security on the entrances, but you're right, the happy couple has a whole army of friends who'll make this sleepy old estate look like Oscars night!' A look of concern crossed his face as he said this, as if he was worried about being indiscreet about the wedding to a total stranger.

'Don't worry.' Lizzie found herself smiling at him. 'I'll keep quiet.' She felt a little flutter in her stomach as Simon smiled back at her.

'Sorry,' he replied. 'I suppose I'm on edge about it all. Serena and Montana have been great about everything; if anything, it's the bloody British Heritage Fund who keep throwing spanners in the works with their compliance demands and their acres of rules about what we can and can't do. I have to keep reminding myself that it's not my estate any more, and they're the ones who are in charge.'

'Sounds like a real hardship.' Lizzie's tone was laced with sarcasm, and she was unsurprised and a little ashamed when Simon's expression shut down immediately.

'I'm sorry,' she said quickly. 'That was unfair. My arm still bothers me when the painkillers wear off.' She raised her wrist an inch to emphasise the point. 'It's making me a bit snappy.'

'Apology accepted.' Simon was smiling again. 'Under the circumstances, I think you're allowed to be a bit grumpy.' He paused. 'Bee said you'd had a car accident?'

'Yeah,' Lizzie replied. 'The culmination of a lousy couple of months. The icing on the proverbial cake.'

Simon grinned. 'Don't mention cake – the one for the wedding has six tiers. Six!'

They stood, rather awkwardly, where their paths had crossed, about fifty metres from the chapel itself. Lizzie, who was torn between wanting to get away from Simon and, weirdly, wanting to keep talking to him, felt in a quandary. She'd deliberately come this way to avoid the possibility of bumping into too many people and now here Simon was, making conversation with her.

'Well, I'll leave you to your walk,' Simon said eventually. Lizzie was surprised to see how awkward he looked. She remembered him as a lanky, slightly shy teenager, but when she'd seen him earlier, he'd seemed much more self-assured. 'Unless, er, you wanted a quick peek at the chapel? Bee's been in a fair bit to work out where best to put the arrangements for the wedding, so you're welcome to come and see it, too.'

Lizzie hesitated. She'd quite enjoyed the chat with Simon, and she was curious to see the interior of the chapel that would be holding the so-called 'wedding of the year'. What harm could a quick look do?

'Thank you,' she said, after another pause. 'I'd like that.'

They began walking towards the chapel again, Lizzie falling into step easily beside Simon. She was long-legged, and their strides matched well.

'So, are you enjoying being back in Roseford?' Simon asked as they neared the chapel.

Lizzie's heart gave a little lurch. 'So far so good,' she said, after a beat. 'It's changed a bit since I was here last.'

'Did you ever come to the hall when you stayed before?' Simon asked. 'It looked a bit different back then!'

Lizzie, shook her head. 'No,' she said quickly. 'Georgina and I didn't really do much while we were here. Mainly just spent time at Bee's place.' The lie, while it felt essential, didn't sit well with her. But it was too late now.

Simon looked quizzically at her, as if he was trying to work something out. But, obviously thinking better of saying anything, he just shook his head. 'Well, I hope you enjoy your stay. The hall's worth a visit if you get a free afternoon.'

'I'll bear that in mind,' Lizzie replied. Eager to move the conversation on, she paused at the entrance to the chapel. 'Are you sure it's all right for me to go in?'

'Be my guest,' Simon replied. 'I've got to do a few checks anyway.' He pushed open the heavy oak door of the chapel, holding it as she moved through.

As Lizzie stepped inside the cool, quiet building, she swore she could feel Simon's eyes following her. She wondered if and when he'd work out where exactly they'd met before. And she didn't have a clue what to say to him when he did.

Before she could dwell on this any longer, though, a piercing, rather patrician voice called out across the chapel. 'Excuse me!' it said, echoing around the empty space. 'The chapel isn't open to tourists. I'm afraid you'll have to leave.'

For the second time that day, Lizzie froze, jolted back twenty years at the sound of that voice. It had changed slightly over the decades, but there was no mistaking it. She reached out and grabbed the back of the nearest pew for support with her good hand.

'It's all right, sis, she's with me.' Simon's voice, close behind her, made Lizzie jump.

No, no, no! screamed the voice in Lizzie's head, although she was frozen to the spot. This was all too much. As if coming back here weren't hard enough, she now had come face to face with Sarah bloody Treloar.

13

As Sarah Treloar walked up the aisle of the chapel towards her, Lizzie felt a burst of adrenaline that nearly made her knees give way. Twenty years rolled back immediately, when she found herself being approached by one of the girls who'd made her life such a misery at school. In that moment, she kicked herself for thinking that she could come back to Roseford and not see Sarah. What the hell had she been thinking? Painkillers had a lot to answer for, as did the smack in the face from the airbag when she'd crashed the car.

'Sarah, this is Lizzie, Bee Clatworthy's niece.' Simon, seemingly oblivious to Lizzie's sudden change in demeanour, approached them both.

Sarah regarded Lizzie with the same quizzical look that Simon had, before she smiled. 'Oh, yes. We were at school together, weren't we? How are you?'

'Fine, thanks,' Lizzie stammered. She tried to pull herself together. She was an adult now, not the shy teenager she'd once been, although telling herself that didn't seem to be helping.

'So what brings you to Roseford?' Sarah, oblivious to the effect that she was having on Lizzie, ploughed on. 'Are you staying long?'

'I, er, don't know yet,' Lizzie replied. She tried to still her breathing. Sarah obviously didn't remember Lizzie as well as Lizzie remembered her.

'Well, give Bee my best,' Sarah replied. 'She's been a miracle worker with the flowers for the wedding.'

'I will.'

Lizzie, not knowing whether to excuse herself or not, made do with walking away a little to peruse, with great concentration, the stained-glass window at the back of the chapel. It gave her a few precious moments to collect her thoughts. She could hear Simon and Sarah checking in with each other about the latest wedding plans, and as she mooched around the chapel, taking in the sights and scents of the beautifully restored building, her heartbeat began to return to normal. Much like Simon, Sarah clearly had no memory of her. It was funny, she thought, how an event could have such a huge impact on one person, but barely register in the lives of others.

Just as she was sidling towards the chapel door, suddenly feeling in need of some fresh air, Sarah's voice broke her carefully constructed bubble.

'Oh, I remember now! Georgina's your sister, isn't she?'

Lizzie spun around, feeling the weight of Sarah's seemingly casual words.

'Yes,' she said calmly. 'She is.'

Something about the tone of Lizzie's voice stopped Sarah in her tracks, and the polite enquiry about Georgina seemed to die in the air between the two women.

Lizzie turned back to Simon. 'I should go,' she said. 'Thank you for letting me take a look around.'

And abruptly, she turned on her heel and strode out of the chapel.

Once outside, she picked up the pace as best she could, but she was in need of some more painkillers, and the uneven momentum made her bones ache.

'Lizzie!' Simon's voice called after her. 'Wait, I'll walk you back.'

Lizzie didn't respond. She tried to speed up, but she felt clumsy and off balance and she didn't notice the slightly raised paving slab until it shifted under her feet and she felt herself falling. Her ankle turned and, with a yell, she hit the ground.

'Christ! Lizzie, are you all right?' Simon had made up the ground between them in the time it took her to go over, and he knelt down beside her, a look of concern etched on his features. 'Did you hurt your arm again?'

Lizzie's breath was coming in short gasps, and she struggled to regulate it. The thought of doing any more damage to herself had sent her into even more of a tailspin. Sucking in great gulps of air, she shook her head. 'No,' she managed. 'My arm's OK. I'm just a bit wobbly on my feet at the moment.'

'Can you stand?' Simon's deep blue eyes regarded her with open concern. 'Let's get you a cup of tea somewhere more comfortable, shall we?' He offered her his hand, and pulled her gently to her feet. His touch was warm, and she felt reassured as he helped her up. He glanced at her, and then gently released her hand as she found her feet again. 'Take it steady now,' he said, his expression still showing concern.

'No damage, I mean, no *more* damage done,' Lizzie said. She gave a nervous laugh. 'Thank you for coming to my rescue.'

'Look, can I buy you a coffee?' Simon asked as they walked. 'That was quite a fall you took, and it doesn't feel right just to let you walk away on your own after that.'

They were drawing close to the small tea and coffee concession that stood at one corner of the manicured lawns to the front entrance of Roseford Hall. Lizzie was aware that they were getting closer to the house, but she tried to put it out of her mind. She smiled quickly at Simon. 'I'd like that. Thanks.'

'Take a seat,' Simon said, gesturing to one of the benches nearby. 'I'll grab us a couple of coffees. How do you like yours?'

In a few minutes, Simon had placed a large takeaway cup in front of her. Lizzie picked it up and took a careful sip. 'Thank you.'

'You're welcome.' Simon glanced at her, then back out across the lawn, where more and more tourists were congregating. She tried to read his expression, but it was carefully neutral. Then he looked back at her, and she saw his eyes soften with concern.

'So...' He paused.

'So?' Lizzie asked. 'That sounds like a question.'

Simon smiled. 'I'm sorry. It's probably none of my business, but you seemed a little jumpy when you were talking to Sarah in the chapel. Is everything all right?'

To stall for a little more time, Lizzie took another sip of her coffee. When she put the cup down, though, Simon was still regarding her with that gentle stare.

'We were at Craven House School together,' Lizzie began. 'I was surprised she didn't recognise me straight away, to be honest. But I suppose there were a lot of girls in our year, and we did come from all over the country.'

'A lot can change in twenty years,' Simon replied. 'I mean, for instance, I haven't always been the suave, sophisticated fella you see before you!' He laughed, undercutting his words with a self-deprecating grin.

Lizzie smiled back at him. 'That's certainly true. Two decades can change a lot.'

'So, you and your sister knew Sarah at school, then?' Simon shook his head. 'I'm sorry... Sarah had a lot of friends back to the house over the years during the school holidays. I didn't pay a great deal of attention to them when I was at home. I was nineteen and *terribly* serious!'

Thinking carefully before she spoke again, Lizzie opted for a neutral approach. 'My sister, Georgina, she was a friend of Sarah's back then. George and I were born within a year of each other. She was older by eleven months. Dad used to joke that the school fees were two for the price of one because of it. I wasn't sure who he thought should have been chucked in as the freebie.'

'It can be rough being in someone's shadow,' Simon replied. 'I went to the same school as generations of my family had. The expectation weighs heavily.'

'It does.' Lizzie paused before continuing. 'Your sister was in the same year as us. She was great mates with Georgina all through year ten and year eleven. Then, suddenly, they stopped hanging out together. In sixth form they barely spoke. Boy trouble, I think.'

'That's why Sarah didn't recognise you straight away,' Simon replied.

Lizzie nodded. 'I recognised her though.' *How could I not?* she added to herself. She thought of the jumper in the carrier bag at Bee's house, wondered if now was the time to elaborate. But then, what good would it do? Pulling herself together with an effort, and taking a large gulp of coffee, Lizzie stood up. 'You've got better things to do than listen to me all day.' She forced a smile. 'Haven't you got loads to organise for the wedding of the year?'

Simon had scrambled to his feet as soon as he'd seen Lizzie move. 'It's been nice talking to you, Lizzie,' he said. 'If you wanted another chat while you're here in Roseford, it would be lovely to see you again. But perhaps without the fall, next time!'

The kindness in his voice made Lizzie want to cry. Simon's gentle nature still seemed the same as it had been twenty years ago. With an effort, she pulled herself away from that particular mental pitfall.

'Thank you, Simon,' she said softly. 'I think I'd like that.'

She looked into his eyes, and saw such understanding there that for a moment she wondered if perhaps he knew more than he was letting on. He certainly seemed to empathise. 'Thank you for the coffee, and for picking me up off the ground,' she said.

Unsure what else to say, she settled for, 'I'll see you around.' And with that, she walked quickly over the grass and out of the Roseford Hall gates, determinedly keeping the hall itself out of her line of sight.

14

Lizzie hurried back up the main street. She'd come so close to levelling with Simon about the tangled mess that passed for her emotions, but something held her back. After all these years, it seemed pointless to go back over it. And it would only cause friction between Simon and Sarah, which, in spite of her feelings towards Sarah, was the last thing she wanted to do. She just had to let things go. Coming back to Roseford might not have been a great idea, especially in her current state, but there were plenty of positives about being here. Not least, spending some time with Bee.

With this in mind, she headed towards Roseford Blooms. Even if she couldn't be of much practical help to her aunt, she might be able to do something in the shop. She'd always found Bee's little store calming; being around flowers, their fresh, meadowy smell, seemed to do something to relax her. As a teenager, when Georgina had been out and about in Roseford, meeting friends and socialising, Lizzie had preferred to be at Roseford Blooms, watching Bee putting exquisite bouquets and arrangements together while she devoured one of the many novels she'd brought down with her to pass the hours. She hoped that a little time spent in the shop now might ease her thoughts.

Bee looked up from the bouquet she was arranging as Lizzie walked through the door. 'Hello, love,' she said. 'Fresh air do you good?'

Lizzie smiled crookedly. 'Sort of.' She looked around at the shop, breathed deeply and felt the atmosphere washing over her. 'Just thought I'd pop by and see if there was anything I could help with.'

'I've just finished the last bouquet of the day – a chap's coming along to pick it up in a little while – but you can check the buckets and see if anything needs getting rid of or freshening up if you like.' Bee expertly wrapped a cone of light green paper around the bouquet, then taped it and secured it with a cream-coloured length of ribbon. She was so practised at it that she barely needed to look as she ran her scissors, flat side down, over the ends of the ribbon to curl them.

'I love watching you do that.' Lizzie sighed. Watching Bee was like seeing one of those videos on YouTube that showed processes like piping hot sticks of rock being formed, or toothpaste being squeezed out of tubes.

'Years of repetition,' Bee replied briskly, sweeping the discarded stems into the compost bin behind the counter.

Lizzie began checking the buckets. Even with one hand, she managed to pull out a few wilting stems. She ran her eyes over the different varieties on display: roses, freesias, sprigs of baby's breath for contrast and texture, all releasing their scents like nature's perfume counter. Pulling out a couple of blooms that were past their best, she transferred them to her other hand, and eventually had weeded out any that wouldn't cut it in an arrangement.

'Thanks, love,' Bee said. 'You always did look in your element with the flowers. Takes me back to when you were younger when you used to spend time in here.'

Lizzie smiled. 'I liked it. I remember you taught me how to make a passable posy, too. Not that I was any good at it.' She sighed. 'I didn't have the same knack you do.'

'Handling flowers is like dealing with people,' Bee said. 'You take what you know, you observe and you listen, and then you add in what you feel.'

Lizzie laughed. 'You make it sound so simple.'

Bee regarded her shrewdly. 'I never said it was easy,' she said. 'But you learn to read flowers and people just as effectively, after a while.'

Lizzie glanced away from her aunt's searching look. She tried to focus on the flowers, and felt that old familiar calm washing over her.

The shrill ring of the landline in the shop broke into her thoughts. Bee swiftly answered it, and took what sounded like a last-minute order. Replacing the receiver, she glanced back at Lizzie. 'Do you feel up to lending a hand with a quick bouquet?'

Lizzie grinned and waved her good hand. 'I've only really got the one at the moment, but you're welcome to it.'

'Right, OK, then.' Bee looked thoughtful for a long moment. 'We can start with a centrepiece of Lavender Lassie and a couple of Jeanne de Montfort, and then build up with some lavender and a couple of the Phoenix Rosa.' She looked expectantly at Lizzie.

Lizzie burst out laughing. 'Can you just run that by me again? And perhaps point to the ones you want? I'm not great on names.'

Bee smiled back. 'That purple one there,' she began. 'And we'll add two sprigs of the white delicate one, that's the baby's breath. And then three deep purple heads... that's the ticket.'

Gradually, Lizzie collected the blooms from the buckets and carefully laid them down on Bee's counter. 'Here you go,' she said.

Bee looked up at her. 'Let's see how much you can remember,' she said softly.

Lizzie remembered the little lessons Bee had tried to teach her years ago. Remarks about colour and texture, as well as scent. As well as how, sometimes, when you knew the rules, you should feel free to bend them a little, in pursuit of something beautiful. For Bee, flowers were a lifelong passion, and it was in these moments that Lizzie could begin to understand that.

'I haven't done this for so long,' Lizzie protested. 'What if I get it wrong?'

'You won't,' Bee replied, then, with a twinkle in her eye, 'and if you do, I'm right here to tweak it.'

Lizzie took a deep breath and focused on the long, elegant stems in front of her. With only one working arm, she'd need Bee's help anyway. She ran a fingertip over the soft, voluptuous petals of one of the roses, tracking down the outside and to the stem. She felt excited about creating something beautiful with the roses as the centrepiece.

'I trimmed the stems this morning, so you should be all right to put them together, then we'll tidy up any that need sorting out at the end.'

Lizzie nodded, lost in the richness of the colours of the flowers. Gradually, piece by piece, flower by flower, the idea she had for the small bouquet took shape, until she'd put them together in an arrangement that she hoped would work. The deep purple Lavender Lassies and crimson Phoenix Rosas were at the centre, then the Jeanne de Montforts, a wilder-looking hedgerow-type rose, formed a protective loop around them, finished with sprigs of lavender and baby's breath. She took a step back after about ten minutes to see how it looked.

'Very pretty,' Bee said as she drew in to look at Lizzie's attempt. 'Although I think I'd have popped the de Montforts in a little tighter. Shall we try it?'

Lizzie nodded, happy to take the constructive criticism.

'Considering I've not done this since I was at school, I'm pleased,' she said. She felt soothed, at peace and as though all of the thoughts that had been spiralling in her brain that afternoon had been stilled in the act of arranging the flowers.

'I'll wrap and put the ribbon on, if you like,' Bee said. 'The customer'll be in in a minute to collect them.'

Lizzie stepped back to allow Bee to get to the counter, and as she did so the shop door opened. 'Ah, speak of the devil.' Bee smiled as the customer walked in.

For the umpteenth time that day, Lizzie's heart did a little lurch, but this time it was because the man coming through the door was a very famous face indeed.

'Hello, Finn!' Bee called. 'It's good to see you back in Roseford. How was filming?'

Giving her aunt a smile that Lizzie remembered beaming out of her TV set when she was in her early twenties, Finn Sanderson, movie star and former teen singing sensation, was quick to reply. 'Really good, thanks, Mrs Clatworthy. I'm glad to be home, though.'

'I'm sure you are,' Bee replied. Turning to Lizzie, Bee introduced her to Finn. 'I don't think you two have met yet, have you?' She furrowed her brow. 'So many comings and goings for this wedding, I've quite forgotten.'

'Er, no, we haven't,' Lizzie replied. 'It's nice to meet you.'

'You too.' Finn smiled down at her. He then caught sight of the bouquet.

'That's perfect. Thank you so much for putting it together at such short notice.'

'You're welcome,' Bee replied.

'Lucy's mom'll love it,' Finn said. 'It's her birthday and we'd ordered a present using Amazon Prime, but it hasn't arrived yet, and she's coming for dinner this evening, so these are great.'

It felt so strange to hear Finn Sanderson talking about such mundane things as Amazon Prime, but, Lizzie supposed, even movie stars had to get their presents from somewhere.

'Well, you wish her a happy birthday from me,' Bee said.

'I will.'

As Finn paid for the flowers, Lizzie couldn't help glancing at him every so often. Although he had aged since he was at the height of his fame, he still had those film-star looks and that wonderful charisma. Lucy was a lucky woman indeed.

Staring at Finn's back as he left the shop, Bee turned to Lucy with a grin. 'Fancy, the first bouquet you've made in twenty years being for Finn Sanderson. Must be fate.'

'I'd never have done it if you'd told me who it was for,' Lizzie replied. 'I mean, what if I'd made a terrible one?'

'You wouldn't have,' Bee said. 'And if you had, I wouldn't have let it leave the shop anyway.'

Lizzie laughed. 'Well, it all turned out well in the end, at least.' She couldn't dispute that she felt a whole lot better now than she had when she'd walked into Roseford Blooms. If only all the solutions to her problems were quite as simple.

15

'Finn! It's great to see you again!' Simon hadn't had much time to ruminate on the conversation with Lizzie, as that afternoon he was meeting his good friend Finn Sanderson to go over some last-minute wedding plans. Finn had a permanent base in Roseford with his fiancée, Lucy Cameron, who owned Roseford Café. He'd taken a couple of weeks' leave before his next movie project in order to provide help and support for his best friend, Montana de Santo, as she married the love of her life. He'd flown back from Los Angeles, where he'd been second assistant director on a film shoot, the night before, and now, determinedly throwing off the jet lag, he was bright and breezy and raring to get back into the swing of things in Roseford.

'It's great to see you too, man,' Finn replied. He stuck out a hand and Simon shook it warmly. They'd met outside the Treloar Arms, the local pub, and headed inside for a drink. Finn, Simon observed, was looking happy and content. A few grey streaks had appeared in his dark brown hair, and he'd put on a couple of extra pounds since he'd filmed the smash-hit Christmas movie, *A Countess for Christmas*, a couple of years back, but it all suited him. Finn and Simon had become firm friends when they'd met while Finn was shooting the film. Despite the fact that Simon had had absolutely no clue who Finn was, the first time he'd met him, the two men had hit it off and been friends ever since. Now, with Finn happily in a long-term relationship with Lucy, the two men got together as often as they could for a drink and a catch-up. Simon was particularly pleased that Finn was on hand as a kind of mediator for the wedding; Finn and Montana went back years, and if anyone could communicate effectively with her, it was Finn.

'So, how've you been?' Finn asked, once they'd got their drinks and walked out to the small beer garden at the back of the pub.

'Oh, not bad,' Simon replied. He smiled ruefully. 'Don't tell Montana, but I don't think I'm cut out to be a wedding planner!'

Finn laughed. 'I bet you'll be glad when it's all over.'

'It's certainly been a learning experience, and no mistake.'

'So not something you think you'll go into as a career, then?'

'Definitely not!'

They drank their pints in momentary silence. 'Although,' Simon added, 'I do like the idea of making my mark on Roseford Hall again in some way. Definitely not weddings, though! Next time, the BHF can take care of that side of things.'

'Must be weird for you,' Finn replied. 'I mean, Roseford Hall was your family home. Do you really think you could hand over the reins entirely some day?'

'Oh, I don't know,' Simon said. 'Sometimes the thought of just walking away feels so tempting, I can't work out why I'm still mired here. Then I think about all of those bloody ancestors and I wonder if I've really got the balls to be the one who lets them down.'

'You wouldn't be letting them down. And you can't stay in the past forever,' Finn said reasonably. 'There must be a compromise you can reach.' He sipped his pint. 'If weddings aren't your thing, then how about some kind of event planning you could get your teeth into? Plenty of festivals happening through the year. Perhaps Roseford could have its own?'

Simon nearly choked on his pint. 'Are you serious? I can't imagine thousands of tents pitched on the grounds. Have you seen the state they leave places in? The BHF would never wear it on their land.'

'Doesn't have to be thousands,' Finn said. 'You could start small, keep control of it. Might give you something to concentrate on, rather than just moping inside your bit of the house, wishing you still owned the whole thing.'

'Who says I've been moping?' Simon said indignantly.

Finn grinned. 'Lucy likes to keep an eye on you.'

'Anyway,' Simon said hurriedly, 'I don't have the contacts for that sort of thing. I wouldn't know where to start.'

'That's what PR and marketing companies are for,' Finn explained patiently. 'And...' he paused mischievously '... I'm sure I could find you a few acts for the inaugural festival, if you wanted me to.'

'What, you'd make a return to the stage?' Simon chuckled. 'I thought you were over all that.'

'It'd hardly be Wembley Arena,' Finn replied. 'If you seriously wanted to get a festival off the ground, I'm sure Montana and I could do a set of our old songs for you.'

Simon was touched. 'Thanks, Finn,' he said. He looked down into his pint briefly. He knew just how much courage Finn would have to muster to sing in public again, and he felt oddly emotional that his friend would do that for him. Apart from one karaoke song in the Treloar Arms a couple of Christmases ago, Finn hadn't sung anywhere but the shower since his days in the smash-hit teen-musical drama *High School Dreams*. He'd developed a bit of a phobia of it, in fact, so Simon knew what a big step it would be.

'Look, man, just give it some thought, OK?' Finn looked Simon straight in the eyes. 'I know how tough it can be when you don't know where you fit. I've been lucky; since that Christmas movie, my life, and my career, have finally fallen into place. I'm now directing my own films, which is a dream I never thought I had the right to have. And meeting Lucy has changed my life in so many ways. Sometimes you just have to take a leap, even if you don't know what's on the other side.'

'I wish I was as brave as you!' Simon smiled back at Finn. He thought, suddenly, of Lizzie Warner, who had come to Roseford alone, and clearly had some of her own dragons to slay.

'You look like you're miles away,' Finn observed. 'Something else on your mind?'

Simon paused. He wasn't quite sure how to reply. He'd enjoyed his coffee with Lizzie that afternoon. In her he'd sensed a kindred spirit, although he wasn't quite sure why. He was intrigued, still, by her response to Sarah in the chapel, and he felt there was more to the story than Lizzie had told him. More than that, though, he'd felt a kind of protectiveness towards her, and he'd definitely like the chance to get to know her better.

Realising he still hadn't answered Finn, he shook his head. 'Ignore me. I'm just being maudlin. I haven't slept too well lately.'

'Well, you know where I am if you need to talk.' Finn finished his pint and then glanced up at the clock on the far wall of the pub. 'I'd better get going. Lucy's mom's coming over tonight for dinner and I said I'd help out.'

'It must be handy having you around to grab things from the top of the kitchen cupboards!' Simon joked. Finn was a little over six feet four.

Finn laughed. 'She puts me to work when I'm back home, yeah.'

Home. Although it clearly filled Finn with happiness, being back in Roseford, the place he now called home, for Simon it felt like a yoke. He'd got to snap himself out of this funk.

'I mean it. Call me if you need to talk.' Finn's face was serious again as they both rose from the table. 'And think about what I said. Perhaps an event here might be a good thing for you to consider.'

'Thanks, mate. I will,' Simon replied. But even as he said it he felt the weight of ten generations of Treloars pressing down on him from their exalted positions, and he wondered if he'd ever get out from underneath their influence.

16

The next days drifted by for Lizzie in a peaceful haze of sunny mornings, the scent of flowers and a real chance to rest and recuperate. Making that bouquet in Bee's shop had altered something: instead of trying to rationalise what had happened to her, both in the past and over the most recent few months, she kept going back to the peace and calm she'd felt when she was putting those flowers together. It was so different from how she normally spent her time, and it had given her an insight into how and why Bee had based her working life in the flower shop. The contrast between working with the flowers and her old life in marketing couldn't have been more pronounced.

At the same time, though, she couldn't help thinking about how Bee could broaden the reach of her business – after all, she was providing the flowers for a Hollywood wedding! Surely that would be the perfect headline for the website that Bee was resisting setting up. Perhaps, while she was here, Lizzie could talk her aunt round – after all, there were very few businesses these days that didn't have some kind of online presence.

Lizzie was feeling better with each day that passed, and she'd almost put her surprise encounter with Sarah Treloar into perspective after a few decent nights' sleep and a couple more shifts at Roseford Blooms. Bee had also mentioned that the village fete, a small affair held in the field beyond the ha-ha at Roseford Hall, was coming up that weekend. Despite her ambivalence about Roseford Hall, Lizzie felt curious enough to want to see what the fete looked like these days. She had a vague memory of it from when she'd been a teenager: a parochial affair where locals displayed their longest carrots and most attractive marrows alongside posies created by schoolchildren and more intricate bouquets by budding floristry amateurs. That, and a series of quaint activities and stalls, made for a jolly, if somewhat twee, afternoon. Lizzie had memories of Georgina chatting to everyone, while she was too shy to venture far from her commandeered seat at the side of the arena, happy to just soak up the village atmosphere.

'So, will you come and help me judge the displays tomorrow?' Bee asked, over dinner.

'Won't you need someone to stay behind and keep an eye on the shop?' Lizzie asked.

'I don't usually bother opening up on that Saturday afternoon, since everyone's down at the fayre,' Bee replied. 'Besides,' she added, 'you've been hiding out in there all week. A bit of sun will do you good.'

Lizzie frowned. 'Am I getting in your way?'

'No, love, not at all,' Bee replied. 'It's been lovely having you in the shop to help me. But there are other things to do in the village, than keep your old aunt company in her shop.'

'You know I'm more than happy with my own company, and yours,' Lizzie said. She raised her cuff an inch off her chest. 'And having this strapped onto me doesn't exactly make me feel much like socialising.'

'I understand that,' Bee replied. 'But an hour or two at the local fayre's not going to wear you out, is it?' She paused. 'I bumped into Simon in the café a couple of days ago, too. He asked how you were.'

A blush warmed Lizzie's cheeks as she met Bee's keen, clear-eyed gaze. 'Did he?'

Bee smiled. 'He seemed worried about you. Is there something I should know?'

Lizzie shook her head vehemently. 'No. I fell over when I was out walking and he picked me up.'

'Oh, my goodness!' Bee exclaimed. 'Why didn't you tell me? Did you hurt yourself again?'

At her look of concern, Lizzie rushed to reassure her. 'No, thankfully. But Simon just happened to be passing by and he took me for a coffee.'

'Really?' Bee raised an eyebrow. 'And how was that?'

'It was fine,' Lizzie replied quickly. Then, realising that Bee was expecting more, 'He was sweet.'

Bee just looked at her.

'Well, OK, more than sweet.' Lizzie smiled. 'I, er, really enjoyed talking to him.'

'He's a lovely boy,' Bee replied. 'I can't think why some girl didn't snap him up years ago.' Her bright blue eyes met Lizzie's and Lizzie couldn't help but laugh.

'It was just a coffee, Aunt Bee. He helped me back to my feet, and he probably just felt sorry for me.'

Bee shook her head. 'Nothing to feel sorry about,' she said briskly. 'You really do put yourself down, sometimes.'

'Yeah, because I'm such a hot prospect with a busted collarbone, no job and nowhere to live right now!' Lizzie kept smiling, though. Bee always made her feel better, in her no-nonsense way. She couldn't feel downcast for long when she was around her.

'Well, you could do a lot worse,' Bee replied. She put her knife and fork together on her plate. 'Strawberries?'

Lizzie nodded. She'd eaten like a Labrador since she'd been in Roseford, but her weakness had been the local strawberries that Bee's friend Helena Martin had been swapping for the odd bunch of flowers. Helena lived in a bungalow in the grounds of Halstead House, a stately Victorian manor at the other end of Roseford. Bee and Helena had become firm friends when Helena had moved to the village some years back, and she was a regular visitor to Roseford Blooms. Helena's former son-in-law, Chris Charlton, and his partner, Stella, ran Halstead House as a writers' and artists' retreat, and Stella was a regular customer, too, as she liked to give each room at Halstead House a centrepiece of fresh flowers when the retreats were running.

As Bee sorted out two generous bowls of strawberries and topped them with clotted cream, Lizzie tried to put Simon's enquiry about her out of her mind. That was the trouble with having no real focus in her life at the moment, she thought. Everything took on more significance than it should. She'd never have been dwelling on Simon, or the past, if she hadn't pretty much lost everything else. Now everything in her life seemed to be on hiatus, it was tempting to linger on things she shouldn't.

All the same, she thought, it had been nice, after the fall, to sit and have a coffee with Simon. He'd been kind to her without prying, and she was intensely grateful for that. Perhaps it would be nice to go to the summer fayre and see him again, if only to clear the air. Tucking into her strawberries, she decided she would. After all, what else was she going to do on a sunny weekend in sleepy old Roseford if Bee insisted that the shop was going to be closed?

17

The morning of the Roseford Summer Fayre dawned bright and sunny. Lizzie had slept well; she was getting used to sleeping with the cuff on, and a cup of Bee's powerful chamomile tea had helped to put her out for the count. As the sun peered through the gap in the forget-me-not-patterned curtains of her room, she stretched her good arm above her head and rolled over. The event officially opened at one o'clock, but Lizzie was going to go to judge the floral exhibits with Bee a little earlier.

After a leisurely breakfast, Lizzie got in the shower, and spent more time than usual deciding what to wear. She knew the peaceful days and restorative nights' sleep while she'd been in Roseford were doing her good, and she wanted to take a little extra care with her appearance. It wasn't because she thought she might bump into Simon and Sarah again...

Settling eventually on a pair of cropped jeans and a flowing floral tunic that she could pull on with ease, she enlisted Bee's help to put her hair up in a messy bun. She giggled when Bee put two decorative long pins that had brightly painted butterflies on the ends into the bun to secure it a little more.

'I remember these from years ago, when I was about twelve,' Lizzie said, smiling at the memory. 'Georgina and I used to love doing each other's hair, but we could never make the hairstyles stay put for more than about two minutes.'

'The secret is not to have freshly washed hair,' Bee said. 'You did yours yesterday, didn't you?'

'Yup.' Lizzie was relieved to get her hair off her neck. It felt as though it was going to be a very warm day, and her usual loose ponytail wouldn't cut it.

As Bee held up a hand mirror so that Lizzie could see the back of her hair, Lizzie nodded in approval. 'I'd never have managed that by myself, collarbone or no collarbone,' she said. 'Thanks, Aunt Bee.'

'My pleasure,' Bee replied. 'You've such beautiful hair; you should experiment with it more often.'

'Not a lot of call for butterfly hairpins in my usual line of work,' Lizzie said dryly.

'Well, things can change,' Bee replied. 'Are you ready to go?'

The judging was to begin at 11 a.m., so Lizzie and Bee had plenty of time to take a leisurely walk down to the field where the fayre was being held.

'Are you sure you don't want me to stay behind and look after the shop?' Lizzie asked as they drew closer to Roseford Blooms. 'I really don't mind. I can sell the pre-arranged bunches and bouquets.'

'No,' Bee replied firmly. 'I've never opened the shop on the afternoon of the village fayre, and I've no desire to start now. Today is all about enjoying the atmosphere and traditions of this place, not putting money in the till. Besides...' she paused, tantalisingly '... Simon would never forgive me if I told him I'd put you behind the counter. I got the impression he was rather looking forward to seeing you.'

Lizzie's face burned at the mention of Simon's name. She found that she was looking forward to seeing him too. She wondered if he, as lord of the manor, was going to be involved in the judging. And with Bee by her side, she didn't feel quite so nervous about walking through the gates of the hall, either. It wasn't as if she had to go inside the house, after all.

Lizzie and Bee headed down past the car park to the field beyond the ha-ha. The ha-ha was a stone wall, built into the slope at the end of the garden, which created the impression of an unbroken sweep of grassland between the house and the horizon. A particular favourite of eighteenth-century architects, it had been restored by the British Heritage Fund as part of their general overhaul of the place when they'd taken it on from the Treloar family. Used mainly now as a space for visitors to exercise their dogs, the field beyond the ha-ha had also hosted a huge artificial ice rink when FilmFlix had shot their smash-hit Christmas movie *A Countess for Christmas* in the house and grounds of Roseford Hall. It was a decent space for events, and had hosted the Roseford Village Fayre for generations.

As Bee and Lizzie approached the field, Lizzie began to realise that this wasn't just the hokey, parochial village fete she remembered from yesteryear. There were many stalls being set up already, and a large marquee housed all of the exhibits that would be judged by a panel of local experts, including Bee. It felt like a summery version of the Christmas Countdown Night that took place on Roseford's main street in the winter, and Lizzie was impressed. Even more so when she saw the piles of glossy programmes that were being readied for sale at £1.50 each. She sensed the hand and professionalism of the British Heritage Fund everywhere.

'It all looks great,' she said. 'And busy, too.'

'Now you see why I don't bother opening the shop,' Bee replied. 'No one's going to be on the main street this afternoon.'

Entering the marquee, Lizzie could see trestle tables stretching in two long rectangles, one inside the other, covered in all varieties of squash, root vegetable, fruit and other produce laid out in neatly serried rows. The runner beans, in particular, looked like a rank of soldiers preparing to take up arms. Lizzie suppressed a smile; the setting reminded her of an episode of *Midsomer Murders*, and she imagined that the competition for first prize in as many categories as possible would, in the fictional world of cosy crime, be enough to wish death on your competitor's veg, if not the competitors themselves.

At one end of the marquee, stretching the whole of the width of the tables, were the many and varied bouquets, posies and wreaths that had been entered for the different classes, all listed in the extensive programme. They had been dropped off earlier that morning, and arranged by the members of the Summer Fayre Committee, one of whom was spritzing each exhibit with a spray bottle to try to keep them perky for the duration of the show.

'So, we've got to award a first place, a runner-up and a highly commended in each class,' Bee explained. 'And it's all judged blind, so there won't be fisticuffs over the cream teas later!'

Lizzie laughed. 'You make it sound so serious.'

'Oh, it is, it is,' Bee replied. 'Never underestimate the wrath of a gardener scorned.'

As they walked down the tables, looking at each and every one of the entries, Lizzie smiled to see how carefully Bee scrutinised them, awarding marks for presentation, colour combination and originality, until she'd chosen the winners across each class. Lizzie was particularly taken by the juniors, who'd all submitted posies on the theme of 'Bee Friendly Bouquets'. These varied from small arrangements that had lavender and sweet peas as their centrepieces, to one who'd interpreted the theme a little more literally and chosen mostly yellow flowers in a black and yellow striped vase.

'Maybe you should offer some floristry sessions at the shop,' Lizzie said as they continued to peruse the exhibits. 'People might like the chance to find out a little bit more about the origins and meanings of flowers.'

Bee glanced at her. 'I'm far too long in the tooth for all that,' she said. 'That's a job for the next owner of Roseford Blooms.'

Lizzie was about to argue, when she was distracted by the sight of Simon entering the marquee. This time, there was no escaping it, her heart really did respond to seeing him. He was dressed in a sky-blue shirt, rolled to the elbows and open at the neck, and a pair of cream-coloured jeans. His blond hair flopped slightly over his forehead, and he was giving a confident smile and greeting to the exhibitors as he passed them. He looked happy, and at ease, and very, very attractive. *The lord in his domain*, Lizzie thought good-humouredly. Trying to get her head together before he reached them, she glanced at Bee's notes.

'You've added that one up wrong,' she said.

'Oh, yes, so I have.' Bee quickly adjusted her scores. 'Just as well you spotted that. Those two entries look like they belong to Josie and Molly, the vicar's daughters. There would have been a steward's enquiry if I'd miscounted those!'

'I thought we were judging blind?' Lizzie said, raising an eyebrow.

'I recognise the vases from last year!' Bee laughed. She glanced down the row of bouquets again. 'Well, I think that's the lot. Did you fancy a quick break for a cup of tea before we finish off?'

'That would be great,' Lizzie replied. 'I'll get them, shall I?' With her heart pounding, she suddenly didn't feel ready to speak to Simon.

'Oh, I'll get them,' Bee replied. 'I think you'll struggle with just the one arm.' Did Lizzie imagine it, or was there a knowing look in Bee's eye as she saw Simon approaching? 'You go and say hello to Simon. I'll be back in a jiffy.'

Before Lizzie could respond, or try to scuttle off after her, Bee had slipped out of the side entrance to the marquee and Lizzie watched as Simon drew closer. Taking a deep breath, realising it was now or never, she walked over to meet him halfway.

18

'Hey,' Simon said as they reached each other. 'So, Bee's roped you into the judging, has she? I'd better not tell you which posies were made by my nieces, then, for fear of nobbling you!'

Lizzie found herself laughing, immediately put at ease by his easy manner. 'You'd be almost too late anyway,' she replied. 'We're just about done, but Bee's gone to grab us a cuppa before we finish the last scores. What are you doing down here?'

'Oh, they've asked me to judge the home-made wine competition,' Simon replied. 'I'm coming down in good time to do it, since the last time I did, I got so pissed on the entries I could barely string a sentence together for the rest of the afternoon!'

Lizzie laughed. 'I'd have paid good money to see that!'

'You can always come and help me, if you like,' Simon said, a look of mischief in his eyes. 'We could split them and safeguard against any mishaps.'

Lizzie shook her head and gestured to her arm. 'For obvious reasons, I'm wary about doing anything that might make me even the tiniest bit unsteady on my feet, especially after the tumble I took the last time I was here.'

'Fair enough,' Simon replied, grinning. The crow's feet around his blue eyes were decidedly attractive, and Lizzie found herself looking into his handsome, open face and suddenly wanting to share a drink with him, even if it was some dodgy home-made wine. There wasn't a trace of the slightly geeky teenager he'd once been. She realised he was wearing his 'public face' today: the supposedly carefree lord of the manor, who was pretending not to mind that he no longer owned the manor.

There was a pause as both of them seemed to wonder where to take the conversation next. Eventually, Simon cleared his throat. 'Your hair looks nice.'

Lizzie blushed. 'Thank you. The pins belong to Bee. Obviously she had to help me with it.'

'Look, Lizzie, I know you're probably not up for a late night, but there's a bit of a barn dance taking place in the marquee after the fayre has wrapped up for the day. Would you, er, like to join me for a very gentle spin?'

Lizzie couldn't help laughing. 'First you ask me to run the risk of falling over pissed, and then you want me to do-si-do?'

Simon joined in with the laughter. 'Well, I hadn't thought about it like that. But dancing isn't obligatory. We could just watch from the sidelines.'

Lizzie decided to give him a break. 'In that case, I'd love to.'

'Great! It starts at eight, so shall I meet you back here?'

Smiling, Lizzie accepted just as Bee returned with two cups of tea, and Simon headed off.

'You're looking more cheerful,' Bee observed as she carefully handed Lizzie her tea.

Lizzie tried to smother the grin that she knew was plastered on her face. 'Am I?'

'Well, don't tell me, then,' Bee replied. 'But Simon looked just as happy. That a coincidence?'

'Maybe,' Lizzie teased. She turned towards the flower displays again. 'Shouldn't we finish judging? Then we can relax and enjoy the rest of the fayre.'

Bee shook her head, but didn't comment further. Instead, after they'd drunk their tea, she passed Lizzie half of the slips of paper to record the last few placings for the flower displays, and they worked their way back down the sections, mostly agreeing with each other as they went. Lizzie had become quite adept at holding paper in the hand with the cuff and writing with the other, after a couple of weeks in the sling. As they made their way through the entries, Lizzie noticed a pair of posies that had what looked like the Phoenix Rosa variety of rose as their centrepieces and wondered if those were the ones that Simon's nieces had made. A few weeks ago she'd never have been able to distinguish between rose varieties; she was obviously learning something at Roseford Blooms.

A short time later, forms handed back to the committee, Lizzie was about to head back to Bee's cottage when she spotted Simon again. He was in animated conversation with two girls, who Lizzie assumed to be his nieces. The taller of the two was grinning at her uncle, and the shorter had a gorgeous-looking syrup-coloured retriever on a lead. The retriever, panting slightly in the heat, looked adoringly up at its mistress, and Lizzie found herself smiling again.

'*Please*, Uncle Simon,' Lizzie heard the younger girl say as she drew a little closer. 'I *really* want to have a look around, but Holmes needs a walk.'

'He's your dog, Elspeth,' Simon replied. 'When I bought him for you, it was on the understanding that you'd feed and walk him. And yet I seem to be the one doing most of the walking these days!'

'I promise I'll walk him this evening,' Elspeth replied. 'But can you just take him now, please?'

From the look on his face, Lizzie already knew Simon was going to acquiesce.

'Give me his lead.' Simon sighed. Then, looking down at the patiently waiting Holmes, said to the dog, 'You'd better be on your best behaviour, old chap!'

Lizzie smiled. She had the sense that Simon really didn't mind at all. She suddenly wished she were brave enough to go and ask to join him on his walk, but, despite their conversation earlier, she didn't feel as though she could. He probably wanted a bit of time to himself before the fayre got going anyway.

As he headed off down the field with Holmes, Lizzie began walking back to Roseford Blooms. There were still a bit of time before the fayre started properly, and she should probably head back to Bee's. She had to make the duty phone call to her parents at some point over the weekend, and she might as well get it over with. Rather now, she thought, than tomorrow when she might be feeling tired from the barn dance. She was feeling better by the day, but the aftermath of the car accident still crept up on her from time to time, and she needed to feel at her best to speak to her parents. At least, having helped Bee out this morning, she'd have a topic of conversation to fall back on.

19

After making the call to her parents, Lizzie had a leisurely afternoon looking around the fayre, which was everything she expected it would be. The head of the organising committee was extorting everyone to spend at the stalls, and, if they hadn't, to buy their barn-dance tickets from the small table that also hosted a raffle. Children rushed about from stall to stall, parents in tow, and the regular ringing of the bell at the top of the 'try your strength' machine competed with the harmonious sounds of the Roseford village choir's medley of Adele songs.

In spite of all this, Lizzie began to feel more than a little nervous about meeting up with Simon that evening. She'd caught glimpses of him during the afternoon, and they'd shared a quick chat, but he was soon buttonholed by other people, and Lizzie had spent her time looking around, trying to get into the spirit of the afternoon. All told, by the time the afternoon was drawing to a close, around a thousand visitors had attended the summer fayre, and it had been idyllic: the perfect example of an English country fayre. Now, the committee would be taking a well-earned rest, and everyone was preparing themselves for a night of cider, dancing and merrymaking to round it all off.

'Don't you go flinging yourself around in all directions, young lady!' Bee said as Lizzie got ready to go back out that evening. 'That arm of yours is still in no state to be messed about with.'

'I'll be careful.' Lizzie smiled back at Bee. 'It's not exactly *Riverdance!*' She looked in the mirror and smiled at her reflection. 'Are you sure you don't mind me borrowing this dress, Aunt Bee?' She had shyly pulled out the brightly coloured maxi from the carrier bag in the cupboard and asked Bee if she could wear it. Bee had laughed when she'd caught sight of it.

'I haven't seen that in years!' she'd said. 'I thought it had gone to the charity shop. Of course you can wear it, darling.'

With a quick wash through, it had dried in no time in the breeze, and, newly ironed, it was the perfect dress for a summer's evening. Lizzie had a denim jacket she was going to throw on top, to make the outfit feel more in keeping with a barn dance, but she was pleased with how good it looked.

'Just you be careful, though,' Bee replied. 'With a few pints of scrumpy inside 'em, even the Roseford locals can be a bit energetic with their dancing. I'd hide behind Simon if I were you!'

Lizzie rolled her eyes. 'I'll bear that in mind.' Ever since Bee had clocked Lizzie having her chat with Simon that morning, and caught her glancing in his direction more than once at the fayre, she'd been casting knowing looks in her direction.

'I'll leave the front door on the latch,' Bee replied. 'Just lock up when you come in.'

'I will.'

Lizzie tried to ignore the butterflies in her stomach as she headed down to Roseford Hall. She could already hear the music from the ceilidh band that had been hired to curate the evening's festivities drifting across from the marquee. As she drew closer, she felt a little tingle in her stomach as she caught sight of Simon, chatting away to a couple of locals. He had a pint in his hand, and he looked relaxed and happy.

'Hi,' she said as she reached him.

Simon's smile was one of genuine pleasure and warmth, and Lizzie felt herself relax a little. 'Hi,' he replied. 'That's a great dress. I hope you're ready for a wild night of, er, quadrilles and square dancing!'

Lizzie burst out laughing as their eyes were drawn to the first few people arranging themselves on the dance floor. 'The only quadrille I can remember is the one from *Alice in Wonderland!*'

'I think there's a first edition of *Alice in Wonderland* in the library of the hall somewhere,' Simon remarked. 'Unless one of my nieces grabbed it before the place was handed over, of course.'

'I'd love to see that,' Lizzie replied. 'It was one of my favourite books as a child.'

'I'll see if it's still there,' Simon said. 'I'm sure I can pinch it when no one from the BHF is looking!'

The music started, and Lizzie was glad she and Simon had sat this one out, as couples started spinning and whirling on the floor. Eventually, though, the dancers settled into their rhythm.

'If this is as wild as it gets, then I think I'll cope,' Lizzie observed. The dancers laughed gamely as the ceilidh band leader tried to arrange them.

'Can I get you a drink?' Simon asked as the band struck up a faster-paced tune.

'That would be great,' Lizzie replied. 'I think I'll have to sit out any numbers quicker than a waltz, anyway!'

Simon laughed, and Lizzie felt herself relishing the sound. It felt good to make him laugh. Her eyes were drawn to him again as he turned back to the bar to order her a pint of Carter's cider. *Just the one,* she swore. She didn't want to do herself any more damage, since the doctor had said she could remove the sling next week. She was looking forward to getting rid of the cuff.

When Simon returned from the bar, they sipped their drinks and chatted, Lizzie began to relax, and when a slower dance came on, 'a couple's ballad to give all you revellers a little break,' she shyly accepted Simon's offer. They put their glasses down on the bar and headed into the centre of the marquee, joining the other couples on the dance floor. Simon smiled and said a quick hello to Stella Simpson and Chris Charlton. Lizzie thought that Chris looked less than amused to be dragged to dance by Stella, but he accepted his fate with good grace.

'Chris and Stella own the writers' and artists' retreat at Halstead House,' Simon said, once they'd drifted away from them. 'I was friends with Chris's late wife, Olivia. We were at uni together.'

'Bee told me what happened,' Lizzie said softly. 'It must have been awful for you all.' Olivia had died suddenly from an aneurysm, leaving a devastated Chris to care for their young son Gabe, and a house that was in dire need of renovation. Chris had lost his wife, and Gabe had lost his mother, but Simon had lost his best friend, so had suffered in his own way.

'A million times worse for Chris, obviously,' Simon replied, 'but yes. I still miss her.' Lizzie felt him tighten his hold on her. She wasn't sure if he'd intended to, but she didn't mind. 'But then he met Stella a couple of years back, and they've made each other so happy.' He shook his head. 'I envy them that.'

Lizzie glanced up at him. She felt completely safe in his arms, as if he wouldn't let her fall. She remembered feeling that once before, all those years ago, when the evening had been so different.

'No one like that in your life, then?' Lizzie asked softly.

Simon looked down at her, and Lizzie's heart thumped so hard she was surprised it didn't leap out of her chest.

'Not yet,' he replied, equally softly. 'But I'm working on it.'

The light caught his eyes, making them sparkle, and the gentle, sultry voice of the ceilidh singer, paired with the achingly tearful tone of the fiddler, robbed Lizzie of a response. She took a deep breath, and their eyes locked. The moment felt loaded with the promise of new discoveries. Lizzie was swept up in it, and, although things had moved quickly, being here, in Simon's arms, felt absolutely right.

'Simon!'

The voice cut through the moment like a knife.

Immediately, Lizzie felt Simon pull back slightly. Coming back to earth, she saw Sarah Treloar standing next to them.

'Sarah,' Simon replied, more than a trace of exasperation in his voice. 'Is there a problem?'

'You could say that.' Sarah wore a serious expression, and for a horrible moment Lizzie thought she was going to call her out for dancing with her brother.

Stepping away from the other couples on the dance floor, Simon kept hold of Lizzie's good hand, bringing her along with him to continue the conversation with his sister whether she liked it or not.

'What's happened? Is it Ma? The girls?'

Sarah shook her head. 'That bugger Holmes got out of the garden again and he's run off. Fleur, Elspeth and I have been searching for him, but we reckon he must be after a bitch. There's no sign of him. I've sent the girls back to the house as it's getting too dark for them to be searching around, but I was hoping you'd come and help me look.'

'I told you to get him neutered, didn't I?' Simon snapped, sounding exasperated.

Sarah rolled her eyes. 'He's on the vet's list for next week.'

'Of course he is.' Simon sighed. He turned back to Lizzie. 'Look, I'm so sorry, Lizzie. I'm going to have to help Sarah look for this bloody dog.'

Lizzie squeezed his hand. 'It's fine. I'm not much good for dancing at the moment anyway.'

'Can I, er, give you a ring?'

'Of course.'

Sarah showed no sign of budging, so Lizzie resigned herself to being the one who had to leave first. A sharp spark of irritation surged through her at the way Sarah had just butted in and called a halt to such a wonderful moment, but Lizzie tried to hush it. It was just bad luck that the dog had escaped, after all.

'Well, goodnight, then,' Lizzie replied. 'I'll see you soon.'

'Soon,' Simon echoed. He looked as though he wanted to pick up where they'd left off, but one look from Sarah put paid to that.

As Lizzie headed back out of the marquee, she sighed in frustration. She and Simon had been having such a lovely time, and it had felt as though they'd begun moving towards something new, something rather lovely. And, just like that, his bloody sister had ruined it. It wasn't the first time Sarah had had a hand in messing up a moment in Lizzie's life.

20

An hour later, having walked back to Bee's, Lizzie was just about to put the kettle on when her phone pinged.

Sorry about that. Bloody dog found and confined to barracks. Is it too late for another drink?

Lizzie smiled, her earlier irritation almost forgotten. She glanced at the clock, remembered she was an adult and texted back a quick response. Within thirty seconds of sending the text, there was a knock at the back door.

'I was hoping you'd say that,' Simon replied.

Lizzie burst out laughing. 'And if I hadn't?'

'I'd have departed from your doorstep with my tail between my legs, much like Holmes now he's back at Sarah's!'

Simon had his hands in the pockets of his jeans and was leaning against the side of the porch, and as he looked up at her in a kind of faux-casual way, Lizzie couldn't help the grin that spread across her face.

'Well, how could I refuse such honesty?' she said. 'I'd invite you in for a cuppa, but Bee's in the front room and I'm probably not allowed to take you to my bedroom, so what do you suggest?'

'Are you up for a stroll back to my place?' Simon asked. 'I've got a bottle of wine in the fridge that I really shouldn't drink alone, and I'm not sure I'm up for any more do-si-doing tonight.'

Lizzie smiled. 'That sounds lovely.' She still couldn't shake the slightly unsettled feeling she had about going back to Roseford Hall, especially after having seen Sarah again, but, temporarily insulated by the heady emotions that getting closer to Simon had evoked, and desperate to see if they'd end up in the same situation again, she figured she could handle it. Grabbing her jacket from her room, and after popping her head around the door of the living room to let Bee know where she was going, she'd soon joined Simon outside.

'Sorry I had to dash off,' he said as Lizzie closed the door behind them. 'I couldn't really leave Sarah in the lurch looking for that blasted dog. She'd have been out all night.'

'Understandable,' Lizzie replied. They walked in step, heading back to Roseford Hall, and as Simon's left hand brushed her right, she kept hoping he'd reach a little further and hold hers. The intimacy of the dance floor seemed to have dissipated a little, and she was keen to recapture that sensation.

The mildness of the night wrapped around them, and, feeling suddenly confident, Lizzie slid her hand into Simon's the next time their fingers brushed. She felt Simon pause slightly, and he turned towards her.

'That feels nice,' he murmured. 'I was, er, really enjoying dancing with you earlier.'

Lizzie squeezed his hand gently. 'I enjoyed it, too.'

The walk took them past Roseford Blooms, and Lizzie glanced back at the shop fondly as they passed. She couldn't deny that she was beginning to feel really at home here, and spending time with Simon was a part of that. They reached the gates of Roseford Hall, which were still open to allow the barn-dance guests to leave, and Simon led her up the driveway. They were heading towards the rear of the hall, and Lizzie's pulse began to race a little more. She'd tried to avoid the main house since she'd been here, and now she was hand in hand with Simon, walking straight towards it.

But, she reasoned, she'd wanted to come back here with Simon. The present was what mattered, not the past. All the same, as they reached the family's private entrance at the rear of the hall, the churning feeling in her stomach intensified. It was silly, she thought. And it was definitely the moment to put such thoughts to one side. What had happened to her twenty years ago in this house had no bearing on why she was here tonight. She was a different person now. And she was here with Simon, who was being so wonderfully charming and considerate. She could handle it.

Following Simon through the door, Lizzie found herself in a cosy kitchen. Simon grabbed a bottle of white wine and then two glasses from a nearby cupboard.

'Shall we drink this on the terrace?' he asked as he turned back to face her. 'It's private enough and we won't be disturbed, unless that bloody dog's escaped again!'

Lizzie smiled nervously. 'That sounds great.'

They ambled out onto the small terrace that overlooked the front of the house. There wasn't a breath of wind in the air and they could still hear the raucous sounds of the barn dance emanating from the marquee some two hundred yards away. A cheer went up as the latest dance finished. Simon placed the wine bottle and the glasses down with a clunk on the cast-iron patio table and swiftly poured out two decent measures. 'Here you go,' he said, passing Lizzie her glass.

She felt the warmth of his fingertips, which was a welcome contrast to the cool of the glass in his hand. She was in great need of the first sip, and, without realising it, the sip became a gulp and she coughed.

In an instant Simon was by her side, a gentle hand on her upper back, clearly intended to reassure her. She leaned into his touch, trying to steady herself. The gulp of wine had unsettled her, and she wiped her eyes quickly.

'Are you all right?' Simon asked gently. And there was something about the tone of his voice that took Lizzie back twenty years. She realised that, if she was going to get closer to him, she'd have to tell him why she was feeling so nervous about being here, in his home.

'Can we talk?' Lizzie asked as Simon led her to one of the chairs.

'Of course.' Simon looked surprised. 'Have I, er, have I messed things up already?' He gave a self-deprecating grin.

Shaking her head, Lizzie tried to smile, but it felt thin and forced. 'No.

You haven't done anything wrong, Simon. It's just...' She paused, trying to find the words that would explain her nervous reaction.

Simon put his glass carefully down on the table, and then knelt in front of her. He took her good hand in his, and looked up at her, his eyes filled with concern. 'It's all right,' he said softly. 'I'm listening.'

Lizzie's eyes filled with tears again, and this time it wasn't because of the wine. She drew a breath to steady herself and tell him. He'd been a part of that night, after all, even if he didn't seem to remember, all these years later.

21

'Talk to me, Lizzie. I'm here.'

The calm in Simon's tone worked wonders to ground Lizzie as she sat on the terrace. Concern and kindness were written all over his face. She gently squeezed his hand.

'You'd better pull up a seat,' she said softly. 'This might take a while.'

Simon looked quizzically at her, but did as she suggested. When he was settled in front of her, his knees touching hers and his hand once again clasped in her own, she began.

'I guess I owe you an explanation about why I'm so jumpy.'

Simon shook his head. 'You don't owe me anything. But if you want to tell me, then I'm here for you.'

Lizzie gave a watery smile. 'Just like you were twenty years ago.'

Simon stiffened. 'Was I?'

Lizzie nodded. 'I don't expect you to remember. It was a bigger deal for me than it was for you. And I look quite different now from how I looked then. But something happened to me in this house. It was a long time ago, but I haven't actually been back through the doors since then.' She gave a shaky laugh. 'I guess it all just got a bit overwhelming.'

'Tell me what happened,' Simon said gently. He was still holding her hand. To Lizzie, it felt like an anchor.

'When I was sixteen, Sarah invited me and my sister, Georgina, to her birthday party. Georgina was the one Sarah and her friends wanted to hang out with. I was just an added extra, someone they could boss around or torment when they got fed up with me tagging along. Georgina was pretty, clever but not a geek, and everyone wanted to be near her. I, on the other hand, was the classic ugly duckling. Socially, boarding school was... not an easy experience. With students coming from all over the country to board, you'd think there would have been a kind of solidarity, but, unfortunately, for me, it didn't really work that way.'

Simon's eyes registered with something that looked like empathy. 'I can identify with that. But go on.'

'Sarah was part of the "In Crowd". They didn't take kindly to people who didn't fit their idea of what was cool, or in fashion.' Lizzie glanced down at herself, remembering what it was like to be part of the outsiders. 'I didn't fit. Therefore, I was fair game.'

From the look on his face, Lizzie could see that Simon was struggling with the notion of his sister being part of such a gang of girls, but he didn't come right out and say it.

'Anyway...' Lizzie swallowed before continuing. 'We both came down to stay with Aunt Bee, and Georgina was in a complete state all that day. She was so excited to be invited to the party. She knew that all of the popular girls had asked all of the boys they thought were fit from the local boys' school, and there was one in particular she really fancied. She was even considering... well, you know.' She paused, and blushed slightly. 'There are a lot of bedrooms at Roseford Hall, after all.'

Simon gave a brief grin. 'I do have a vague memory of being the night-watchman that evening, and turfing out a few couples from places they shouldn't have been.'

'I guess you must have thought it was all a bit pathetic, really,' Lizzie said. 'I mean, you were, what, nineteen at the time? We must have seemed exactly what we were, stupid school kids who thought they knew everything.'

Simon shook his head. 'Well, I wouldn't quite put it that way. At least it gave me an excuse to ditch *King Lear* for a night. Shakespeare is pretty heavy going when there's music pumping round the house.'

Lizzie, despite herself, gave a laugh. 'I'd have far preferred to have hidden out in a room with a book, if it's any consolation.'

'I wish I'd known,' Simon said, softly, his eyes shining brightly in the moonlight. 'I'd have whisked you off and we could have discussed the Bard together!'

'You did enough,' Lizzie said, her voice suddenly trembling again. 'Do you really not remember?'

Simon paused, and the silence between them stretched tantalisingly for a few moments. He moved a little closer to her, still, obviously mindful of her fragile state. 'Why don't you try to remind me?'

Lizzie felt reassured by his presence, and squeezed his hand. 'I was bored at the party,' she said haltingly. 'I didn't know many of the girls, and I wasn't really sure about the boys. I was always the ugly duckling to Georgina's perfect swan, and while she could talk, and make people feel good by turning her attention on them, I just didn't know what to say, to anyone.' She gave a slight bark of laughter, and covered her mouth self-consciously. 'I even tried to escape and find the library, to get a bit of peace and quiet until it was time to leave. Parties weren't my thing. I felt stupid in what I was wearing, and, if I'm being honest, I was just fed up. I told Georgina I was going to go back to Aunt Bee's, but she persuaded me to give it another half an hour, at least. I could never refuse her anything back then, so I agreed.'

A shiver ran down her spine, and a sick feeling rose in her stomach when she remembered what had happened next. Clearly sensing her discomfort, Simon squeezed Lizzie's hand a little tighter, tacitly encouraging her to go on.

'I should have just gone back to Aunt Bee's,' Lizzie whispered. 'But I didn't want to leave her alone. She was chatting up this guy from St Jude's, and I knew he had a bit of a reputation as a player. I figured, if I hung around, at least if it went wrong, I could help her.' She gave a short, bitter laugh. 'I had no idea what I was letting myself in for.'

'What happened, Lizzie?'

Lizzie shook her head, trying to form those awful memories into some kind of coherent whole.

'I was sitting in the corner of the library. I'd got fed up of the music and

I didn't want to drink any more, so I found a spot in there and decided to wait it out until Georgina and I could leave. Anyway, then this girl, Nina, came into the room and started talking to me. She was one of Georgina's friends, but I'd always been a bit suspicious of her. She was one of those girls who seemed to just fit in with everyone, but she liked to make life difficult for those who didn't. She told me that one of the boys who'd come to the party really liked me, that he wanted to talk to me but he was too shy to ask me himself, so he'd asked her to see if I wanted to go out with him.' Lizzie paused. She needed a moment to ground herself in the present, away from the mortifying sensations that talking about those long-buried memories was evoking.

'What happened?' Simon prompted gently.

'Well, even though I was fed up, I felt, oh, I don't know... flattered. I hadn't had much experience with boys at that point, and I felt lonely enough at the party that a bit of me just wanted to try to fit in. For a stupid moment, I wanted to be part of the "In Crowd". Georgina had disappeared, and I thought it might be nice to be included in something. When Nina said she'd give me a makeover before we went to talk to the boy, I thought it would be a great idea.'

Lizzie took a sip of her wine to fortify herself against what was coming next. She could feel the hot flames of mortification running over her at the memory, and she felt embarrassed about recounting it all to Simon.

'Nina took me off to the room where she was staying. She insisted that I got out of the dress I was wearing and she gave me an extra one she'd packed. I remember being so embarrassed when I put it on because it was really tight, and short. I remember thinking at the time that there was no way it would have properly fitted Nina, or George, let alone me, but I went along with it.' Despite herself, she gave a brief laugh. 'Teenagers can be stupid sometimes, can't they? I definitely preferred covering myself up. I was always so much taller and broader than Georgina, I felt self-conscious if I wore anything low cut, or too far above my knees.'

'So what happened next?'

'Nina did my make-up, but she didn't want me to see what I looked like. She kept telling me it would be like one of those makeover shows on the TV that we all watched in the common room at school in the evenings, and that I could see when she was done.' Lizzie paused. 'If I'd had any idea what she was doing, I'd have stopped her. But, stupidly, I trusted her.'

Seeing the look on Simon's face, which veered between empathy and incredulity, perhaps that Lizzie could be taken in so easily, Lizzie tried to explain. 'These were girls who'd alienated me since I'd started school, but they were my sister's friends. I just wanted a little bit of what she had.'

'I can understand that,' Simon said quietly. 'Wanting to belong, and be part of the herd, can be something that consumes you.'

Lizzie nodded. 'Well, I went along with it. And when she told me to give her my glasses, that I'd look so much better without them, I agreed to that, too.'

Lizzie, needing to move from the cast-iron bistro chair, stood up and looked over the stone wall that bordered the verandah. 'How stupid can you get?' She gave a quiet laugh. 'But, you know, I thought at last I was going to be part of the gang.'

Simon stood as well, and moved so that he was next to her. 'I'm guessing this doesn't end well,' he said gently.

'You'd be right.' Bracing herself against the cool stone of the verandah wall, she turned to face Simon. 'Nina led me down to what I think used to be your old family living room. The lights were off in there, and at that point I think I knew that something wasn't right. I'd been telling myself all the way through that because Nina was George's friend she wouldn't do anything to hurt me, but I couldn't have been more wrong.' She shuddered at the memory. 'Nina brought me in, holding my hand, and I knew that there were people in there, but without my glasses, and with the lights out, I couldn't see. I tried to ask her what she was doing, but the second she'd put me in the room, she'd let go of my hand. She told me to call out to find Theo: that he was there, in the room waiting for me. Stupidly, I did. Then, before I really knew what was going on, all the lights came on.' She turned back to Simon, who'd taken her hand again.

'Nina shouted something as she turned on the lights, about me having a gorgeous makeover, and didn't I look fabulous, but I knew, at that moment, that I'd been set up. That I looked awful, and the worst part was, I couldn't even see their faces properly.' She stifled a sob. 'But even though they were all so fuzzy without my glasses, I knew they were all there. All of Sarah's friends, and the boys from St Jude's. And they were laughing at me. I'd become even more of a joke than I was already.' Lizzie covered her face with her hands, the shame of what had happened washing over her. Twenty years might have passed, but this was the first time she'd spoken about what had happened, and it felt, for that moment, as raw as it had back then.

Simon moved closer, and enfolded his arms around Lizzie. He felt solid, and reassuring, and she leaned against him, drawing strength from his closeness. It had been so draining, recounting all of it, but she realised with some surprise that she was feeling a little lighter because of it.

'I'm so sorry, Lizzie.' Simon's tone was as appalled as his expression. 'If I'd known any of this, I'd have stopped the party there and then.'

'They were stupid, vicious kids,' Lizzie said. 'And that was what it was like back then. I was fair game, they thought.'

Simon didn't reply and Lizzie could see that he was struggling with something. 'Go on,' she said softly. 'You want to ask, don't you?'

'Christ, Lizzie, I don't know how to.' Simon's eyes were suddenly hollow. He drew a deep breath. 'Was... was my sister, Sarah, involved in this?'

Lizzie let the pause stretch between them for a long moment before she spoke. 'I've thought about it on and off over the years,' she began. 'And after all this time, I'm still not a hundred per cent sure. There were so many people in the living room, and I didn't have my glasses, that I really can't be certain. She might have been a bystander, or she might have known about the plan. I just don't know. The only thing I do know is that George wasn't in the room.' Lizzie gave a brief grimace. 'She told me later, when she got back to Bee's, that she'd spent most of the evening with the boy she'd wanted to get off with, and I wanted to believe that was true so much that I didn't question her. I was so ashamed that I didn't tell her what had happened, and if Nina filled her in later, well, she never told me.'

'So how did you get out of there?' Simon asked.

Lizzie gave a sad smile. 'That's where you come in.'

'Me?'

'Yup. I ran out of the room, and, stupidly, like all of those girls in the films, I ran as far upstairs as I could. I made it to the roof terrace before I realised how dangerous it was up there.'

'And that's where I found you,' Simon said, the memory finally clicking into place. 'I do remember now.'

'You gave me your jumper. I was pretty shivery, and that stupid dress barely covered anything. I think you thought I was just cold. I meant to return it to you the day after, but I must have left it at Bee's place, and was in such a hurry to get away, I forgot to ask her to take it back to the hall for you.'

'I liked that jumper, too,' Simon teased gently, but when he saw Lizzie's stricken face, he relented. 'I'm kidding. I don't even remember which one it was.'

'A black lambswool one,' Lizzie replied. 'It had holes in one of the elbows and was stretched all out of shape.'

'Ah, yes,' Simon said. 'Holes in the elbows from resting on pub tables trying to read the set novels, and out of shape because I kept putting it on the wrong washing cycle at the university launderette! I remember it well now...'

'I found it in one of Bee's cupboards,' Lizzie said. 'Do you want it back?'

Simon laughed. 'For nostalgia's sake, perhaps, but there's no need.' Then, suddenly serious again, 'But why didn't you tell me what happened on the night?' Simon asked. 'You ran away again, if I remember correctly.'

'I'd just been humiliated in front of most of the people in my school year,' Lizzie reminded him. 'The last thing I wanted was to stay here any longer than I had to. I wanted to get out of Roseford Hall and never look back.'

'Can't say I blame you,' Simon said. 'But, for the record, I would have seen you home, at least. And come back and dealt with those kids. And I'd never have treated you the way they did.'

Lizzie nodded. 'I know. You were very sweet. But I couldn't handle it, after what had happened. I needed to escape.'

'It's all coming back to me now,' Simon said carefully. 'I turned around and you'd vanished. And I'd just about convinced myself that it had all been a figment of my imagination. Would've believed it, too, if it hadn't been for that jumper.'

Lizzie gave a slightly choked laugh. She remembered the comfort she'd taken in that simple gesture, as she'd stumbled back to Bee's cottage, and thrown herself into bed, willing it all to have been some awful dream. Georgina had returned hours later, eyes alight with the thrill of new love, and had tried to talk about the evening, but Lizzie hadn't been able to cope with her sister's exuberant high spirits; she'd feigned sleep until Georgina had given up. They'd left the next day, and as time had gone by Lizzie had felt less and less able to confide in her sister; where once, they'd shared everything, now Lizzie felt that indefinable glass wall between them, which she'd never really managed to break. Twenty years on, there was little point. She still didn't know if Georgina had been aware of the plot to set her up. She hadn't had the strength to ask at the time, and now it seemed ridiculous to ask.

So why had she brought it up with Simon now? Obviously, being back in Roseford had made her think about it all again, as she'd known it would from the moment Aunt Bee had sent her the invitation to stay. But perhaps talking about it, laying the ghosts to rest, was what she needed to finally let go of it all. And perhaps, because she was getting closer to Simon, she wanted to be able to move on.

'I just felt it was time to face what happened to me head-on,' Lizzie said, only realising once the words were hanging in the air that she'd spoken them out loud.

Simon looked at her curiously. 'That sounds like the answer to a question only you could hear.'

Lizzie shook her head. 'Sorry. I got lost in my head there.' She smiled. 'And I'm so sorry to dump this on you. I guess that was the last thing you were expecting when you invited me back here for a drink!'

Simon drew closer to her. 'I wasn't expecting anything,' he said gently. 'I just wanted to spend a little more time with you.' He paused, and, seeking permission tacitly from her, he took her hand again. 'I like you, Lizzie. I like you a lot. And I'm so sorry that the one abiding memory you have of my family and my home is such an awful one.'

'But you did your best to help, all those years ago,' Lizzie murmured. 'And I did appreciate it.'

'I never realised Sarah was part of such a horrible group,' Simon continued. 'I'm so sorry that you had to go through all of that.'

Lizzie shrugged, and her collarbone gave a warning not to repeat the gesture. 'You weren't to know. Teenage girls can be pretty feral.'

'All the same, I wish I had known.'

There was a pause, and Lizzie felt as though the moment was loaded with something else. Drawing closer to him, she tilted her gaze upwards, to find that he was looking down at her with the same intensity. Her lips parted, and the hand that was still clasped in Simon's slowly travelled up his arm, fingers brushing across his shoulder and neck, to rest in his hair. Gently, mindful of both her own arm and the emotions that being in this house with him evoked, she stretched upwards, until, in the space of a few rushing heartbeats, her lips met his in a careful but exquisite kiss. At her own pace, she pressed herself against him, and his arms slid around her waist as the kiss grew deeper, until, eventually, both of them drew back, breathless and flushed.

'Wow,' Simon murmured. 'That really was worth waiting for!'

Lizzie smiled, her own mouth still only a centimetre or two from his. 'I'm glad to hear it.'

'I wasn't expecting that,' Simon continued, his breath warm on her face as they lingered between kisses. 'Not after what you've just told me.'

Another couple of kisses punctuated the moments before Lizzie replied. 'It was a long time ago,' she said eventually. 'And maybe this is helping me to move on, in a way.'

Simon nodded. 'I hope so.'

And standing there, kissing Simon in a house that had once held so much significance for her, for entirely different reasons, Lizzie found herself daring to hope that things were going to get better.

22

'Someone's happy this morning!' The voice came from behind him as Simon, humming under his breath, finished unloading the dishwasher. 'Is there something I should know?'

Simon's head jerked up at the sound of Sarah's voice. 'Would it kill you to knock before you come in?' He put the stack of dinner plates, which he'd very nearly dropped, onto the worktop.

'Oh, sorry,' Sarah replied. 'I mean, it's not as if this used to be my house too, or anything.' She grabbed the kettle, and, filling it briskly with cold water, flipped the switch. 'I just thought I'd come over and see how you are, oh, and thank you again for your help with Holmes last night.'

'No problem,' Simon replied evenly. He felt his face growing a little warm as he remembered how wonderful the much-delayed kiss had been with Lizzie later that evening, but he wasn't prepared to elaborate on that with Sarah. Some things he wanted to keep to himself. There was, of course, an elephant in the room that he needed to discuss with her, though. He had hoped he'd have a little more time to think about how to broach the subject, after Lizzie's disclosure last night, but it didn't need putting off.

As Sarah made two cups of tea, and chatted idly about the plans for the wedding, and a couple of other events that Roseford Hall was hosting over the coming weeks, Simon tried hard to focus, but all he could think about was what Lizzie had told him, and how it had altered his perspective of Sarah considerably. Even allowing for the fact that time might have enlarged Lizzie's grievances, Simon was inclined to believe her account. What bothered him was what exactly Sarah had known about the plan to harass and embarrass Lizzie.

'Thanks,' he said as she passed him a mug of hot tea and they both sat down at the table. His stomach rumbled. He hadn't had breakfast yet. He was happy, therefore, when Sarah produced a couple of Chelsea buns from a paper bag.

'Thought you might want a bit of sugar to tide you over,' she said, passing him one.

'So,' Sarah said, once she'd had a couple of bites of her own huge cake. 'Is there anything you'd like to tell me?'

Suddenly the mouthful of soft pastry seemed to be taking Simon an eternity to chew and swallow. He took a gulp of tea that was entirely too hot and did little to ease his predicament.

'There was something I needed to talk to you about, actually.'

Sarah raised an eyebrow. 'Oh, yes?'

'It's about Lizzie Warner.'

'Don't tell me you've proposed!' Sarah laughed. 'I mean, she's only been in the village a couple of weeks, hasn't she?'

Simon shook his head. 'Mum might be desperate to marry me off, but I'm not into rushing quite that much.' He toyed with the handle of his tea mug.

'The thing is, Sarah... while it's Lizzie I want to talk to you about, it's not in the way you might think.'

He paused.

Sarah gave a short laugh. 'She's not asked you for money, has she? Haven't you made it clear that we don't actually *have* any?'

Simon shook his head impatiently, irritated that Sarah was refusing to take him seriously.

'Look, she told me, about something that happened here years ago. I need to know just how... involved you were in all of it.'

Sarah looked confused. 'What are you saying?'

Simon took another sip of his tea before continuing. Rapidly, he relayed the story that Lizzie had told him the night before, trying not to downplay or over-dramatise, despite his conflicted emotions.

As he drew to a close, there was a long silence.

'God, Simon,' Sarah began. 'I mean... what do you want me to say? It was twenty years ago.'

'I want to know your side of the story,' Simon said calmly. 'Everyone makes mistakes, and everyone's been a stupid teenager, but did you know about all this, back then?'

Sarah dropped her gaze to her mug. 'You don't understand how it was when we were teenagers. How hard it was to fit in. To not be the one that stood out. That school... there was just so much pressure.'

'That doesn't exactly answer my question.'

Defiantly, Sarah looked back up at him. 'Don't. You were just so fucking oblivious to everything, weren't you? To how awful it was to be surrounded by all of those girls, judging you, making you feel small for the slightest thing. Of course I tried to fit in, and I won't have you condemning me for that.'

'And did *trying to fit in* mean victimising other people?' Simon replied. 'Other people who were just as vulnerable as you, if not more so?'

'Oh, please,' Sarah retorted. 'You've got her version of something that happened decades ago. It wasn't as bad as all that.' Something in Sarah's eyes gave her away though, and Simon immediately knew that it had been *exactly* as bad as Lizzie had made out.

'I believe her,' Simon said softly. 'I know that upsets you, sis, but I do. So the question is, how much did you know?'

The silence stretched interminably between them.

'I knew that Nina was up to something,' Sarah said quietly. 'I knew that Lizzie had only been invited because Georgina had. I didn't know what exactly Nina had planned until she brought Lizzie into the living room and switched on the lights. And for that I'm sorry.'

'You could have gone after Lizzie!' Simon said brutally. 'Instead of sitting by, watching her become the victim of Nina's bullying. You could have stood up for her, Sarah. Why didn't you?'

'You make it sound so simple!' Sarah exclaimed. 'Have you no memory of what it's like to be a teenager? And it was so long ago, Simon. Don't you think I've thought, over the years, about how we treated Lizzie? Don't you think I already feel bad enough? If I could change it now, I would, but I can't. It happened. We were a horrible group of girls. We allowed something terrible happen. But it's done... over. There's nothing I can do.'

'You can apologise to Lizzie for your part in it.' Simon stood up from the table. 'It's not too late for that.'

As he walked from the room, he paused. Then, more gently, he added, 'And I do get it, Sarah. You weren't the only one who found school a nightmare. Maybe those scars stay with us a whole lot longer than we think.'

Later on, as he perused the invitation from Cross Dean School for the thousandth time since he'd received it, he wondered if it might just be time to face his own fears.

23

In the week leading up to what Simon had only half-jokingly dubbed 'The Wedding of the Year', both Lizzie and Simon were preoccupied with their different roles in the proceedings. Lizzie was helping Bee out with the floral arrangements. Some could be done a few days in advance, so long as they were kept cool and hydrated, and some would have to be done the night before, and finished off on the day.

The long, hot summer continued; long, sunny days led into warm, sweet nights, infused by the scents from Bee's garden drifting in through the window as Lizzie dozed. Since their kiss, her mind kept replaying the moment with Simon. They'd kissed a great deal that night, but both had stopped short of taking things further. Simon, ever the gentleman, had walked her back to Bee's cottage later that night, with a promise to call her. They'd spoken and texted since, but hadn't managed to spend any significant time together. Being in the same village but unable to snatch more than a few moments together was deliciously frustrating, but it seemed unavoidable, as the last preparations for the wedding were under way.

Unfortunately, Simon had been caught up with yet more admin to do with the chapel, and the arrangement of the day, and she'd been working alongside Bee, learning more and more about the day-to-day running of Roseford Blooms. Bee had a student from Cannington College with her to assist her with the vast floral demands of the wedding and, with Lizzie acting as an extra pair of hands, they were all kept busy.

Lizzie had to concede she was enjoying being part of the business and she was feeling more and more at home in Roseford Blooms. Watching Bee, admiring her artistry as she brought to life the concepts that Serena and Montana wanted for the wedding, was not only therapeutic but inspiring. Lizzie found herself wanting to spend more time in this world where flowers were not just admired for their beauty, but also had meaning, and when she found a book on the Victorian language of flowers on the shelf at Bee's house, she devoured it.

This did not go unnoticed by Bee. Late afternoon, on the day before the wedding, Bee paused in her creation of the buttonholes.

'You're nearly as fast as I am with these now,' she said, wrapping the green finishing tape around the one she was working on and popping it into the box. 'You've really got the hang of them.'

Lizzie smiled. 'It's a lot easier now I've got rid of the sling.' The hospital had advised her to keep it on for at least two weeks, but she'd passed that deadline and was now learning to be without it whenever she could. She still had to be careful: an injury to the collarbone took longer to heal when you were an adult, and it ached if she did too much, but she was relieved to be out of the collar and cuff.

'Well, I think you've got an eye for them. And these roses really are quite beautiful.' Bee picked up another flower from the pile on the counter and briskly started to prepare it. 'They're a variety I haven't used before, but apparently the colour matches the brides' dresses to a tee.'

'I should imagine everything's been thought through to the nth degree.' Lizzie laughed. 'I mean, Montana de Santo isn't going to risk a hair out of place, is she?'

Bee smiled. 'I met Montana a few times when she was filming in Roseford. She's actually a very sweet girl. But she does know what she wants, and, like any bride, she wants her day to be perfect. And Serena, of course, I've known since she was born. They make a lovely couple.'

Lizzie put the finishing touches on the buttonhole she was working on and popped it into the box. 'I'm looking forward to seeing them,' she said. 'And I know they'll love all of these beautiful creations.' Before she reached for another rose, she looked towards Bee. 'I've really enjoyed helping out in the shop, Aunt Bee. It makes me wish...' Lizzie trailed off, suddenly unsure about sharing her thoughts.

'What does it make you wish?' Bee asked gently.

Lizzie shook her head. 'Oh, I don't know. And it's probably a stupid idea anyway. You can't teach an old dog new tricks, after all.' She began putting the buttonhole together.

'Well, I don't know about old dogs, but you certainly seem to be learning a lot while you're here,' Bee replied. 'And I'm glad you're enjoying it.'

Lizzie smiled. 'Yes,' she said. 'I am. I really am. It's good to be working with something that I can see and feel taking shape in my hands. It's so different from what I did before, which was all about marketing products that other people had envisioned. Creating things with flowers reminds me how rewarding that process can be.'

'I think it's doing you a lot of good,' Bee observed. Then she laughed. 'Of course, on a winter's day, when you have to keep the shop cool to stop the flowers from wilting, it's not quite so idyllic, or having to improvise because your key delivery hasn't come in and you've a wedding or a funeral arrangement to make.'

Lizzie laughed, too. Helping Bee was one thing, but it was a long way from actually running the business. Playing about with buttonholes had been fun, but there was far more to it than that. But perhaps she could learn, if Bee was willing to teach her? It wasn't as if she'd been inspired by anything else lately, career wise. In fact, ever since she'd sold her share of Warner-Basset, she'd been trying to decide what to do with the rest of her life. Maybe being part of a venture like Roseford Blooms would be the change she'd been looking for?

Then reality asserted itself. She was staying in Bee's spare room, she had no base of her own, and she might have a lot of money in the bank right now but much of that would have to go to find her a new place to live. Some pipe dream about a career change was just out of the question.

24

The day of the wedding arrived, and it meant an early start for the florists. Lizzie rearranged the last of the flowers on the end of the pew at the back of the chapel, and gave them a final spritz from the spray bottle that Bee had given her. She stepped back to admire her handiwork. Not bad for an amateur, she thought, proudly. Bee, of course, would have the final say, and was carefully checking over the arrangements they'd brought in earlier, making sure everything was perfect.

'That's lovely, darling,' Bee said as she approached. 'We'll make a florist of you yet!'

'I'm not so sure about that,' Lizzie replied, although she did feel pride in a job well done, and a glow of pleasure at Bee's words. She wasn't used to being praised for any of her efforts by her immediate family, it simply wasn't their way, so Bee's regular and effusive feedback felt strange, but rather lovely.

Simon popped his head around the heavy chapel door at that moment, and Lizzie felt her stomach do a little flip. He looked smarter than usual in his well-cut navy-blue suit, with a plain white shirt underneath the jacket and a richly toned gold tie in a perfect Oxford knot. He'd scrubbed up rather well again, Lizzie couldn't help but notice.

'Everything all right in here?' he asked as he walked towards Lizzie and Bee.

'Everything's fine, Simon,' Bee replied, her smile seeming to reassure Simon just as much as her words. 'Given the temperatures that have been forecast, the flowers needed a touch more water, but we're all on track.'

'Good to hear it,' Simon said. 'The guy from the British Heritage Fund is due any minute, so I'll meet him at the front gate and bring him down, so he can tick off his checklist or whatever else he sees fit to do. Hopefully he'll bugger off as soon as he's done that, and we can all get on with the business of enjoying the day.'

Simon looked nervous, Lizzie thought. Too nervous just to be meeting some pen-pusher from the BHF. She wondered what else was on his mind, but wasn't sure if she should ask him in front of Bee. There must be so much to think about running an event like this. She was used to high pressure in her job – her *previous* job, she corrected herself – but the sprawl and scope of Roseford Hall and the tension between the wedding organisers and the BHF must take some navigating.

'I'm sure he won't want to hang around any longer than he has to,' Bee, who always seemed to find ways to soothe people, said. 'Even with the guests being as, er, famous as they are.'

'Don't remind me.' Simon rolled his eyes. 'There's security on the gate just in case, and one or two others will be dotted around, but hopefully no one will kick off and try to gatecrash proceedings.'

Lizzie laughed. 'Don't worry, if rabid fans try to storm the castle, I'm sure we'll handle it!'

Simon grinned back at her. 'Well, back in the day, Montana and her co-star Finn apparently inspired some pretty "creative" behaviour from their admirers, if what Finn's told me is anything to go by.'

'Did I just hear someone take my name in vain?' Another figure appeared at the church door, and Lizzie couldn't help a gasp, even though she'd met him when he'd popped into the flower shop the other day to get the bouquet for Lucy's mother. Finn walked into the church, and for a moment Lizzie was dazzled by that aura of charisma that seemed to surround him. She wondered if that feeling ever went away, and what it must be like for Finn.

'Oh, hey, Finn,' Simon said. 'How's our wedding party doing?'

'They're all just about managing to keep a lid on it,' Finn replied. He was dressed immaculately in black pin-striped trousers and a beautifully cut tailcoat, with a cravat in the palest rose pink at his throat. Lizzie smiled at the thought that, with a top hat on, he'd be about seven feet tall.

'Well, I've got to meet this bloke from the BHF and bring him down for a final inspection, but that hopefully won't take too long, and then we can all relax and enjoy ourselves! Maybe,' he added playfully, 'you'll be able to get out of that penguin suit at some point, too!'

Finn laughed. 'Montana threatened to put me in a taffeta bridesmaid's dress if I didn't behave myself.'

'Now that I'd have paid good money to see!' Simon quipped.

Lizzie watched Finn as he looked down the aisle, taking in the flowers arranged at the end of each pew, the displays on the sills of the mullioned windows and the two beautifully presented collections of roses and freesias either side of the ceremony space. 'This all looks wonderful. Montana will be knocked out when she sees it.'

Lizzie smiled back at him. His politeness and enthusiasm seemed completely genuine, and she instinctively liked him.

'I'm glad you like it,' Lizzie replied. 'My aunt Bee is the real genius; I'm just an amateur who's happy to lend a hand.'

'Well, it looks great.' Finn smiled again, then turned back to Simon. 'I guess I'd better get back to the wedding party, unless there's anything I can do to help?'

'I think we've got it all under control,' Simon said. 'But I'll head back out to the gate with you and see if that BHF guy's here yet.'

As they said their goodbyes, Lizzie realised that neither had taken a buttonhole from the box by the church door.

'Simon, wait!' she called after them. 'You might as well have these now, before the rush.' She picked up two exquisite ivory-coloured roses from the box and passed one to Finn to pin on his lapel. Simon reached for his, but fumbled getting it into place.

'Do you want me to pin it for you?' Lizzie asked. 'Bee's taught me a quick trick.'

'Thanks,' Simon said. Was she imagining it, or did he flush slightly as she drew closer to him, slipping her fingers under the lapel of his jacket and gently pinning the spray onto it? She paused for a moment longer than was necessary, before releasing him again and meeting his gaze.

'That should do it,' she said.

'Thank you,' Simon said again, and their eyes locked until Simon coughed nervously. 'I'll, er, see you a bit later?'

'See you later.' Lizzie smiled at him. As he left the chapel with Finn, she watched them both in animated conversation and wondered how the two of them had become such great friends. Simon was so unworldly, and Finn was such a huge star, they seemed an improbable pair. But they were both wonderful men and obviously enjoyed each other's company.

'I don't think I've ever seen Simon so nervous,' Bee's voice interrupted Lizzie's musings as she joined her by the chapel door.

'Well, if Simon doesn't get this wedding right in the eyes of the BHF, they're not likely to clear any others in the chapel, are they?' Lizzie reasoned, her eyes still following the receding backs of Simon and Finn.

'Not about the wedding – he's been nervous for weeks about that.' Bee looked shrewdly at Lizzie. 'When you were pinning on his buttonhole.'

'He probably thought I was going to stab him with the pin!' Lizzie laughed, but her face started to burn. Every encounter she'd had with Simon seemed to lead to an unsettling set of emotions and standing so close to him just now had been no different. She had to get a hold on herself; she wasn't in Roseford forever, and she didn't want to get caught in the net of the past. All the same, she reflected, she couldn't help but be pleased by Bee's observations.

25

Simon glanced at his watch as he walked towards the gates of Roseford Hall. Finn said goodbye until later, and ducked through the gate, hurrying back off in the direction of the Treloar Arms, where one of the brides-to-be, Montana de Santo, and her bridesmaids were preparing themselves for the big day ahead. Finn was acting as best man for Montana. 'Not chief bridesmaid, then?' Simon had teased.

Simon glanced at his watch again. He didn't really want to waste time hanging about at the gate, and hoped that the BHF contact, a guy named Mike Walcott, would arrive soon. To reconfirm to himself that he had the right details, he swiped to his email on his phone again and was just rereading the correspondence when a voice broke into his concentration.

'Simon, my man, good to see you. This place is just as crappy to get to as I remembered, though.'

Simon nearly dropped his phone. The voice, cutting into his reverie, took him back years. Over twenty years, actually. He hurriedly pocketed his phone and then looked towards the owner of the voice.

'Jago?' he said carefully. 'Jago McAvoy? What are you doing here?'

Of all the people who could have turned up on this day, Jago was the absolute last person he wanted to see. Jago had made Simon's life a living hell when they'd been at school together, and when Simon had left Cross

Dean for the last time, Jago was one of the people he'd hoped vehemently never to see again. And now, here he was, standing in the grounds of Roseford Hall, smirking confidently as if they were both teenagers again. Not to mention what the bastard had put Sarah through as well, he thought darkly.

'Mike Walcott couldn't make it, had a bout of sickness late last night, apparently, so I've stepped into the breach. Since I knew where the place was, I said I'd take this inspection on.'

Simon felt keenly as though Jago was assessing him with every word. The years suddenly seemed to have rolled back, and he felt shaken and decidedly wrong-footed. Simon shook Jago's hand numbly when it was offered, but when he tried to speak, he found that his mind had gone blank.

'Well, shall we get this over with?' Jago said, by way of not-so-subtle prompting. 'I've got a family barbecue to get back to this afternoon and I want to get back on the bloody M5 before the tourists crash and have it closed again.'

'Sure, sure,' Simon said. His heart was racing inside his ribcage, and the adrenaline was spiking in his veins. He was not that boy from school, he reminded himself swiftly, as, on autopilot, he guided Jago up the driveway and across to the chapel.

As the two of them walked, Jago kept up a fairly constant monologue that required only the briefest of responses and occasional nods from Simon. It was only when Jago asked after his sister, Sarah, that Simon tuned back in.

'She's fine,' Simon replied. 'Two girls of her own, now.'

'But I heard the husband buggered off,' Jago pressed. Simon remembered him always having a nose for gossip. 'What'd you do? Drop a sconce on him or something? The last time I saw this place, it was falling apart.'

'As you can see, it's a lot different now,' Simon said stiffly. 'And frankly, Jago, that's none of your bloody business.'

'All right, all right, keep your hair on.' Jago flashed Simon a far too self-assured smile. 'I just wouldn't have minded saying hello, that's all.'

Simon remembered how heartbroken Sarah had been when Jago had dumped her just before her A levels, and immediately started trying to think of a way to get a message to her that he was on site. Perhaps he could send her a quick WhatsApp when Jago was doing his rounds. After Sarah's divorce, Simon had felt incredibly protective towards his sister, and he wanted to keep Jago as far away from her as possible.

They were nearing the chapel, and Simon felt instantly soothed seeing Lizzie and Bee coming out of the main door.

'All set,' Bee said as they met outside. 'I've left Lizzie with another spray bottle, just in case anything needs pepping up before the ceremony.'

'Thank you so much, Bee,' Simon said. Then, to Lizzie, 'I'll save you a seat in the church.' Finn had raised a speculative eyebrow when Simon had asked him if Lizzie could come to the wedding as his plus one, but he'd checked with Montana and Serena, who had a little space from a couple of last-minute cancellations, so were fine with it.

'Thanks,' Lizzie replied.

'I'll see you later,' Simon said.

'Yes,' Lizzie replied. 'You'd better go and keep an eye on your friend there. I take it he's the one doing the checks for the BHF?'

'He's no friend of mine,' Simon said bleakly. He reached out a hand and touched her forearm. 'I hope he won't be here long.'

Lizzie smiled quickly at him. 'See you in a bit.'

As Lizzie left to get smartened up for the wedding, Simon made it his mission to get Jago McAvoy out of Roseford as soon as he could.

26

Hours after the formalities of the wedding were over, Lizzie still had to pinch herself when she looked around the marquee and saw so many famous, and incredibly glamorous faces. As if having a bride like Montana de Santo wasn't enough, Montana's close friends were a selection of the cream of the Hollywood crop, as well as those who seemed, refreshingly, rather more ordinary. The wedding photos would be a *Who's Who* of twenty-first-century movie making. Montana and Serena were incandescent with joy, and the two brides had barely left each other's side for a moment. And as the day had gone on, the 'non-showbiz' guests and friends had mingled with the more famous ones, and the atmosphere had been everything they could have wished for.

Lizzie could see some people chatting, tired but happy after a long day of celebration. On the dance floor off to her right, in front of the DJ, who was doing a sterling job of encouraging a few last dances out of people, was Finn Sanderson. He was dancing in a kind of cute trio with both Lucy and her ten-year old-daughter, Megan, who was, from the look on her face, torn between loving every minute of the situation and thinking it was all a bit lame. Lizzie could remember those sensations well, herself. Finn, tailcoat long since discarded and white shirt untucked, looked every inch the off-duty movie star. That image was further compounded as the music changed to a slower number, and Megan scuttled off to fill up on more wedding cupcakes. Lucy, a look of absolute contentment and love on her face, settled into Finn's arms, and, locked in each other's embrace, they swayed gently to the music.

Lizzie regarded them with a mixture of delight and envy. It had been so long since she'd danced that way with someone. She and Paul had been to their fair share of friends' weddings, of course, but he'd never been a dancer, and had preferred to drink and chat. Finn and Lucy's love story was everything she'd ever secretly wanted, and seeing their obvious happiness, and that of the newly-weds Montana and Serena, who'd just stepped onto the dance floor and were dancing together, the absolute picture of love and joy, Lizzie's sense of envy grew stronger.

'May I have this dance?' A voice broke into her ruminations. Glancing up, tearing her gaze away from the couples on the dance floor, Lizzie saw Simon smiling down at her.

'I don't really dance,' she said, a note of defensiveness in her voice.

'Well,' Simon replied, 'neither do I, but it appears to be the expected thing to do at a wedding reception, and I'm rather fed up of doing the Macarena by myself.'

Simon, too, had shed his suit jacket and his formal tie was loosened, the top button of his crisp white shirt undone. He looked gorgeous, sexy and, Lizzie felt with a sudden stab of longing, infinitely desirable. A lock of fair hair had fallen over his forehead, giving him the look of an older, blonder Rupert Brooke, and, just for the moment, Lizzie wanted to believe in the fairy tale.

'Don't leave me hanging, Elizabeth Warner,' Simon said. 'Or the song'll be over by the time we hit the floor.'

Smiling, Lizzie stood up. 'Well, since you put it that way...' They made their way over to the dance floor, where the slow song was now in full flow. Simon asked a tacit question with his eyes, Lizzie nodded, and in moments she'd slid into his arms. As she drew closer to him, she felt the heat from his body, and the scent of his woody, spiced cologne. She was tense in his arms, not just because her left arm felt vulnerable, only recently out of the sling.

'Try and relax if you can, Lizzie,' Simon whispered into her ear, the gentleness of his tone making her choke back a nervous laugh. 'I promise I won't step on your toes.'

'Wouldn't matter if you did,' Lizzie replied softly. 'I changed into trainers hours ago.'

'I thought you seemed shorter,' Simon murmured. 'I wish I'd done the same.'

The warmth and gentleness in his tone was helping Lizzie to relax, and as she moved slightly closer to him, she didn't resist the urge to rest her head on his shoulder. Turning her gaze to the side, she smiled at Lucy, who was looking dreamily across, lost in the moment. As their eyes locked, though, Lucy raised a curious eyebrow. Lizzie couldn't help a grin in return.

The DJ, clearly sensing the mood of the dancers, rather than pick up the pace with a more upbeat song, followed the dying embers of the slow dance with another mellow tune, and Lizzie tightened her arms around Simon, hopefully giving him the signal that she was more than happy to stay where she was for another few minutes.

'I'm so glad you were with me today,' Simon murmured into her ear. 'Thank you for being my plus one.'

'My pleasure,' Lizzie replied softly. She lifted her head from his shoulder and met his gaze, which looked tender and open in the soft light from the twinkling fairy lights hanging across the marquee. 'I enjoyed it.'

'You did brilliantly, too,' Lizzie said. There was a pause as they regarded each other. Lizzie saw Simon's eyes widening as she drew closer to him, and her lips parted in delicious anticipation. Their first kiss, born out of heightened emotions and disclosures, had been the anchor she'd needed in her emotional storm. This next one, she hoped, would be sweeter, filled with promises of things to come. She stretched up on tiptoes and brought her mouth to Simon's. 'Would it be too forward of me to say I want to spend the night with you?' she murmured between increasingly passionate kisses.

For a long, blissful moment, Simon relaxed into her arms but, a few seconds later, he disentangled himself gently from her, putting a little space between them. When he opened his eyes, she saw an apology there.

'What's wrong?' she said softly. 'Did I overstep the mark?'

Simon shook his head. 'It's not you,' he said quietly.

Lizzie laughed, a trace of bitterness in her tone. 'Did you honestly just say that?'

'I'm sorry, Lizzie.' Simon shook his head. 'Look. Can we go somewhere and talk?'

Lizzie sighed. 'It's been a very long day. I think I'll just go home.' The sting of rejection from Simon pulling so summarily away from her was the last thing she needed at the moment. Had she misread the signs so badly? Had she taken a risk in asking to spend the night with him, when he clearly didn't want that?

'No, Lizzie, please don't go. That's not what I want.'

'You could have fooled me,' Lizzie shot back. She felt the humiliation washing over her. She should have just kept quiet. Now she had to deal with the fact that Simon had pulled back from her, and she knew she'd be replaying that moment in her head until the small hours.

'Let me walk you,' Simon persisted. 'It's really uneven out there.'

Lizzie laughed. 'So chivalry isn't dead after all.' She stepped off the dance floor with as much decorum as she could muster, unwilling to make a scene in front of the other wedding guests. 'But I'll be fine. I'll see you.' Even more glad, now, of the trainers, she strode out of the marquee and into the night.

27

'What was that all about?' Finn asked as he approached Simon, his arm still around Lucy. 'Has the infamous Treloar charm run dry?'

Simon shook his head. 'I think I just made the biggest cock-up of my life.'

'I'm sure it can't be that bad,' Lucy said soothingly. 'I mean, you're not an idiot, Simon.'

'Jury's out on that one,' Simon muttered. 'And I think I need a drink.'

'Well, the bar's still well stocked, so you're in luck there,' Finn replied. Simon saw him glance at Lucy, and a line of communication passed between them.

'I'll, er, just go and try to prise Megan away from the cupcake stand before she makes herself sick,' Lucy said. She touched Simon's arm as she passed. 'It'll be all right, Simon.'

'Come on,' Finn said. 'Let's get those drinks.'

A few minutes later, Simon had the remnants of a bottle of Krug and Finn had grabbed himself a non-alcoholic beer. They settled themselves at a table, far away enough from the disco so they could hear themselves think, and Simon, after a good slug straight from the bottle of champagne, sighed.

'I don't know why I pulled away from her,' he said. 'She's gorgeous, and funny, and she's single. What the fuck is wrong with me?'

'If it didn't feel right, then there's no point pushing things,' Finn said. He took a sip from his beer bottle. 'You're only setting her up for heartache later, otherwise.'

Simon shook his head. 'The stupid thing is, I want to be with her. But then everything started running through my head again: what if it was a mistake? What if it was just too much wine and too much good music?'

'Man.' Finn gave a short laugh. 'I thought I had the monopoly on self-doubt. You take it to a whole new level.'

'Thanks,' Simon replied dryly. 'But the question is, what do I do about it?'

Finn looked him straight in the eye. 'Go after her,' he said simply. 'If you have feelings for her, then tell her. Don't waste this opportunity.'

'Easy for you to say,' Simon replied. 'You're shacked up with the love of your life, on the way to the second biggest celebrity wedding of the year.'

'And you're just making excuses,' Finn replied smartly. 'So, stop talking to me and have this conversation with Lizzie.'

'I don't think that's such a good idea,' Simon said.

'And that's your problem.' Finn sighed. 'You need to stop thinking, Simon. It's a beautiful night, and ten minutes ago you had a wonderful woman in your arms. Get her back.'

Simon took another long gulp of the Krug, for Dutch courage, put the bottle down on the table and stood up. 'If this backfires, I'm coming back to find you,' he said, looking down at Finn.

'Good luck,' Finn said. 'Just tell her how you feel.'

Simon exited the marquee, and hurried back towards Roseford Hall's gates. There were quite a few people sitting on the benches that bordered the manicured lawns of the grounds, chatting quietly. The sounds of relaxed laughter drifted on the humid evening air. Simon raised a hand briefly as a couple hailed him on his way past. He fumbled in his back pocket for his phone, and fired off a text to Lizzie, hoping she'd pick it up. Then, he kept walking towards and through the gates of Roseford Hall.

Heading towards the village centre, he hurried as fast as he could up the street, trying to see if Lizzie was up ahead. She could well be back at Bee's

by now, but he wasn't sure he was brave enough to face the kindly inquisi-
tion from Lizzie's aunt if Lizzie had told her why she was upset. Upping his
pace a little more, he hoped he'd catch her before she got home.

As he approached the village square, his heart, already elevated from
the pace, gave a protracted thump at the sight of a figure sitting on the
bench by the war memorial.

'I was hoping to find you before you got back to Bee's,' he said gently as
he approached the bench.

Lizzie looked up at him, and her face was illuminated by the warm
golden glow from the street light. At once he knew that he'd been a
complete fool when he'd pulled away from her.

'I thought about going back to Aunt Bee's,' she said quietly, 'but I wasn't
quite ready to. Not yet.'

'I'm glad you didn't,' Simon said. He gestured to the empty space beside
her on the bench. 'May I? I'd like to talk, if that's all right?'

Lizzie's eyes flashed defiantly. 'I think you made your feelings pretty
clear on the dance floor, actually.'

Simon felt the lurch in his heart at the directness of her words. 'Actually,
Lizzie, I think that's the last thing I did.' He took a deep lungful of the night
air to try to calm his thoughts.

'I'm sorry,' he said as he drew closer. 'I was an idiot.' He looked her
straight in the eye, looking for signs that she was considering his words. He
reached out and took one of her hands in his. 'I suppose that so many years
of feeling like everyone's watching my every move as Lord Treloar has
made me awfully cautious. Or maybe just awful,' he added, as an
afterthought.

'You're not awful, Simon,' Lizzie replied. He felt a huge sense of relief
when she didn't withdraw her hand from his. 'You just need to work out
what you want.'

Simon laughed gently. 'I'm getting there.'

'And how do you feel?' Lizzie asked. 'I don't want to be messed around,
Simon. I had enough of that with Paul. It really felt as though we were
making a connection, over the past few weeks. That's why I took the risk
and asked you if you wanted to spend the night with me.' She paused. 'I
don't say that to everyone I kiss, you know.'

Simon felt his cheeks starting to flame, both in embarrassment and with other, more wonderful thoughts. 'I get that,' he said. 'And I'm flattered that you would be so direct with me.'

'But you're not interested,' Lizzie cut in, pulling her hand away. 'That's fine. It was just a few kisses. No big deal.'

Simon saw her eyes glistening in the lamplight before she turned away from him, and he felt a thrum of frustration that she could so easily misunderstand him.

'No, Lizzie,' he said firmly. 'That's not it at all. Quite the opposite, in fact. I really, *really* want to spend the night with you. More than just one night, if I can. And I'm sorry that I pulled away from you and gave you completely the opposite impression.' He paused, and gently raised a hand to her shoulder, until she turned back to look at him. 'My best friend, Olivia, always used to say that I'd need a woman to shove a banner under my nose before I realised she was interested in me, and I'm afraid she's right. So you did exactly the right thing by being direct, even though it took me by surprise.'

To his immense relief, Lizzie smiled. 'Well, then,' she murmured as she closed the gap between them, 'consider this the direct approach.' As her lips met his, this time he didn't pull away, and felt a heady, reckless desire to do just the opposite. He wanted her in his arms for a much longer time than a park bench in the middle of Roseford would allow.

'Is this clear enough?' Lizzie murmured against his mouth.

Simon, lost for words, simply deepened the kiss, until he felt Lizzie's arms around him, and they were both breathing heavily.

'Come home with me,' Simon said. 'I don't want you to go back to Bee's tonight.'

Lizzie regarded him levelly. 'And you're absolutely sure this time?'

Simon nodded his head vehemently. 'Yes, Lizzie. Yes, I am.' His hand, slightly shakily, traced its way from Lizzie's cheek to the nape of her neck as he pulled her towards him for another kiss. 'I want you. If you want me... I'm here.'

'Then we'd better get somewhere a little less public.' Lizzie smiled as they pulled back from one another again.

Simon nodded, stood up and took Lizzie's hand. 'That sounds like a wonderful idea.'

28

The moon and stars overhead were the only observers as Lizzie and Simon made their way back to Roseford Hall. As if to remind them both that there were still some people around, though, a muffled cheer floated across from the marquee.

'Serena and Montana must be heading back to their hotel,' Simon said. 'I suppose that means the party will wind down soon.'

They crossed the front lawn of the house, heading for the door to Simon's quarters at the back of the house. Lizzie could sense Simon's excitement and apprehension, which she suspected were as great as her own. His eyes sparkled as he turned to kiss her again, before putting his key in the lock to let them both into the house.

Simon pushed open the front door, and reached for the switch in the entrance hall. When the area was flooded with a bright, piercing light, Lizzie blinked to let her eyes adjust. As she was acclimatising, she felt Simon's hand tighten in hers.

'Elspeth!' Simon exclaimed as the figure of a young girl was revealed, huddled in the wooden justice's chair, a relic that Simon had rescued from another part of the house, that sat in the hallway. 'What are you doing here? Shouldn't you be with Fleur and your mother?'

The girl, visibly upset, looked up at Simon. 'Uncle Simon! I'm so glad you're here!' Struggling up from the chair, where she'd clearly been for some time, she ran over to Simon and threw her arms around him.

'What's wrong, sweetheart?' Simon said, once she'd released him a little.

Elspeth gave a huge sniff. 'Fleur's been horrible to me all evening,' she said, wiping away a stray tear. 'She told me no one liked me, that I was just a little kid and I should go and play with Montana's nieces. But they're all loads younger than me and it was boring! Mum's been too preoccupied chatting to some bloke from the BHF, and in the end I just got fed up and decided to come and wait for you to come back. I saw you leave the party, and thought I'd get you to make me some hot chocolate. I used the spare key under the flowerpot to let myself in. Can I stay here tonight?'

Lizzie saw Simon's back stiffen, and wondered if it was the frustration of his romantic plans being thwarted by his niece, or the mention of Jago, whom they'd both assumed had buggered off home hours ago. Above Elspeth's head, Simon gazed skywards, and then back at Lizzie. Lizzie gave him a small, understanding smile.

'Come on, shrimp,' Simon said to Elspeth. 'I'll sort out the hot chocolate and then I'll get hold of your mother, wherever she might be.'

'But can I stay here? I don't want to go back home tonight.'

Simon paused, and in that moment Lizzie knew that he was doing battle with the two sides of himself: the part of him that was a loving, concerned uncle, wanting to do the best for his niece, and the part of him that desperately wanted to spend time with Lizzie.

In the end, Lizzie stepped in. 'I'd best be off,' she said. 'I'll, er, see you some other time to talk about what we were, er, discussing earlier?'

Simon's look of disappointment and frustration would stay deliciously in her memory, Lizzie thought. She was in absolutely no doubt that, had Elspeth not been there, she and Simon would have been embarking on a wonderful night together. She felt the same emotions as Simon told Elspeth to go to the kitchen, and that he'd be there in a moment.

Turning back to Lizzie, he moved her gently back against the dark oak panelling of the entrance hall. 'God, my niece has the worst timing!' he growled as he leaned to kiss her again. Lizzie could feel that barely contained arousal as they moved their bodies together, and she couldn't resist pushing herself even closer, until they were both breathless and aching for more.

'Goodnight, Simon,' Lizzie said, once she could draw breath again. 'I'll see you soon.'

'You'd better,' Simon replied. 'All the hot chocolate in the world isn't going to make up for not spending the rest of the night with you.'

'Are you coming, Uncle Simon?' Elspeth's voice emanated from the back of the house.

Simon raised a suggestive eyebrow at Lizzie, and she burst out laughing. 'Hold that thought,' she said softly. Leaning up to kiss him once more, she pulled open the front door and walked down the pathway to the main gate.

What an evening, she thought as she began the walk up the hill to Bee's cottage. The doubts about how Simon felt about her had been thoroughly chased away by the fire in the kisses they'd shared. She only hoped that they'd get the chance to finish what they'd started soon.

29

Simon woke blearily the morning after the wedding.

Elspeth, contrary to her tired appearance when he'd found her at Rose-ford Hall, had kept him talking long into the night, despite his best efforts to send her to bed. He supposed he shouldn't have put quite so much sugar and whipped cream in the hot chocolate he'd made her, but he had to admit it had been nice to spend some time with his youngest niece, even if it meant having to say goodbye somewhat prematurely to Lizzie and miss out on the incredible night he was sure they would have had together. He'd phoned Sarah, who'd been grateful for his intervention. Fleur and Elspeth's relationship had been under strain lately, as one became a teenager and the other was still more interested in playing games. Simon hoped that, eventually, the sisters would become close again. Sarah seemed pleased that Elspeth had come to Simon, and thanked him for having her.

Rolling over in bed, he was also quite glad that he hadn't spent the rest of the night making a dent in the stocks of champagne in the marquee. He'd had a fair bit through the day but not enough to leave him with a hangover. A slight fuzziness of the head was to be expected after a long day and late night, but things could've been so much worse.

As he got up, he ran an idle hand through his hair, threw on an old pair of jeans and a T-shirt and his knackered old trainers and went to chivvy

Elspeth along. She'd stayed in the bedroom a couple of rooms away down the corridor. It used to be the room that she shared with her elder sister back when they all lived in the family quarters of Roseford Hall, and he hadn't yet got around to doing anything else with it. So, short of making the bed up last night, it hadn't been much hassle to have her sleeping over.

But she needed to get back to her mother and sister or Sarah would soon be ringing to find out where she was. He wasn't looking forward to having that conversation. Sarah had always struggled to completely understand the personality and motivations of her youngest daughter, and Elspeth, having run away back to the old family home late last night, wouldn't have done a great deal to aid that understanding.

As he headed down the corridor, Simon's thoughts again drifted back to Lizzie and he resolved to send her a text as soon as he dropped off Elspeth. Perhaps they could meet for breakfast and, he thought hopefully, maybe even pick up from where they'd left off last night.

As he walked into the room where Elspeth was sleeping, he wasn't surprised to see that she still had the covers pulled up around her ears.

'Come on, lazybones!' he called just loud enough to elicit a groan from his niece. 'It's time to get you back to your mother.'

In response, Elspeth rolled over and put the pillow over her head. 'Can I just stay here a bit longer?'

'Normally I'd say yes, you know that, but I've got too much to do this morning, such as making sure that the chapel is sorted out before the hall reopens on Monday, so you'll have to move it, squirt!'

Reluctantly Elspeth struggled out from underneath the duvet, stretched and reached for the dress that she'd taken off the night before. Simon had lent her one of his T-shirts to sleep in and it fell almost to her knees.

'Can I have some breakfast before I go?' Fleur asked.

'Only if you're quick. Your mum'll be expecting you back.'

'I doubt it,' Elspeth replied. 'The amount of wine she had last night I doubt she'll even have surfaced yet.'

Simon winced at the way Elspeth said that. The actions of adults through the eyes of a child had a harsher patina than was probably the reality. Children, especially those approaching being teenagers, seemed to see things in black and white, but Simon knew that Elspeth's view of Sarah wasn't reality; it was the supercharged emotional response of a child on the cusp of adolescence.

'We both know that she'll be looking forward to having you back,' Simon said. Elspeth just rolled her eyes, and mooched past Simon in the direction of the kitchen.

A short time later, Simon was walking Elspeth back to Sarah's cottage on the edge of the Roseford estate. The sun was warm, and the light breeze in the air meant he couldn't help but feel optimistic. He'd definitely get in touch with Lizzie after he'd dropped Elspeth back home. They had a whole day to pick up where they'd left off.

Elspeth kept up a steady stream of chatter as they walked, and Simon only half listened. In the distance, he could see the marquee company beginning to dismantle the huge white canopy, and the catering team loading the last of the boxes of glasses and crockery. The wedding had been such a long time in the planning, and now, in a few hours, Roseford chapel and the grounds would be returned to normal. He was sure this was just the first of many celebrations that the chapel would see, but this one would always be special.

The huge white canopy of the marquee was being carefully packed away as they skirted the field. Simon couldn't help thinking back to the conversation he'd had with Finn about staging some kind of festival in the grounds. If Roseford Hall could host a wedding, surely it wasn't a huge leap to host a bigger event? He resolved to give it some thought when he'd mopped up the last bits and pieces from this weekend. After all, Finn had offered him his support, which was something to be taken very seriously.

As they drew closer to Sarah's cottage, which she'd recently named, to Simon's amusement, Riverside View, due to its proximity to the more often than not dried-up stream that ran through the bottom of her garden, Elspeth darted up the garden path calling for Holmes.

Hearing his young mistress's voice, Holmes came bounding out of the house, meeting Elspeth halfway. His high-pitched, joyous bark of welcome at the sight of her never failed to make Simon smile.

'All right, boy?' he said as he stooped to ruffle under the dog's chin. Holmes gave him a big, dopey grin and the lively spring of the dog's step suggested that Sarah hadn't taken him out for a walk yet. Simon decided to see if Sarah wanted him to take Holmes out for his morning constitutional; it would give him the perfect excuse to walk by Bee's cottage and see Lizzie in person.

As he trailed behind Elspeth and into the house, he heard the dull hum of two voices, one male, one female, coming from the kitchen. Heading towards them, he was momentarily distracted by a new photograph of Sarah, Fleur and Elspeth on a side table in the hall, obviously taken on a photoshoot when the bluebells were in bloom. They looked happy, relaxed and very much a family unit. He felt a pang then, of something that felt unnervingly like envy. Had he missed the boat to have moments like this with children of his own? He wasn't getting any younger, after all.

The smell of coffee brewing in the kitchen drew him back away from the photograph, and as the voices grew more distinct, and the sound of Sarah's laughter rang out, he wondered who it was that she was talking to that would make her laugh like that. He hadn't heard her this happy in a long time. As he entered the kitchen the greeting on his tongue died. Sitting comfortably on a stool pulled up to the island in the middle of the kitchen, looking to all intents and purposes as though he owned the place, was Jago McAvoy.

30

'Oh, Simon, hi,' Sarah said as she turned back from her coffee machine and brought two cups over to the kitchen island. 'I hadn't realised you'd be coming back with Elspeth. Thanks for having her last night.'

Simon stared at his sister. It wasn't often worlds failed him, but this wasn't a situation he'd ever expected to encounter.

'Can I get you a coffee?'

Sarah's question broke into his racing thoughts. 'Er, not right now, thanks, sis.' He threw her a questioning glance, but she seemed to be avoiding his gaze.

'That was quite a night,' Jago said. 'If I'd known you threw such great parties down here, I'd have made the effort to visit sooner.'

Was Simon imagining it, or did Jago's tone seem to be issuing a challenge? Something along the lines of *Go on, mate. Ask. I dare you.* The fact that Jago was still wearing the clothes he'd arrived in yesterday, but his shirt was rumpled and had a couple of buttons undone, was sending a clear message about what had happened under this roof after the wedding.

'Are you all right?' Sarah asked. Uncharacteristically for her, she suddenly looked nervous, and more than a bit guilty.

'I'm fine,' Simon replied, a little too quickly. He couldn't help raising a speculative eyebrow at his sister, who flushed and averted her gaze again.

'Well, I'd best be off,' Jago said, after knocking back his coffee. Simon hoped it would scald him. Jago turned back to Sarah. 'Walk me out?'

Sarah glanced at Simon again, and then nodded. 'Sure.'

As they left the kitchen, Simon's irritation seemed to grow in proportion to the smugness in Jago's cheerily thrown out, 'See you, mate.' He decided to reconsider the coffee.

He was just pouring a most welcome cup of Americano, and sweetening it with a much-needed spoonful of sugar, when Sarah came back into the kitchen.

'I know what you're going to say,' she said, grabbing her coffee from the island and leaning back against the kitchen units. 'So don't bother.'

Simon shook his head. 'Sarah... Jago's a complete tosser. I can't believe you let him stay here last night. What the hell possessed you?'

'Loneliness,' Sarah retorted. 'A need for human contact?' She paused, her face flushing. 'Or maybe I wanted to lay an old ghost to rest? Take your pick.'

'But he screwed you up when you were eighteen!' Simon exclaimed. 'He nearly made you fail your A levels, you were in such a state. Why the hell would you want to spend any more time with him?' He glanced around, mindful that Fleur or Elspeth might be listening in.

'That was nearly twenty years ago,' Sarah retorted. 'And, frankly, Simon, I'm a free agent and a grown woman. What I choose to do is absolutely none of your business.'

Simon shook his head. 'Fair enough. But you'll forgive me if I'm just a little shocked that you had such a huge lapse in judgement. I mean, Jago? Really?'

'I hadn't intended for it to happen,' Sarah said quietly. 'But we got chatting, and I realised that I still really fancied him. Fleur went off to a friend's house for a sleepover after the wedding and when you texted me and said Elspeth was sleeping at the main house, this rebellious part of myself just took over.' She paused. 'There was a bit of me that wanted to show him what he'd missed all these years.'

'Well, I hope it was worth it,' Simon muttered.

Sarah grinned. 'I hate to say it, little brother, but it was.'

Unwilling to hear any more details about his sister's night of passion with Jago, Simon put his coffee cup, mostly untouched, down on the island. 'Are you planning on seeing him again?'

'Oh, I don't know,' Sarah said, a trace of defensiveness in her voice. 'I'll see how it goes.'

'Is that wise? I mean, you don't really know anything about him.' As he said it, he realised that he was probably overstepping the mark. Sarah *was* an adult, after all. But he couldn't help his concern. They might both be in their thirties now, but Sarah was still his sister.

'Don't worry,' Sarah said carefully. 'I'm not the stupid teenager I used to be. I'll be careful.' She smiled briefly. 'You don't need to fret.'

'I hope not,' Simon replied. As the pause stretched, he cleared his throat. 'Well, I'll be off, then. I was going to see if you wanted me to give Holmes his morning walk, but now you're up, you can handle it yourself, can't you?' With that, all thoughts of using the dog as an excuse to visit Lizzie forgotten, he walked briskly out of the house.

Elspeth was playing with Holmes in the garden as he thundered down the path, and he forced a smile as she waved him goodbye. Of all the people Sarah could have hooked up with, why did it have to be bloody Jago?

Striding purposefully towards the centre of the village, Simon tried to walk out his frustrations. Sarah was perfectly entitled to spend time with whomever she wanted, after all. He couldn't help but acknowledge that the feelings of frustration also stemmed from having his night with Lizzie cut so short by Elspeth's arrival. And that he'd unwittingly made things easier for Sarah and that wanker Jago to have their own night of passion off the back of it.

Almost without realising it, he walked through the village, and his feet seemed to take him up the hill to Bee's cottage. He wondered if Lizzie would be up for a cup of coffee. He definitely felt as though he needed it, or something stronger, despite the early hour. It was only when he was opening the front gate and heading up the garden path that he remembered how scruffy he looked. The old T-shirt and jeans he'd thrown on were hardly 'hey, let's pick up where we left off last night' material. Especially when last night he'd been in a *really* good suit. Simon wasn't vain, by any stretch of the imagination, but nor did he want to look like a total slob in front of Lizzie.

He stopped dead on the path, wondering if it was too late to scuttle away and try again when he looked smarter. But as he was in the process of deciding, the front door opened and out popped Lizzie, smiling broadly at the sight of him.

'Hi!' she said, as brightly as her grin. 'I was just about to text you. You must have read my mind.'

Simon, despite his embarrassment, found himself smiling back. 'I was out and about, dropping Elspeth back home, and I thought I'd see if you fancied a coffee.' He patted the back pocket of his jeans absently, only then realising that he'd obviously left his phone in the kitchen.

Lizzie looked quizzically at him. 'Everything all right?' Was he imagining it, or did she glance him up and down?

'Yeah, fine.' He looked back at her. 'Just doing the old phone-check-patting dance. Are you familiar with it?'

Lizzie laughed. 'I think I know the one.'

Simon decided to seize the moment, regardless of his scruffy attire. 'So, would you like to grab a coffee with me?'

Approaching him, Lizzie took a moment to answer. She glanced up at him from under her lashes and there was no mistaking the look in her eyes. Simon's pulse quickened.

'After where we left things last night, I was rather hoping for something a bit more adventurous than a coffee,' Lizzie murmured. 'If you're on the same page, still, of course.' She traced a hand over Simon's cheek, and he found himself leaning into her touch like a cat.

'I'd love that,' Simon replied, his body responding immediately to her touch, and the tone of her voice. 'So I suppose the question is, do you want to make it your place or mine?'

Lizzie grinned up at him, a naughty glint in her eye. 'Well, my bed in Bee's spare room is only a single. We might be better off back at yours.'

He was smiling back broadly as Lizzie's warm, gentle mouth met his. After a kiss they both wanted to savour, they began a brisk walk back to Roseford Hall.

31

Lizzie cast a quick glance at Simon, who looked adorably unkempt and scruffier than she'd seen him thus far. His faded T-shirt, with the remnants of the logo of some rock band from the 1990s, was clean but creased, and his jeans were a medium blue wash, softened through age. He looked quite different from the carefully presented figure of yesterday. In fact, his appearance reminded her of the teenager he'd been that fateful weekend she'd come to stay in Roseford. For some reason now, though, that memory didn't haunt her so much.

'What?' Simon asked, clearly catching her appraising look. He unlocked the private entrance to Roseford Hall and they hurried through.

Lizzie grinned. 'Oh, nothing. It's just that I haven't seen you looking so casual before.' She drew closer, pressing herself against him and feeling the heat from his torso emanating from under his T-shirt. 'I like it.'

'I'm glad,' Simon replied, a husky note in his voice. He reached towards her and wrapped an arm around her waist, bringing her even closer to him as he leaned back against the whitewashed wall.

Lizzie stood up on tiptoe and brushed her lips against his. 'I take it you've already had breakfast,' she said playfully.

'Am I going to need a lot of energy?' Simon said, teasing Lizzie's mouth with the warmth of his own.

'Well, put it this way, I made sure I had an extra round of toast when I got up this morning!' Lizzie gave a giggle and she was shocked at how carefree she sounded. But then so much had happened in the space of so short a time, she really did feel as if she was healing, and not just from a broken collarbone.

The kisses they shared became deeper and with them the playful mood shifted into something entirely more intense. Lizzie's free hand reached up through Simon's unkempt blond hair, ruffling it even further. She shivered as his right hand moved its way under her shirt, stroking and caressing her back, and she felt the beginnings of a slow tingling warmth rolling through her. In response, she pressed even closer to Simon, standing between his parted thighs and feeling how aroused he was through his jeans as he pressed back.

It was soon clear that kissing the life out of one another in the hallway was an entirely impractical idea. Simon gently disentangled himself from Lizzie and she immediately felt the loss of warmth against her own skin.

'Shall we, um, take this somewhere a little more comfortable?' he murmured, still kissing her despite introducing a little distance between their bodies.

'Definitely,' Lizzie replied. She looked up at Simon and saw that the pupils of his dark blue eyes were wide with lust, and there was a flush to his cheeks that she found infinitely desirable. 'If you're sure that we aren't going to get interrupted by your sister, her daughters or their dog!'

'I've banned them all from the house,' Simon said, giving a little laugh. 'We definitely will not be disturbed this time.'

Hand in hand, they made their way out of the kitchen and up a small set of stairs to Simon's bedroom. Situated at the back of the house, overlooking the walled garden that had once grown produce for the estate, it faced south-east and the sun was already shining through the tall window. Despite its elegant proportions, the bedroom was reassuringly normal and functional-looking in contrast to the highly dressed and arranged rooms that comprised the public parts of Roseford Hall.

Lizzie felt some of her residual anxiety dissipate as she caught sight of a homely looking duvet cover on a modern king-sized bed. She laughed out loud.

'What is it?' Simon looked perplexed.

'Oh, I don't know.' Lizzie grinned before continuing. 'I kind of figured that the lord of the manor would sleep in an ancient mahogany four-poster job, not a modern king-size divan with a flowery duvet cover!'

'Have you ever actually slept in one of the "heritage" beds in this place?' Simon joined in her laughter. 'Because I can assure you, while they look wonderful, you won't get a wink of sleep in them.'

Lizzie raised an eyebrow. 'I wasn't aware that we were actually planning on sleeping.' She took Simon's hand. 'If we're still thinking the same thing, that is?'

In response, Simon pulled her gently over to the bed. The room was so high up that there was no need to draw the curtains, and no need to worry about being interrupted. The top window was open, and Lizzie could hear the birds chirping outside, and the arrival of the first tourists of the day.

They sank down onto the bed, and Lizzie, mindful of her injury, was grateful when Simon allowed her to take the lead. He lay back against the duvet, and she settled herself next to him, rolling onto her good side to begin a long, leisurely line of kisses, beginning at Simon's mouth and trailing over his neck, while he arched in pleasure at the touch of her lips. She tasted the sweet-saltiness of his skin, and nuzzled deeper into the crook between neck and shoulder, before he turned his head and their lips met again.

Soon, Simon's T-shirt that Lizzie had observed with such amusement had been discarded by the side of the bed, and Lizzie saw for the first time just how well built Simon was. She'd had a fair inkling, from their near misses, but the sight of him, lying back against the pillows, made her draw in a quick, involuntary breath. The leanness of his body was underpinned by some definition, a flat stomach and a scattering of dark blond hair across his chest. Her eyes trailed down over his abdomen and further, and she wanted to explore every last inch of him.

Straddling his jeans-clad thighs, Lizzie took a moment to unbutton her shirt and throw it to the floor. She'd invested in a front-fastening bra after her car accident, and she carefully undid the clasp and removed that, too, noticing how Simon's eyes widened and he shifted slightly beneath her. His hands, tanned from a summer of being outside on the Roseford estate, reached for her, caressing and stroking her breasts, and she felt herself responding to his touch.

She swiftly undid the brown leather belt of his jeans, and popped the button. She relished his sigh as she slowly, tantalisingly, pulled the zip and then shifted again as he rose to pull his jeans off. Sliding off him briefly, she quickly undid her own jeans and then lay back on her side next to him.

'God, you're everything I imagined you would be,' Simon breathed as they became entwined again. Lizzie could feel his arousal through the fabric of his boxer shorts, and she pressed against him, willing those last, thin layers that separated them to disappear. Still mindful of her collar-bone, she carefully reached down and they both removed the last barrier of clothing, wriggling under the duvet and the crisp white cotton sheet after they did so.

Simon ran a warm hand over Lizzie's neck, and gently brushed her collarbone. Despite the fact that she didn't need to wear the sling any more, Lizzie still tensed slightly as he did so.

'I don't want to hurt you,' Simon murmured. 'Feel free to do what you want to do. And if you don't want it, to tell me to stop.'

Lizzie nodded. 'I will.' She leaned down and kissed his hand, and then, rising up on her good arm, she began to trail kisses down Simon's chest, over his abdomen and further. She heard him release a shuddering sigh as her mouth made warm contact with his hardness, kissing and caressing until his hand on her shoulder guided her back to the top of the bed.

'Careful,' he said breathlessly. 'I don't want to go off half cocked!'

Lizzie giggled. 'I'm sure you've got it all under control.'

In response, Simon's blond head dipped below the sheet, and Lizzie found herself being explored by fingers and tongue until she herself was tingling and on the edge.

'You are *very* good at that,' Lizzie breathed as her hips moved to meet Simon's gentle, erotic caresses. She could feel herself building inexorably towards a deep, pulsing climax, and as she pushed over the edge, Simon's warm breath and expert hands held her there.

'Come here,' she whispered.

Pausing briefly to grab a condom from his bedside drawer, Simon glanced down at her, and she immediately interpreted the question.

'You're sweet,' she murmured. 'Lie down and I'll let you know if it gets uncomfortable.' She was touched that, clearly concerned about crushing her and doing additional damage to her collarbone, he wanted to give her the control. She slid a thigh around his waist where he was lying on his side, and carefully guided him into her, the exquisite sensation of their bodies becoming joined enough to elicit a moan from Simon, who was more than ready. As they began to move, Lizzie found a rhythm that suited them both, and Simon's hand began to caress her once more, until she was gasping and clenching around him. As he came, she felt herself fall with him, and for a long moment they just held fast, relishing the sensations and the wonderful heat.

A little time later, Lizzie lay snuggled into Simon's chest. Her stomach, suddenly, gave an almighty rumble.

'I thought you said you'd had breakfast,' Simon chided gently, placing a kiss on the top of Lizzie's head.

Lizzie giggled. 'I guess we must have built up an appetite!' She propped herself up on one elbow and looked down at him. 'Do you have any plans for lunch?'

'Anything, so long as it's with you,' Simon replied, and then grimaced. 'Sorry. Can I put that down to post-coital sappiness?'

Laughing again, Lizzie gave him a kiss. 'Forgiven.' Settling back down again, she felt, for the first time since she'd been in Roseford, as though she was truly moving forward.

32

After a warm shower, and a cup of tea while she was getting dressed, which Lizzie greeted with great amusement, responding to the spotty mug with the observation that no one had ever brought her tea after sex before, but she supposed it fitted Roseford Hall perfectly, Simon and Lizzie decided to get some fresh air. Most of the businesses in Roseford were closed on a Sunday, but there were still plenty of people about, and Simon had been extended an invitation to the informal post-wedding buffet to be held in the Treloar Arms that afternoon.

'Isn't the village pub a bit of a parochial venue for a shindig for the wedding of a world-famous movie star?' Lizzie asked as they headed down the main street towards the pub.

'Montana stayed at the pub during the filming of *A Countess for Christmas* a couple of years ago, and Serena grew up in the village, with it as her local, so they thought it might be a nice place to celebrate,' Simon replied. 'Most of the hangers-on will have departed to the four winds, so it's a select gathering of friends and family, but I'm sure the happy couple won't mind if you gatecrash, since you were my plus one for the wedding anyway.'

'Are you sure?' Lizzie replied, brow furrowing. 'I wouldn't want to intrude.'

'You'll be most welcome.' Simon stopped and pulled her close.

All the same, Lizzie felt nervous, and a little underdressed in her white shirt, sandals and jeans as they approached the pub. Simon had thrown on a better pair of jeans and a shirt after he'd got out of the shower, and she wondered, again, if she should head home and put something more dressy on before they joined the party at the pub.

'You look wonderful,' Simon reassured her before kissing her again. 'It's casual, honestly.'

'Then why did you get changed?'

Simon smiled ruefully. 'I've got a rep to protect round here. Band T-shirts and my worst jeans wouldn't cut it.'

Lizzie burst out laughing. 'Did you just quote *Grease 2* at me?'

Simon looked bewildered. 'Did I? I don't think I've ever seen it.'

Shaking her head, Lizzie decided not to try to explain the reference right now. She'd already realised how unworldly, in terms of popular culture, Simon could be; it was something she'd have to get used to. Something she hoped she'd have the time to get used to.

They walked into the bar of the Treloar Arms. Lizzie smiled when Simon was greeted from all sides by the landlord, some customers and some of the wedding guests, who were making their way through to the function room, which led out via a large set of bifold doors to the picturesque back garden of the pub. She immediately realised why he wanted to look less scruffy. Despite the fact that this was supposedly a 'casual' gathering, the guests all looked as if they'd stepped straight off the pages of *Hello!* magazine.

'I thought you said this was going to be casual,' Lizzie muttered. She felt vaguely irritated with Simon; his obliviousness in certain situations was obvious now, and she really would have appreciated the chance to glam up a bit more. Especially when Montana de Santo herself rushed up to them as they entered the conservatory, with a beaming smile on her face.

'Simon, darling, so glad you could make it!' Montana said, kissing Simon on both cheeks as if they'd not seen each other for years, instead of at yesterday's wedding.

Before she knew what was happening, Lizzie found herself greeted just as enthusiastically, and being enclosed in a hug by the new bride.

'Lizzie, thank you again for the wonderful flowers. I'm so glad Simon brought you along to the party.'

'I hope I'm not intruding,' Lizzie, flustered but feeling slightly more at ease, replied.

'Not at all. If you hadn't come, I'd have told Lord Treloar here to go get you.' Montana, flushed with happiness, glanced behind them. 'No Bee, though?'

Lizzie smiled. 'She's gone to visit a friend today. But I'm sure she'll love to know she was missed.'

Montana tucked an arm through Lizzie's as if they'd known each other for years, and Lizzie found herself being led across the room to where the champagne was placed on a side table. 'Now, let me know if there's anyone you want to meet,' Montana said, a mischievous gleam in her eye. 'Let's see if we can't make Simon a little jealous.'

Lizzie's face burned. 'Is it that obvious?' she whispered.

'Honey, I've known Simon a couple of years now, and he's smitten, I can tell. According to Lucy, Finn's fiancée, she's never seen him so bowled over by anyone as he seems to be with you.' She paused. 'But there's no harm in testing that out, is there?'

Lizzie laughed. 'It's early days, Montana, but it is lovely to be here with him, and such an amazing crowd.'

Montana sighed, but kept grinning. 'Fair enough. And Serena would murder me if I, er, stuck my oar in where it wasn't wanted.' Obviously a bit self-conscious about using the colloquialism, Montana broke the moment by passing Lizzie a glass of champagne. 'But in the meantime, drink up and grab some food. There's plenty here. Dave's done us proud.'

'Thank you, I will,' Lizzie replied, knowing that her two minutes with the famous bride were probably up. Simon rejoined them a moment later, and then Montana drifted away to see the other guests.

'Everything all right?' Simon asked. 'Montana wasn't giving you the third degree?'

'She's lovely,' Lizzie replied. She shook her head. 'I still can't get my head around the fact that I was at her wedding.'

'She is,' Simon replied. 'And a whole lot more normal that you'd give her credit for, given the guest list here!'

Glancing around, trying not to make it too obvious, Lizzie was agog at seeing so many famous faces still hanging around for the morning-after party. It was like a roll call of Oscar nominees, television stars and those working behind the camera. She raised a hand in greeting, though, to one of the familiar faces that she knew fell into the category of someone with a 'normal' job: Lucy. As Lucy, with Finn not far behind, came over to join them, Lizzie relaxed a little.

Was she imagining it, or did a significant look pass between Finn and Simon as the four of them moved together?

'How are you doing?' Finn asked them both.

'Well, thanks,' Lizzie replied. She smiled as Simon reached down to give her hand a squeeze. There was that look between the two men again, and Lizzie wondered if words had been had last night, and whether she had Finn to thank, in part, for the diffident Simon coming to find her after she'd walked off the dance floor.

'How are you holding up after all of this wedding malarkey?' Simon asked.

'I'm just glad someone else is doing the catering!' Lucy joked. 'It's nice to be able to relax and enjoy myself.'

'Amen to that,' Finn replied. 'And it's great to see Serena and Montana so happy.'

'It is,' Simon replied. They took another moment to observe the newly-weds, arms around each other, talking to a famous director and her husband, and the lead actor in the last film that Montana had co-starred in. 'They look absolutely lit up, even after a night partying.'

'They're not the only ones,' Lucy observed, a twinkle in her eye.

Simon, Lizzie noticed, didn't answer, but he shifted a little closer to her. She was grateful for his presence, and reassured that she was being accepted into this group of friends.

As if on cue, Sarah Treloar joined them. Lizzie tried to stop her heart from racing, but she still couldn't help tensing, and Simon clearly noticed, he was already so good at reading her.

'Hi,' she said as she turned to Lizzie. 'How are you doing after the last couple of days?'

'Oh, not too bad,' Lizzie replied, trying to keep a light tone in her voice. 'It's been lovely to be a part of it.'

Sarah regarded her thoughtfully, and as the others began to make conversation, she drew a little closer to Lizzie. 'Look, can we have a word when you're ready?' she asked in an undertone.

Lizzie nodded. She'd half suspected this moment would come, once she'd told Simon what had happened to her, and his sister's part in it. 'Sure.'

'Thank you.' Lizzie looked directly at Sarah for the first time, and was shocked to see the relief and gratitude in the other woman's eyes. Perhaps this wasn't going to be such an awful conversation, after all.

33

A couple of minutes later, Lizzie and Sarah walked outside to the pretty walled garden at the back of the pub. The sun was out in full force now, but thankfully Dave, the landlord, had had the foresight to pull out the canopy shade attached to the building and open up a few of the parasols on the generous wooden pub benches.

Simon, realising that this was a moment that the two women needed to navigate on their own, had excused himself on the pretext of going to get something from the very generous buffet lunch that had been provided by the brides. He had, however, tacitly checked in with Lizzie with a gentle touch in the small of her back and a kiss on the cheek before wandering away. She was sure she hadn't imagined that whispered 'good luck' that had tickled her ear as he'd moved away once again.

The two women sat down at a table a little away from the rest of the guests who were seeking sunshine on that glorious lunchtime. Lizzie noticed that Sarah looked nervous and suddenly felt an absurd need to be the one to reassure her. Given their history, this was ridiculous. If anything, Lizzie was the one who should need the reassurance, but something about the way Sarah kept twisting the stem of her champagne flute suggested she was the one on the back foot.

'I'm sure you can guess what it is I wanted to talk to you about,' Sarah said after taking a deep breath.

'I assume that Simon has been talking,' Lizzie replied as she took a quick sip of her own glass of champagne. 'I suppose I should be angry with him for breaking confidences, but under the circumstances, and after all this time, it feels pointless to get cross about it.'

Sarah stared down into her glass for a long moment before she spoke again. 'Until he reminded me about that night, I'd forgotten it had ever happened. That's kind of how it is with school, isn't it? You don't forget the things that affect you, but you don't recall the things that affect other people, even if those things were terrible.'

'Funny,' Lizzie replied. 'I seem to be able to recall pretty much everything about you and your gang of friends. The clothes you wore, the hairstyles you had, the boys you fancied and the things you did to make my life so difficult.' She gave a short laugh. 'But I take your point. I'm sure you don't have any memory of me.'

From the flushed expression on Sarah's face, Lizzie knew she'd hit the nail on the head. 'But that's what it's like on the outside. I bet you can recollect all about my sister, Georgina, though. She was, after all, one of the *chosen ones*.' Even Lizzie was surprised by the bitterness in her own voice as she mentioned her sister's name.

Lizzie saw something flaring in Sarah's eyes at that last remark.

'Oh, Georgina. I remember the way everyone looked at her and how bloody jealous I was of her. How I only invited her, and you, of course, to my party because then I knew the St Jude's boys were guaranteed to turn up.'

Lizzie felt a flare of defensiveness about her sister, and it was a sensation that surprised her. She'd always resented Georgina's popularity; why did it rankle, therefore, that Sarah had openly admitted that she too had been taken advantage of for Sarah's own ends?

'So you were using her, then?' Lizzie said quietly. 'You weren't really her friend?'

'Was anyone anyone's friend back then?' Sarah said bleakly. 'Weren't we all just trying to survive?'

'Oh, don't give me that!' Lizzie retorted, fired up by the conflicting feelings about her sister and *finally* talking to Sarah about that night that haunted her. 'Your notion of survival at school is a whole lot different from mine, I can assure you of that.'

Sarah sighed. 'For the record, I'd no idea Nina was going to humiliate you like that. But she'd pressured me to invite you to the party as well as Georgina, and, like an idiot, I went along with it because I wanted to please them. I was young, and stupid, and I'm deeply ashamed that what happened to you happened in my family home. And for all that, I'm sorry, Lizzie. I really, really am.'

For years after it had happened, Lizzie had rehearsed how she'd react if she ever came into contact with Sarah or her friends again. She'd imagined that she'd be full of cutting remarks, desperate to hit back against Sarah for the trauma she'd endured that night, for being embarrassed in front of everyone, in that awful dress and terrible make-up. But now, she merely felt a kind of calm emptiness. It didn't seem to matter any more to get back at Sarah; they were both adults, and they'd both lived twenty years of their lives in between then and now.

Finally, realising that Sarah was waiting for some kind of a response, Lizzie spoke again.

'It was a horrible thing,' she began. 'And you and your friends had so much power to stop it from happening, if you'd bothered to. But you didn't.' She took a sip from her nearly empty glass just to break the moment a little before she continued. As Sarah tried to interject, Lizzie held up a hand. 'No. I'm not finished. Twenty years is an awfully long time to wait for an apology, but, to be honest with you, it's not as if I've been wasting my life because of it all. Simon did a lot that night to try to repair things, even though, bless him, he hadn't a clue what had happened. And I've gone on and done what most people try to do: lived my life on my terms. Being back in Roseford has made me face it, but it doesn't make a huge amount of difference to my life as it is now.'

'And I am sorry for my part in it,' Sarah repeated. 'I should have gone after you. I should have stood up to Nina and called out her shitty behaviour. But I was a coward, and I was afraid I was going to be next.'

'Self-preservation?' Lizzie said bleakly. 'I think I can understand that.'

Sarah nodded. 'I'm glad you came back here, and that we could address it. Maybe we can try to be friends, or at least be kind to each other while you're here?'

Lizzie fought the urge to laugh. Accepting an apology was one thing, but she wasn't sure if she'd ever be 'friends' with Sarah Treloar. That being said, an awful lot had changed for her this year. Perhaps it wasn't entirely out of the question.

'Maybe.' Lizzie smiled. She knew that was enough to let Sarah off the hook a bit, as she saw Sarah visibly relaxing.

At that moment, Simon, laden with two plates of food from the buffet, approached the table. He cocked an eyebrow at them both. 'Am I interrupting?'

Lizzie glanced at Sarah, who smiled tentatively back. 'I don't think so,' she said. Then, focusing on the food, 'Is one of those plates for me?'

Simon nodded and gave them both a quick, relieved smile. 'If you want it. I wasn't sure if you had any allergies, so I thought I'd go for a general selection.' He plonked the two plates down on the wooden table with a clunk. 'Sorry, sis,' he added, turning to Sarah. 'I only had enough hands for two helpings.'

'Typical,' Sarah grumbled good-naturedly, but Lizzie could hear the relief in her tone. 'I'll, er, grab some myself.' She looked back at Lizzie as she stood up. 'Would it be all right if I came back and joined you?'

Lizzie, without even looking at Simon, smiled gently. 'Yes,' she said. 'It would.'

34

The next morning, Simon turned the invitation from Cross Dean School over and over in his hands. He still hadn't sent his RSVP, and in truth he still wasn't sure which way to jump. Yet again he wondered why he didn't just chuck the thing in the bin; he didn't owe anything to that place, and he had no desire to go back there and relive the awfulness of his school days. But there was something about Lizzie facing her own demons that made him hesitate. She'd been brave, and confronted the traumas of her past; shouldn't he try to be brave, too? With a sigh, he put the invitation down on his desk again.

His gloomy thoughts were alleviated by the deluge of positive social media posts about how wonderful Montana and Serena's wedding looked. Roseford Hall, its chapel and the grounds really did look great on camera, and the carefully curated 'official' shots that Montana and Serena had selected, as well as the more candid ones taken by various guests, cast his home in a wonderful light. There was so much to be positive about, and although he knew that credit was mostly due to the British Heritage Fund, he still felt a sense of pride.

It wasn't such a leap for the idea of the festival to come creeping back into his mind after seeing all of the positive images of the wedding on social media. While the British Heritage Fund now owned Roseford Hall, the chapel and the surrounding gardens, the Treloar family still owned several acres of fields beyond the immediate gardens, which, hitherto, had been rented out for grazing to local farmers. It didn't provide much of an income, but it meant that the family still had some notional claim on the land. It had been ruled out for building on, as it was agriculturally tied, but Simon had been formulating a few ideas about what he'd like to do with the land in the longer term. Grazing was fine as far as it went, but he was feeling increasingly as though he'd like to leave a bit more of a mark on what was left of his family estate.

Of course, he hadn't discussed any of this with Sarah or his mother. Sarah probably wouldn't have any objections, but his mother was another matter, and, despite the fact that he'd inherited his father's title upon his death, his mother still had some share in the leftover land.

Simon, despite his unworldliness in some areas, was no fool. He knew that he could sit out his days in Roseford Hall, being the figurehead of an estate that he no longer owned, being employed as the site manager. He knew he'd probably be perfectly content doing that. But contentment was different from happiness, he thought. Contentment had got him this far; maybe it was time to take a risk.

Feeling a frisson of excitement, he clicked open a file on his laptop and waited for it to load. As the document splashed up on screen, he reminded himself of the details that he'd sketched out after that initial conversation with Finn some weeks ago. One word jumped out at him from the screen: RoseFest. If nothing else, he thought wryly, he'd hit on a great name.

A knock at the door drew him out away from the screen.

'Come in,' he called. His mother had a habit of popping over each morning to catch up on things, and keep a largely figurative hand on the tiller, but this time, it wasn't her. Instead, Lizzie walked in.

'Hey,' he said, rising quickly from his chair and rounding the desk. She'd gone back to Bee's after the post-wedding party yesterday afternoon, and although they'd exchanged a couple of texts after that, she hadn't suggested meeting up today.

'Hi, you.' Lizzie smiled as he drew closer. They shared a long, warm kiss, and Simon tasted coffee and toothpaste on Lizzie's breath. 'Got time for a coffee? I've brought you one just in case.' She reached down to the hessian tote bag she'd placed by her feet when he'd come across the office for the kiss, and pulled out a cake box and two Thermos mugs of coffee. 'Lucy let me borrow the mugs, so long as they make it back to the café at some point.'

'That sounds great,' Simon replied. Lizzie opened the cake box and passed Simon his coffee. She made her way over to the window behind his desk and looked out over the grounds.

'I can see why you chose this office!' she joked as she turned back to Simon, who, having skipped breakfast again, was tucking into his rosewater cupcake with gusto.

'Lucy knows how to bake,' he said, once he'd taken a sip of coffee to wash down the cake. 'But if you make this a habit, I'll be the size of a house by Christmas!'

Lizzie laughed. 'No danger of that, with all the running around that you do.' The light from the window cast her in a soft, warm glow, and Simon was suddenly struck by exactly how strongly he felt for her, even in the short time they'd known one another. He reached out a hand and pulled her down onto his lap, relishing the feeling of holding her close again, after a night's absence.

When they broke apart, both of them were more than a little breathless and flushed, and the sound of Lizzie's nervous laugh made his heart race.

'I'll never get any work done at this rate,' he said, trying to take a deep breath and to still his thumping pulse. It would be so easy to dump everything he had to do today and escape back up to his private rooms with Lizzie. But, regrettably, he had things to attend to.

While he was still thinking about all the things he'd rather be doing with Lizzie than sitting at his desk, he realised that she'd been glancing at the screen of his laptop with interest.

'Sorry,' she said, looking back at him when she realised that she probably shouldn't be looking at his screen. 'The name caught my eye. What's RoseFest?'

Simon, suddenly embarrassed, reached for his mouse. 'Oh, nothing,' he said. 'Just something I've been thinking about to try to diversify my own interests in this place.'

'May I?' Lizzie asked.

'Sure.'

Lizzie shifted position again on his lap and turned back to the laptop screen. Simon could see her eyes scanning the document, her brow furrowing slightly as she took in the information. When she had finished, she turned back to him.

'Is this really a possibility?'

'It's just an idea,' Simon replied. He felt a blush colouring his cheeks, as if he'd been caught looking at something he shouldn't. 'It's a bit pie in the sky, really, and I've no idea if the British Heritage Fund would allow it so close to the estate anyway.' He tried to shrug it off. 'Had a conversation with Finn a few weeks ago and started chucking a few ideas down... probably not worth thinking about.'

'Then why *are* you thinking about it?' Lizzie gestured to the screen again. 'Shouldn't you be, I don't know, checking the drainage in the lower field or something?'

Simon laughed. 'You're far too young to make *that* reference.'

'There is such a thing as Amazon Prime,' Lizzie replied. 'And don't ignore the question.'

Simon sighed. 'Finn and I went for a drink before the wedding. I mentioned I was keen to have a project of my own that I could manage, to kind of leave my own mark on Roseford. He suggested some kind of event, or a festival, and it's an idea that keeps coming back to me. The wedding made me want to think about and tweak it a little more. Made me wonder if it was a possibility. If I could actually create something here.'

Lizzie smiled down at him, and, although he still felt embarrassed, he could see the warmth and enthusiasm in her eyes.

'I think it's a great idea,' she said softly. 'And it seems like this is a bit more than just some scribbled notes after a few drinks. They actually make sense!' She looked again, and Simon saw her brow furrow in thought. 'The field's a great space, and if you could get the BHF on board to host a few indoor events as well, you'd have the makings of a great little arts festival.'

'Thanks,' Simon replied. 'But it'd be a lot of work, and that's if the BHF are happy with the idea. There's so much red tape involved, just in the risk assessments. It'd probably take twenty years to get it all approved, by which time I'd be far too long in the tooth to set it in motion.'

'But no one's saying it has to be a huge, Worthy Farm style extravaganza in its first year,' Lizzie said. 'I mean, Glastonbury had to start somewhere, right?'

Simon really did laugh out loud at that. 'I think the residents of Roseford, as well as the BHF, might have something to say if I turned RoseFest into the Glastonbury Festival!' He shook his head. 'I was thinking of something far less ambitious in the first instance. A small arts festival, perhaps. Some music, some literary stuff, some activities for the kids? Oh, I don't know.' He slumped again. 'It's only a bunch of words on a page, after all. Probably won't come to anything.'

'It won't if you keep thinking like that,' Lizzie said. 'Nothing ever does.'

'And where would I even start?' Simon continued. 'I know the BHF has its contacts for events, but the idea is to retain as much control of it as I can, to make it *my* contribution to the future of the estate. I don't want it just to be another carefully curated BHF event.'

'So it's something to make you feel better?'

Simon felt stung. 'No. Well, not entirely. It's... oh... I don't know, something that I can build on, and maybe my family, one day, can call their own, if they can't actually lay claim to Roseford Hall any more.'

'Legacy, then?'

'Sort of, yes.'

There was a pause between them, and Lizzie seemed to be mulling over their conversation. Simon reached for his coffee again, and Lizzie shifted slightly as he did so. He realised he'd put his cup down on the invitation from Cross Dean, and the heat from the cup pulled the invitation with it as he lifted it.

Lizzie grabbed the invitation as it fluttered off the bottom of the cup. 'Wow. This looks... interesting, too.' She glanced from the invite back to him. 'Are you going to go?'

'Are you seriously asking me that question?' Simon laughed. 'It wasn't the greatest time of my life, to put it mildly. I would rather stick red-hot pins in my eyes than go back there.' He was rattled enough by Lizzie's enquiries about RoseFest. He cursed himself for not chucking the bloody invitation in the bin the moment it had arrived.

Lizzie's shrewd gaze made him fidget a little underneath her. 'Really?'

She raised an eyebrow. 'I mean, after everything I've told you about what happened to me here?'

Uncomfortably aware that he'd witnessed Lizzie laying her own ghosts to rest, but he was too afraid to exorcise his own, Simon tried to formulate a response, but found his brain severely lacking. 'It's not the same,' he muttered.

'Isn't it?'

'No.' Simon leaned forward to kiss Lizzie again, but she saw through his ploy to distract her immediately, and, after a brief touch of lips, she drew back from him.

'So, what you're telling me is that it's no big deal for me to face my demons, but when it comes to your own, you're just going to let them fly out of hell while you hide under the bed?' Lizzie's turn of phrase was amusing, but she clearly wasn't going to be deflected. 'Don't you think that's a bit rich?'

Simon leaned back in his chair and gazed briefly up at the ceiling. 'It's not like that, Lizzie.'

'Isn't it?' Lizzie, refusing to be put off, got off his lap and perched to one side of him on the desk. 'From where I'm sitting it seems pretty much the same to me. You've got one night at Cross Dean to contend with; one night to face all of those idiots and show them just how little an impact they've had on your life. Then you can walk away and come back here, and carry on. And you're telling me you can't do it?'

Simon was getting used to Lizzie's ability to cut straight to the heart of an issue, but it still irked him somewhat. Not everything was as black and white as she made it sound. 'It's not only about one night,' he said softly. 'There are people who are going to be there who made my life a sheer bloody hell for seven years. And it isn't about facing demons; it is about trying to survive. You told me that Sarah and her friends did the same to you, but at least you had an ally in your sister. I had no one. There was no one I could talk to – no one I could go to and tell what was happening. Jago McAvoy and his bastard friends saw to it that every single line of escape I had was cut off and now you expect me to go back there, smile and make polite conversation with the very people who made all that happen?' He could feel his throat constricting; he could feel the onset of the panic he'd felt as a teenager almost every single day when he'd woken up in his bed at Cross Dean threatening to engulf him once more and he hated every last moment of it.

Lizzie kept looking at him. 'My sister was there in body, rather than spirit,' she said quietly. 'I'm not sure she ever really had a clue what was going on, and, if she did, she didn't make it any better for me.' She leaned forward and pushed back a lock of blond hair that had fallen over Simon's forehead, then Simon felt her lips against the same space. His breath hitched once again at the contact.

'But isn't there a tiny part of you that wants to show them that, despite everything they put you through, you came out of it, lived your life, made a success of things and won?'

'Did I though?' Simon laughed humourlessly. 'I mean, did I really, Lizzie?' He raised a hand to her face as she pulled back to look at him again. 'Is this winning? I handed over my birthright to the nation. Couldn't even get that right.'

'Oh, for god's sake!' Lizzie's frustration was evident in her tone. 'I'm so sick of this pity party, Simon. You have so many chances to really make your mark here. Everything you helped to do for this wedding shows that. What if you walked into Cross Dean and used it as an opportunity to get some backers for RoseFest? There are plenty of people who'd jump at the chance to be associated with something like that. Use the reunion to your advantage. Do some networking and make it work for you. Don't walk in there with some victim mentality, like you're still the same boy they bullied. You're not. Just now, when we were talking about RoseFest, I felt like you really had something, and it could become your legacy for this place. But legacies don't just fall into your lap. You of all people should know that. You need to decide if RoseFest is what you really, really want. And if it is, then go to Cross Dean and spread the word.'

'And if it is?' Simon replied. 'What then?' He was hugely aware of the pressure and warmth of Lizzie's hand, now resting on his arm, and he could see the flush on her cheeks. Their eyes locked and he let her move a little closer to him, rather than bridging the gap himself. She put her other hand on his shoulder, and he felt the softness of her touch as she slid her palm up to the back of his neck.

'Then,' she breathed, 'you take chances, seize opportunities. Make things happen the way you want them to.' He could see her eyes widening and feel the way she breathed in as they moved together, and when she pressed her lips gently to his own, the softness of the kiss ignited his senses.

The kiss deepened, became more intense as Lizzie slipped back onto his lap again. Simon felt Lizzie's hand slide up through his hair, and he brought his own fingertips to her cheek, delicately brushing her flushed face. It felt like a moment of magic that he didn't want to end. Eventually, though, they broke apart and Simon suddenly knew what he had to do.

'Come with me?' he said softly. 'I can take a plus one to the reunion. Come with me and hold my hand?'

Lizzie laughed rather nervously. 'Well, when you put it like that...'

'If you want to come, I would really like you to be there.' He paused. 'For networking purposes, of course.'

Lizzie smiled up at him. 'I'd like that.' She leaned forward and kissed him again. 'Now, I'd better leave you to it. This was only meant to be a flying visit, and I said I'd help Aunt Bee out in the shop today, since she's a bit behind with the orders after the wedding.'

'Of course.' Simon released her and she clambered off his lap. 'Will I see you later?'

'I hope so,' Lizzie replied. 'Shall I text you? We could meet for a drink?'

'Sounds good.'

As she kissed him goodbye, his eyes fell on the Cross Dean invitation. Perhaps he *could* do it, he thought. And it would be a good opportunity to put the word out about a potential RoseFest. Turning back to the document once more, he reread it, and a plan began to form in his mind. Maybe it wasn't such a pipe dream, after all.

35

Lizzie headed back to Roseford Blooms with a spring in her step. The tingle of excitement she felt about her growing relationship with Simon was garnished with something a little more cerebral. Simon's notes, though they contained a fair few gaps, had the outline of what could, potentially, be a brilliant idea, not only for him, but for Roseford, too. After a month or so when she'd hadn't thought about work, she suddenly found herself bursting with ideas that she could share with him, if he wanted her input, that was. Between that and her thoughts about Roseford Blooms, she could feel the part of her brain dedicated to her career really firing again.

Lizzie jumped when her phone beeped with a message. She was expecting it to be from Simon, but her smile abruptly faded when she saw the name that flashed up on screen.

Hi, sis! Am at Bee's house with Mum and Dad. Are you coming back soon? X

Lizzie's heart sank to her shoes. So they'd finally come to see her, had they? And the three of them, at that. She glanced at Roseford Blooms as she neared the shop, wishing she could just rush in and close the door behind her, hide from the rest of her family behind the banks of flowers, but, she figured, it was best to face them head-on.

As she passed the front door of the flower shop, Bee popped out of it.

'I gather you've heard,' she said dryly, looking at Lizzie's face.

Lizzie smiled grimly. 'Yup.'

'I'm sorry, darling. Your mother phoned me half an hour ago and asked me where the spare key was. I had to let them in. I tried to phone you but it went straight to voicemail and I've never been good with phones.'

'It's all right,' Lizzie replied. She warmed up her smile a little in response to Bee's worried expression. 'I had to face them sometime. Might as well be now.'

'Do you want me to come with you?'

Lizzie shook her head. 'No. You've got enough to do here. I was going to help you, but under the circumstances...'

'You go on,' Bee replied. 'But let me know if you do want me to come back to the house.'

'I will.' Impulsively, Lizzie reached out and gave Bee a hug. 'Thank you.'

'Get on with you,' Bee replied. 'I'll see you later.'

Lizzie nodded, squared her shoulders, and headed up the hill to Bee's cottage.

From the moment she opened the front door, she knew hurrying had been a mistake. The five-minute walk from Roseford Blooms to the cottage had in no way prepared her to face the rest of her family. She'd barely spoken to them since saying goodbye to her mother at the flat after she'd been discharged from the hospital, apart from the odd call to let them know where she was, and now all three of them were seated in Bee's cosy living room, like some kind of middle-class inquisitorial squad.

'Elizabeth.' John Warner spoke first. He rose from the armchair he'd settled in to wait, and walked towards her. Stiffly, he leaned forward and gave her a kiss before her mother did the same. 'How are you?'

'I'm fine, Dad.' Missing a beat, as always, she added, 'And you?'

'Fine.'

John sat down again, and gestured to the empty seat on the sofa, next to Georgina. Lizzie, nettled by being given directions in the place she was currently calling home, acquiesced nonetheless. As she sat, Georgina gave her a brief grin. 'Hey, sis.'

'Hey, George,' she replied. 'It's, er, good to see you.'

Georgina shot her an ironic smile as Lizzie echoed the same words. Lizzie knew that her sister knew *exactly* how good it was, and the answer was not good. Not good at all.

'I see you've got rid of the sling,' her mother observed. 'You must be on the mend.'

'It still hurts a bit if I overdo it,' Lizzie replied. 'But it's a lot better than it was.'

'Glad to hear it.'

There was another uncomfortable pause before her father spoke.

'So, what are your plans, now that you're feeling better? You can't hide down here forever, you know.'

Lizzie sighed inwardly. She might have known her father would cut to the chase. Ever a practical man, he'd have been working on a solution to her 'problems' pretty much since she'd sold her half of the business.

'I don't really know, Dad,' she replied. 'Since the car accident, I've had a lot of time to think, but I don't just want to jump into something else.'

'That's all well and good, but you can't trade on Bee's hospitality forever, either. You might as well come back with your mother and me for a week or so, give Bee a break.'

'I'm not a kid, Dad!' Lizzie's temper flared. 'I've been helping Bee since I've been here. She doesn't need to look after me.'

'That's as may be, but you can't expect to keep living here rent free. You'd be taking advantage.'

That hurt. She hadn't offered Bee any rent since she'd arrived, but Bee hadn't asked. Lizzie felt a sliver of doubt creeping through her brain. Perhaps she shouldn't have stayed here so long? But surely if Bee had wanted her to leave, she'd have said something?

'It's not as if you've been keeping in touch with us,' her mother interjected. 'A few calls when you left hospital isn't good enough, Lizzie.'

'I'm sorry.' At her mother's tone, Lizzie hung her head. 'I didn't want to worry you. And I had some things to figure out.'

'Well, you don't need to worry about that now,' John said briskly. 'You're coming back with us this evening, and I've got you an interview with Howard Harper's PR company on Monday. He owes me a favour. He's agreed to interview you for a post, starting immediately.'

'What?' The word was out of Lizzie's mouth before she could stop it. 'No! I don't want to go back with you. And I certainly don't want to go and work for Howard. That's where I started when I graduated. It'd be a retrograde step.'

'Well, what other choices are there?' John snapped. 'You've sold your business and the money from that won't last forever. You've got to get back to work sooner or later. Might as well be sooner.'

Lizzie drew a deep breath. 'If and when I do decide to go back to work, Dad, that's my decision. Not yours. And I certainly won't be going to work for Howard.'

'Georgina, can't you try to talk some sense into your sister?' John turned to Lizzie's sister, who was pointedly examining her nails in the face of such a heated conversation.

'What do you want me to say, Dad?' she asked. 'I told you she wouldn't listen. That it would be a waste of time coming here. She'll do her own thing, as always.'

Lizzie rounded on her sister. 'Are you serious?' Her voice rose as she saw the insouciant expression on Georgina's face. 'I've always done everything I was bloody supposed to! Kept my head down, done as I was told, and where has it got me? You want to talk about doing what you want, then why don't we talk about you?'

'This isn't about me,' Georgina said quickly.

'For bloody once!' Lizzie's blood was up, and she felt light-headed, despite the sustenance from the cake and coffee she'd eaten with Simon not half an hour ago.

'If you'd only kept us in the loop, darling,' her mother said, 'we wouldn't be here right now, urging you to sort things out.'

'Things? This is my life, Mum! There's nothing to sort out. And if there was, I'll be the one to do it. There was absolutely no need for you to come here.' Lizzie, who'd sat forward during the exchange with her father, slumped back against the cushions of the sofa as the dizziness threatened to overwhelm her.

'That's as may be, but we're here now, so you might as well pack your things.' John Warner could be very difficult to argue with when he was in full flow, and Lizzie realised that she'd have to fight hard if she wasn't going to end up in the back of his Volvo XC90 that afternoon, on the way back to Surrey and an interview with Howard Harper.

'No, Dad,' she said quietly, but firmly. 'You've tried to manage every step of my life since I was born, from where I went to school to what I did for a living. And I've gone with it, to the point where I became very successful. But enough is enough. I chose to sell Warner-Basset. I chose to come here to recover after my car accident. And I'm choosing to stay here, now.' She held up a hand as her father started to interrupt. 'And I'm thankful, Dad, that you've spoken to Howard, and offered me somewhere to go, but I'm happy with those decisions.'

John Warner stared back at her for a long moment. 'And that's your final word?'

Lizzie nodded. 'It is.'

John turned to his wife and other daughter. 'Come on, then. Let's go.'

'There's no need to go yet, Dad,' Lizzie said. 'You've only just got here.'

'Well, we can't really stop,' Lizzie's mother replied. 'We're on our way to Bruton to pick up Hugo and Effie from school summer camp.'

Lizzie felt the dagger prick of rejection sharply. So this hadn't been a special visit, then. It had been a pit stop on the way to pick up Georgina's two children. Why had she expected it to be anything else?

Pulling herself together, she rose from the sofa. 'Well, it was good of you to drop by,' she said, eventually. 'Send my love to Hugo and Effie.'

As her family made a swift departure, Lizzie closed the front door of Bee's cottage and leaned against it. Had she really just stood up to her father for the first time in her life? To her shock she found she was shaking.

36

Simon had fired off an email to Cross Dean as soon as Lizzie had left, filled momentarily with confidence after their conversation. It was only later on, when the endorphins had stopped fizzing, that the doubts started to set in again. It was all very well in theory, but in practice? Did he really have it in him to go back there?

He shook his head in irritation. He was a grown man with bigger responsibilities. He didn't need to worry about what happened during his cussed school days. Lizzie was right; it could be a valuable networking opportunity to gauge some interest and find some backers for RoseFest. It was time to look to the future, after being mired for so long in the past.

Simon's phone pinged with a WhatsApp message. Heart leaping that it might be Lizzie, he was almost as pleased when he saw the message was from Finn, asking him if he was free for lunch.

Texting back that he had time for a sandwich and a cuppa, as his virtual in-tray was starting to mount up, he agreed to meet Finn at the BHF tea and coffee concession in about an hour. He knew Finn was heading off to the airport tomorrow, and was pleased that his friend wanted to check in with him before he left. After he'd answered a few more emails, it was time to meet Finn, and he locked his office and headed out into the sunshine.

'Hey!' he said as he caught sight of Finn, who'd already got a couple of coffees in. 'Have you recovered from the celebrations?'

'Just about,' Finn replied, passing Simon a latte. 'Got time to walk and talk?'

'Sure.' Still fortified by the cake and coffee that Lizzie had brought him, he wasn't too bothered about more food. 'Are you all set for your trip?'

Finn nodded as he sipped his own coffee. 'Yeah. There's something I wanted to ask you before I left.' Finn glanced around briefly, making sure no one else was in earshot. 'Not many people know yet, but since I'm headed out of the country for about six weeks, I was wondering if you could do me a favour?'

'Of course,' Simon replied. 'Name it.'

They walked a few more paces until they were ambling along the ha-ha, which separated the manicured gardens from the fields beyond.

'Can you check in on Lucy while I'm gone?'

'Is she all right?' Simon asked. 'She's not ill or anything?'

Finn shook his head. 'No, nothing like that.' He paused. 'She's pregnant.'

'Mate! That's brilliant news. Congratulations!' Simon glanced around again, and lowered his voice, even though there wasn't anyone nearby. 'When's she due?'

'End of February,' Finn replied. 'We, uh, we weren't completely sure until a couple of days ago, but we decided to do a test, since I'm headed off to Iceland tomorrow to assist on a new movie. Turns out the nausea she thought was a stomach bug was morning sickness.' He raised an eyebrow. 'We haven't even told my mom yet.'

'Well, I'm honoured you've told me,' Simon said. 'Does Lucy know you're asking me to check in?'

Finn looked sheepish. 'Not exactly. She's insisting she's perfectly fine, and she's got plenty of help in the café, but I thought it wouldn't hurt to have you keep an eye on her while I'm gone, too.'

'Let me guess... she's a whole lot more relaxed about it than you are?'

'She's done it before. I haven't.'

'Fair enough.' Simon grinned at Finn. 'But let her know I'm here if she needs anything. I don't want to come across as taking an unhealthy interest!'

'I will. Thanks, man.'

As they walked back towards Roseford Hall, Simon felt a pang of something that seemed like envy. Finn and Lucy seemed to have everything sorted out now; they had each other, their careers, a secure future and now were going to meet a new addition to their family, which already comprised themselves and Lucy's daughter, Megan, whom Finn adored. He had a sudden vision of himself in the future, with Lizzie by his side, and a couple of kids of their own, enjoying all that RoseFest had to offer. But at the moment it all felt like a dream. Filled with renewed determination to look at the RoseFest project again that afternoon, he said goodbye to Finn, looking forward to catching up with him when he got back from Iceland.

After a busy afternoon, mostly clearing up the last of the admin from the wedding, Simon sat back in his chair and stretched his fingers above his head. Having cleared his immediate in-tray, he cracked open the RoseFest file again and scanned it, even though he'd read it so many times he virtually had it memorised.

Was there something in it? Could he make it work? Feeling rather foolish, he opened his web browser and did a search for 'how to run an event on British Heritage Fund property'. He figured, if he was going to use the field the family still owned, he might as well go all in and see what the restrictions were for using parts of Roseford Hall's land as well. He scanned the information on the website, and then copied and pasted the email address for further information into his RoseFest document. So far so good. Then he stopped short, feeling even more foolish as it occurred to him that he didn't have the first idea about how to write a business plan. Watching the latest series of *The Apprentice* certainly hadn't given him any ideas, and, with a pang of frustration, he realised he was still a long way off forming anything coherent that he could present to the BHF.

Simon hated asking for help. It was a flaw in his character that he'd tried hard to overcome through the years, but it had made the decision to hand Roseford Hall over to the BHF even harder. He'd been used to being self-sufficient, emotionally and practically, and the idea of having to seek advice for a project that felt so personal was making his insides squirm uncomfortably. His best friend, Olivia, whom he'd known at university, used to berate him constantly for not seeking help until it was too late, and she was one of the few people he'd opened up to and trusted. Her death a few years ago had devastated him almost as much as it had her husband, Chris. Chris had found love again, eventually, with Stella Simpson, and they co-ran the writers' and artists' retreat at the other end of Roseford. They'd taken a chance, reached out and trusted each other. Simon was tired of being cautious. But he needed to learn to ask for help. And merely googling 'how to write a business plan' didn't cut it.

But perhaps there was someone who could help. He pulled out his phone and sent a text, asking Lizzie if she'd like to meet later for a drink. As he was typing, he suddenly had a great idea about what they could do that evening. Asking Lizzie to meet him at the gates of Roseford Hall at eight o'clock, he wondered if he had time to get to Roseford Café for some supplies.

37

Through blurry eyes, Lizzie tapped the message from Simon as it appeared on her home screen. It had taken her a long time to calm down after the dressing-down from her father, made worse by the fact that they'd only come to see her on the way to somewhere else. *Story of my life*, she thought. So why did it still hurt so much? She'd always known she'd been the second fiddle to Georgina, but now she had been left in no doubt that she was barely in the bloody orchestra. Her father's attempt to micro-manage her into another role where he could keep an eye on her seemed well intentioned, but Lizzie couldn't help feeling it was done more out of a need to re-establish order than any real concern for her future. He'd always been like that. He'd always needed a plan. And she'd gone along with it. But no longer.

Simon's text, cryptic as it was, did at least raise a smile. She wondered what he had in mind for the evening. In hindsight, they'd rushed into bed together, high on the emotions. It would be nice to spend a bit more time getting to know each other, to be sure that what they both felt was genuine attraction and not lust.

She had a bit of time to compose herself, too. She was contemplating what to wear – Simon hadn't given her any details about what they'd actually be doing that night – when she heard the front door opening and Bee calling her name.

'I'm here,' Lizzie replied, scrubbing at her face, trying to eradicate any evidence of the upset of the day. The last thing she wanted to do was go over it all again.

Bee popped her head around the bedroom door. 'Are you all right, love? Feeling tired?'

'A bit,' Lizzie replied. She couldn't quite meet Bee's enquiring gaze.

Bee made her way into the room and sat down next to Lizzie on the bed.

'Don't be nice to me or I'll cry again.' Lizzie sniffed.

Bee sighed. 'Your dad's been up to his old tricks?'

Lizzie nodded. 'He just wants to control everything. Georgina can cope with it, but I can't any more. Not after everything that's happened.' She looked up at Bee. 'I'm sick of trying to play the game. I need some space to be myself.'

Bee sighed. 'I know it doesn't seem that way, but he means well. He grew up with nothing; he just wants the best for you and your sister.'

Lizzie gave a laugh. 'I don't know how you can say that when he's been so consistently vile to you over the years. He never could understand how you could settle for a "little" life as he sees it.'

'I know.' Bee smiled sadly. 'And I'd be lying if I said we hadn't had our arguments about it. But your mother, my sister, chose him, and he's tried, in his own way, to give her a good life. Even if that life is quite different from the one I chose.'

'Well, he's not making decisions for me any more,' Lizzie said firmly. 'I don't need his help.'

Bee smiled. 'I'm glad to hear it.'

Lizzie turned to Bee and looked her in the eye. 'He did make me think about one thing, though,' she said. 'If I'm going to stay here any longer, I need to start paying you some rent.'

'Don't be daft!' Bee laughed. 'I'd never ask you to do that.'

'I know, but I'm going to do it anyway,' Lizzie replied. She looked sheepish. 'That's if you don't mind me staying a bit longer? I'd kind of like to hang around, if that's all right with you?'

Bee put an arm around her. 'I said when you came you could stay here as long as you wanted,' she replied. 'But instead of paying rent, why don't you do something more useful for me?'

'Like what?' Lizzie replied.

'Like setting up that website you've been nagging me about for ages, so I can advertise a bit more widely.' Bee held up a hand as Lizzie tried to interrupt. 'Now I'm not saying I'm going to start *selling* online—' she looked vaguely horrified at the notion '—but perhaps it's about time I joined the twenty-first century and put myself and my business out there a bit more. You could help me do that, couldn't you?'

Lizzie gave a brighter grin. 'Of course I could!' she exclaimed, suddenly excited, and overwhelmed with ideas. 'Let me give it some thought and I'll draw up a mood board of ideas. I'm sure we could come up with some great concepts for a USP for Roseford Blooms.'

'A US what?' Bee asked. 'Now you can see why I need a little advice to update things!' She stood up from the bed. 'That's better,' she said. 'You're smiling again now. So, what would you like to do for dinner?'

Lizzie suddenly felt guilty. She'd been out and about a lot over the past few days, and she'd already accepted Simon's invite. 'I'm sorry, Aunt Bee, I'm going out tonight.'

'Oh, yes?' Bee raised an eyebrow. 'Anywhere or anyone I know?'

'Simon's invited me over to Roseford Hall.' Lizzie felt the blush creeping up her cheeks again.

'Well, that's definitely a reason to bow out on your old auntie.' Bee smiled. 'Enjoy yourself.'

'I will,' Lizzie replied. 'And thanks, Aunt Bee. You always did know what to say to make me feel better.'

Bee's smile faltered a little. 'Sweet of you, darling, but I don't think that was always the case.' She glanced at the small armchair by the window that had Simon's jumper slung over it. Lizzie suddenly had a feeling that Bee had known more than she'd let on about that fateful night twenty years ago, although she didn't know how. Standing up from the bed, Lizzie gave her a hug. 'It's true,' she murmured. 'And I'm sorry it's taken me so long to realise how important you are to me.'

As they broke apart again, Lizzie felt immeasurably better. Perhaps things were starting to fall into place for her, after all.

38

That evening, Lizzie took extra care with her appearance. She brushed out her hair until it was shining, and, while still wearing jeans, she picked her best top out of the wardrobe to pair with them. It was rather loose fitting, as she was conscious that her collarbone was still healing. The dusky pink colour complemented her skin tone. Bee had lent her an amethyst butterfly pendant, which rested gently on her décolletage, and she spritzed a little of her favourite floral scent on her wrists and behind her ears.

At around quarter to eight, she left the cottage and walked down the hill to the main street, stopping off at Southgate's Stores on the way to pick up a bottle of Chilean Chardonnay, cool from the fridge. Niall, the owner and manager of the stores, convinced her to add a bottle of sparkling water as well, claiming that it was locally sourced from a secret spring just the other side of the Quantocks.

'It's a new line we're trying out,' he said. 'Let me know how it is.'

'I will.' Lizzie smiled. She was half convinced it was blarney, but promised to pop back in with her thoughts in a day or two.

As she approached the now locked gates of Roseford Hall, she caught her breath when she saw Simon waiting on the other side of them. He was dressed in a crisp white shirt and dark blue jeans, which offset his slightly tanned skin to perfection. She hadn't noticed before just how the sun had bleached his dark blond hair a little lighter, and he looked every inch the relaxed English squire. The fact that she'd already seen this man completely undone added to the heat of the emotions she felt for him, and she felt the colour rising in her cheeks again.

'Hi,' she said as she approached.

'Hi, yourself.' Simon smiled as he pulled open the gate, let her through and then locked the padlock again. 'Glad you could make it.'

'Me too,' Lizzie replied.

As they walked back to the hall, Lizzie contemplated telling Simon about the conversation she'd had with her family that day, but thought better of it. She'd been over it enough in her own mind, and with Bee. She didn't feel like revisiting it again.

Simon must have noticed her lack of focus, though, as he paused before they entered the house.

'Everything all right?'

Lizzie snapped back to the moment, and she smiled. 'Yes. Everything is definitely all right.' She was intrigued as he led her through the house and up the wide, light stone-coloured staircase that ran through the centre of it. She'd been expecting him to take her back to his private quarters, and was surprised that they were taking a very public route to the top floor.

'Where are we going?' Lizzie asked.

'You'll see,' Simon teased. They reached the top of the staircase and turned right onto the top floor. Formerly, the space where they stood, the Long Gallery, had been crammed with furniture and cast-offs from the rest of the house, the detritus of a family who just hadn't known how to declutter ten generations of hereditary titles. Now, under the influence of its new owners, it had been cleared, a length of rush matting applied from end to end, the walls cleaned and strategically placed oil paintings in gilt frames lined the space. The effect was stunning, especially with the early evening sun gilding the upper end of the gallery.

'It's amazing up here!' Lizzie breathed. 'What a transformation.'

Simon grinned. 'I wish I could take the credit for that, but all I did was dig out the ancestors for the walls!'

They began to walk down the Long Gallery, Lizzie taking in the portraits as they went. She was amazed, even with several generations between them, how much Simon resembled his forebears. One painting in particular, of a young man in a World War I army uniform, blue eyes captured for all eternity in a solemn gaze, seemed to peel away the layers of time, and unite Simon with his past in the most poignant way.

'Ah, yes, Great-great-uncle Edmund,' Simon said quietly. 'Of the three Treloars who went to the Great War, he was the only one who didn't return. The other two, including my great-grandfather, survived. This was painted after his death.'

'I think I could tell that from the way it looks,' Lizzie replied softly. There was such wistfulness in Edmund's eyes; the sadness of a life not completely lived. Cut too short by forces far greater than himself. She found herself contemplating the man in the painting, and wondering who he'd have been, what he'd have achieved, if he'd had the chance.

Seeing Simon next to the painting was an eerie reminder of the brevity of life. Moved by the juxtaposition, she stepped forward and kissed him, hard.

As they moved apart once again, Simon's face registered surprise. 'Had I known that would be the effect of showing the family etchings to you, I'd have brought you up here ages ago!' He laughed nervously, and Lizzie joined in.

'Sorry,' she said. 'It's been a bit of a day.'

'Want to tell me about it?'

Lizzie shook her head. 'I'm not sure. It's complicated.'

Simon stopped and took her hands in his. 'No pressure, but I'd like to help if I can. You can tell me anything, Lizzie.'

Encouraged by the compassion in his eyes, Lizzie smiled up at him. 'I know that,' she said softly. 'You proved it when I told you about what had happened to me at that party. But this is years and years of history, Simon.' She looked down the Long Gallery again. 'Although I suppose you might know something about that!'

Simon grinned and raised an eyebrow. 'I might have some idea.'

'I guess I've always felt as though I didn't quite fit into the neat little box my family wanted to put me into,' Lizzie said. 'And for most of my life I've done my best to squeeze in, to be what they think I should be. My sister, George, was better at all of that. She still is. I started my company to try to make my parents proud, and for a while I think they were, but they can't seem to get to grips with the fact that I want, no, I *need* to do things differently now. If it was up to Dad, I'd go back into marketing, do a nine-to-five job and be more *convenient*, but I feel as though that's not me any more. I tried to tell them that, and they really didn't take it well.'

'Change can be scary,' Simon said reasonably. 'And you've been through a lot in the past few months. Might they just be looking out for you?'

'I'm sure that's a big part of it,' Lizzie conceded. 'But I've always found their approach quite claustrophobic. Their idea of looking out for me is to try to make all of the decisions for me. When I was younger, it was reassuring, but now I really feel like I need to put some distance between them and me. Being in Roseford has opened my eyes to that.'

'But you struck out on your own when you created your business,' Simon said. 'You've already said your parents were proud of you for that?'

'Yeah, they were,' Lizzie replied. 'But it also frightened them. Until Paul and I had made a real success of Warner-Basset, in financial terms, they were trying to persuade me to go and work for someone else, for a bigger company where I'd be more secure.' She gave a short laugh. 'Dad's even set up an interview for me with one of his friends at a company I worked for years ago, he's that concerned I'll chuck everything away.'

'You're not going to take him up on it, I assume?' Simon raised an eyebrow.

'Nope.'

'So what are you going to do?'

'Oh, I don't know!' Lizzie replied. 'For the first time in my life, I don't have a plan, and it actually feels quite nice. I know it won't last forever, but while it does, I'm going to try to enjoy it.' To underline that point, she leaned up on tiptoe and kissed Simon.

'Amen to that,' Simon murmured, 'if it gets me more responses like that.'

They broke apart and continued their walk down the Long Gallery, and as they reached the middle, Lizzie noticed that, in one of the bay alcoves that looked out onto each side of the gardens, there was a picnic basket, a folded blanket and a bottle of champagne in an ice bucket.

'Are we allowed to eat up here?' The rule-follower in her reared its head.

Simon gave her a mischievous look. 'Well, I won't tell if you won't,' he replied. He took her hand. 'What the BHF doesn't know won't hurt them.'

They laid out the blanket, and Simon began to unpack the basket. Lizzie noticed the beautifully cut smoked salmon and cream cheese sandwiches and slices of Victoria sponge with thick, whipped double cream were wrapped in discreetly labelled Roseford Café packaging and suppressed a smile. Lucy had done them proud.

Finding herself hungrier than she'd anticipated, she wolfed down a couple of the sandwiches. Simon had twisted the cork off the top of the champagne, and, although he'd joked about firing the cork down the length of the Long Gallery, he'd shot it into his hand. 'Wouldn't do to take out any of the ancestors,' he said, pouring two flutes and passing Lizzie one.

'So, I've been thinking about what you said this morning about Rose-Fest,' Simon said, once they'd had their fill of the picnic. 'And I just don't know where to start. It seems like such a mad thing to try to plan.'

'Well, it won't be straightforward,' Lizzie replied. 'But then what is, that's worth achieving?'

Simon leaned back on the picnic blanket, propping himself up on one elbow. 'Easy for you to say,' he said. 'You haven't got the weight of these guys all looking down on you, waiting for you to fail. Again.'

'Don't you think that's a bit of a cop-out?' The champagne had already loosened Lizzie's tongue, and she knew she was probably being less diplomatic than she should, but she persisted anyway. 'Maybe it's time you thought bigger, instead of passively accepting that you'll only ever be a spare part around here.'

Simon looked surprised, and a bit affronted. 'Maybe I'm just terrified that if I cock this up, everyone'll be pointing the finger and saying, "Look, there's Simon Treloar, the one who had to get rid of the family home, and he can't even handle setting up a poxy festival."' He stood up suddenly and began to pace towards the top of the Long Gallery.

'Are you sure it's disappointing other people you're so afraid of, and not letting yourself down?' Lizzie retorted, standing up to follow him. 'I mean, heaven forbid you should show any weakness; be anything less than perfect, Simon.'

Simon stopped abruptly, as if her words had lashed his back. 'Perfect?' He gave a hollow laugh. 'Now you're being daft.'

'Am I?' Lizzie, sensing that she'd hit a nerve, tried to swallow down her residual frustration. Shouting at Simon wasn't the answer, but his diffidence was so frustrating. She took a few steps towards him, until she could reach out and touch his shoulder. She could feel the tension in his body as she rested her palm on his back, and as he turned around to face her, she could see the conflict in his eyes.

'I'm not perfect, Lizzie. You of all people should know that by now.'

'Who is?' Lizzie replied. 'But no one's asking you to be, Simon. Least of all me.' She gave a half-laugh, half-sob. 'I've spent my whole life trying to measure up to someone who was. Georgina was the "perfect" one as far as everyone was concerned. Me? I was just the understudy. So I worked harder, pushed further, did everything I could to make my family proud. And where did it get me? A broken collarbone, no job and a tiny bedroom at my aunt's house with absolutely no clue about what to do for the future.' She shook her head. 'I'm as lost as you are.'

'But you can rebuild yourself, and your career,' Simon shot back. 'You sold your company, remember? What do I have? An English degree and house I don't even own any more.' He raised a rueful eyebrow. 'I'm not exactly a marketable proposition, by any stretch of the imagination.'

'Oh, will you just stop?' Lizzie's anger was rising again. She hated hearing the apathy and defeat in Simon's tone. 'You don't realise how bloody lucky you are, do you? If you wanted to, you could sit here, in your private apartment in the house you grew up in, for the rest of your life, being the family liaison for the BHF. You'd never have to step outside your comfort zone, and you'd lead a perfectly happy life. Frankly, no one would blame you if you did. But you've got the chance to put your own stamp on this place, to create something wonderful, that people will remember, if you're brave enough to do it.'

Simon shook his head. 'I'm really scared, Lizzie. I mean, when you say it out loud it all seems so stupid and so simple. If I put my mind to it, I have pretty much everything at my disposal I would need to launch RoseFest and yet I'm absolutely terrified to take that first step. The BHF are likely to be completely on board and, thanks to Finn Sanderson and Montana de Santo, I've got headliners Glastonbury would be proud of. But—' he gestured uselessly down at himself '—do I look like a festival organiser? I don't even own a pair of fucking flip-flops! Most popular culture of the past twenty years has completely passed me by while I was trying to keep this place afloat and I have no idea how to create a festival out of thin air. For all I know, some marketing whizz will come in, give me really shitty advice, take all my investment and it'll be an utter humiliation.'

Lizzie couldn't help smiling at how flummoxed Simon was. 'It's really not that bad,' she said. 'I know sometimes you come across as a throwback from the early twentieth century, but I really think you should have more faith in yourself than that.' She raised an eyebrow. 'And, while I wouldn't describe myself personally as a marketing whizz, I've been in the business long enough to know what does and doesn't suit a client. I'm not saying I'll be your marketing consultant, but I can certainly make sure whoever you do employ will do the right thing by you.'

Simon took a step closer to her. 'And if I asked you to be my marketing consultant?' he said softly. Lizzie could see the tenderness in his eyes.

'You couldn't afford me,' she murmured.

Simon grinned. 'Then please can you hold my hand if I decide to do this? Seriously, Lizzie, I just need someone to talk to.'

Lizzie smiled back. 'Of course. And you've got all of those potential backers at the Cross Dean reunion to butter up, as well.'

Simon groaned. 'Don't remind me. I still can't quite believe I've agreed to put myself through that. You know I'm only going because I'll have you by my side,' Simon reminded her, then reached down and took her hand. 'I think you know how much I'm going to need that.'

Lizzie felt her frustration with Simon beginning to dissipate. She knew how scared he was, about taking this next step in his life and facing his past back at Cross Dean, and her irritation began to turn into sympathy. She wanted to help Simon bring this project to fruition; but it was more than that. She wanted to be there, supporting him, maybe even loving him, while he did. Even after this short time, that much was becoming clear.

'I promise I'll be with you every step of the way,' she said softly. She leaned up and placed a kiss on his lips. 'Now, there's still some champagne to finish, isn't there? And I assume you'll need my help to remove all traces of this illicit picnic from here, if you're not to get thrown out of your own house!'

'I'm pretty sure that would be grounds for eviction, if the BHF has anything to do with it!' Simon responded.

39

The following Saturday, the Cross Dean reunion did not begin well when Simon and Lizzie were caught in a fifteen-mile tailback on their way to the small bed and breakfast Simon had booked for them. Since the school was in the heart of the Buckinghamshire countryside, it would have been too far to drive there and back in one night, and both of them had, initially, been looking forward to the change of scene. Despite Simon's strong reservations about going to the event in the first place, having Lizzie by his side was definitely helping to calm the torrent of nerves that kept bubbling up periodically. As they crawled their way through the traffic on the motorway, though, those nerves began to resurface.

Simon noticed that Lizzie, too, had been very quiet as they'd got closer to the venue. He glanced over at the passenger's seat, and observed that she had her head turned to look out of the window, one hand absently massaging her collarbone.

'Are you all right?' he asked gently. Somehow, focusing on her well-being took his mind off the reunion, calming him a little.

Lizzie looked round at him and gave him a tired smile. 'I'm fine. I could do with a loo stop, though, once we get through this traffic.'

'No problem,' Simon replied. They'd been in the car nearly two hours;

he could do with a break himself. He noticed she was still pressing her collarbone as they both looked ahead, trying to gauge how far the traffic now stretched. Thankfully, they finally began to move, and Simon spotted a sign for the motorway services coming up in another mile.

As the traffic gathered speed, Simon pulled into the inside lane and then onto the slip road, and they were soon stretching their legs. While he was waiting for Lizzie, Simon grabbed a couple of takeaway coffees for the next leg of the journey, and dithered over some pastries to go with them. He wasn't particularly car proud, but he wasn't sure if he fancied sugar and crumbs all over the seats of his Range Rover. Deciding they could eat them before they set off, he bought two Chelsea buns and then headed back to the entrance hall of the services. He spotted Lizzie coming out of the small branch of Waitrose with a packet of strong painkillers and a bottle of water in her grip.

'Is it hurting you still?' Simon asked as she swallowed a couple of the pills and took a good swig of the water.

Lizzie nodded. 'I must have slept oddly last night. It's been giving me hell since I woke up this morning.'

'Why didn't you tell me?' Simon said gently. 'You didn't have to come with me if you're in pain.'

Lizzie looked up at him. 'I didn't want to leave you in the lurch. And these'll take the edge off, anyway.' She smiled briefly, although Simon could tell it was strained. 'The doctor did warn me healing was going to take a while. It's just bad timing it hurts today, that's all.'

Simon reached out and pulled her close in a very gentle hug, trying not to aggravate her collarbone any further. 'If it's still bad this evening, then you can rest up in the B & B. Don't force yourself to come out and endure this thing with me.'

Lizzie looked up at him, and he felt his heart expanding with love for her. 'Honestly, I'm a big boy... I can handle it myself.'

'I know.' Lizzie's smile got a little steadier. 'But I promised I'd be there with you, and I will be. Now, shall we get back on the road? We've still got a little way to go.'

As they climbed back into the Range Rover, Simon reflected on how much easier this all felt with Lizzie next to him. And also, how much he wanted to be by her side protecting her when she needed it, too. Perhaps it was because of what she'd shared with him about that night back in their teens, but he found himself wanting to be there with her for everything, good and bad, from now on.

About an hour later, they pulled into the car park of the Silverton House Bed and Breakfast and briskly retrieved their luggage. Simon had hung his suit carrier on the handle of one of the back seats, and was juggling that, his holdall and Lizzie's overnight bag by the time she'd stepped down from the Range Rover.

'Give your suit to me.' Lizzie grinned, clearly appreciating Simon's chivalry. 'I'm feeling a bit better now the painkillers have kicked in.'

Simon handed it over, and got a better grip on their bags. 'Thanks.'

They headed to the front of the charming, Victorian house where they were staying, and checked in with the friendly and welcoming owner. During their picnic in the Long Gallery, Simon and Lizzie had talked about the sleeping arrangements, and Simon had booked them a room to share. They were pleased to be led to a generously sized, light and airy room that overlooked the back garden of the property.

'This is lovely, thank you,' Lizzie said as the owner left them to it. She ambled over to the sash window, which had been pulled up to let in the summer air, and breathed in the scent of honeysuckle and English roses that tumbled over the garden walls and packed the borders of the freshly mown lawn.

Simon looked at her for a long moment, enjoying the sight of her. Despite the circumstances, and still feeling nervous about what was to come, he slipped behind her, wrapping his arms around her waist and gently leaning down to kiss the side of her neck, breathing her in as she arched against him in pleasure.

'That feels good,' she murmured, before turning around to kiss him on the mouth. Her lips felt soft and warm, and as the kiss deepened, his body immediately responded to the press of her torso against his.

'What time do we have to be at the school?' Lizzie asked breathily.

'Not until seven,' Simon responded between kisses that were growing more heated. As he pulled back slightly from her, he felt his desire surging at the look in her eyes. It was clear that they were both thinking about how to best spend that time, and that their thoughts were heading in exactly the same direction. Simon pulled the curtains across the window, and allowed himself to be led to the huge, brass bedstead. As they collapsed down onto the thick, white duvet, they began discarding their clothes, and soon they'd lost all track of time.

40

Later on, after a shower, Lizzie lay in a white, fluffy towel on the bed where she and Simon had spent most of the afternoon, watching Simon slipping into his dinner suit. The cut of it was exquisite, and she was reminded again of what a great figure he made when he tried. Despite where he lived, and what he did for a job, it was sometimes easy to forget that he was Simon Treloar, Tenth Lord of Roseford, even if his circumstances were now a little different from his forebears'. But there was something about the straight lines of his back as he stood, the way he, when he chose to, carried that heritage with pride, that seemed so natural. It was also deeply at odds with his admissions about what had happened to him during his time at Cross Dean. Everyone wore some kind of protective psychological armour, she thought, and she had the feeling that Simon's had been years in the making. She also knew that he was going to need it tonight.

'Do you need any help with the bow tie?' she asked as he pulled it from the inside pocket of his suit carrier.

'No, thanks.' Simon threw a grin at her over his shoulder. 'I've got it down to a fine art. Wouldn't mind a hand with the cufflinks, though.'

Lizzie tucked her towel around herself and stood up from the bed. 'Of course.' She took the small jewellery box that Simon passed her and opened it. The cufflinks, silver inset with sapphires, glinted back at her when she opened it. 'They're gorgeous,' she breathed.

'One of the few family heirlooms left unhocked,' Simon replied dryly. 'I guard them with my life.'

Carefully, Lizzie slipped the left one into the buttonhole in Simon's crisp white cuff. The colour was exquisite against the fabric. Then, quickly, she did the right.

'Thank you,' Simon said. His eyes were similar in colour to the sapphires, and Lizzie found herself staring deeply into them as she looked up at him.

'Any time.' Then she glanced at the clock on the wall. 'I'd better get my skates on.'

'I'll, er, go down to the lounge and wait for you,' Simon replied. 'Unless you need my help with anything?'

'I should be fine,' Lizzie replied. She leaned up and kissed him. 'See you in a bit.'

As he softly closed the bedroom door behind him, Lizzie swiftly did her make-up and then slipped into the dusky pink dress that she'd bought for the occasion. It was a colour that suited her. She pulled up the zip, thankfully at the side and not difficult to reach with her still tender arm, and then slipped on the shoes she'd bought to match. Both shoes and dress had come from the newly opened shop in Roseford, which had saved Lizzie hours of trawling through websites and waiting for something to be delivered. The owner of the shop, Polly, had a great eye, Lizzie had to admit, as the chiffon of the dress fell flatteringly to just below her knees, and the shoes were the perfect complementary shade.

She wrapped her hair into her go-to style for going out, a messy, asymmetrical Dutch braid, with several tendrils of her dark hair framing her face to soften the look, and took a deep breath. She was glad she'd made the effort; it might sound a little old-fashioned, but she wanted Simon to feel proud to have her on his arm tonight.

Checking she'd got everything she needed in her handbag, she grabbed her jacket from the hook on the back of the door and pulled the bedroom door shut behind her. She walked to the steep staircase and took a moment to compose herself. She wasn't sure why she was nervous; it wasn't as if she knew anyone who was going to be there tonight, after all. It actually felt quite good to be the moral support in this situation, to have no agenda other than to be there for Simon.

As she descended the stairs, she heard Simon in the lounge having a chat to the owner of the B & B. He was so good with people, it was difficult to imagine him as the boy who lacked confidence at school.

She walked through the doorway into the lounge and was gratified to see Simon doing a double take.

'Hi,' he said, smiling broadly. 'You look absolutely wonderful. That's a knockout dress.' He put his drink down on the bar and walked towards her, leaning forward to kiss her cheek.

'Thank you.' Lizzie glowed with pleasure. 'I'm glad you approve.'

'Can I get you a drink? I'm having a spot of Dutch courage myself, while we wait for the taxi.' He gestured to his glass on the bar. 'Ron here assures me that this is the best single malt this side of the Irish Sea, and I'm inclined to agree with him.'

'I'm fine for the moment, thanks,' Lizzie replied. She was wary of mixing booze with painkillers, and she'd had another couple before she'd come down. Her collarbone was pleasantly numb right now, but she didn't want to take any chances. 'Can I have a sip though?'

'Of course.' Simon passed her the glass, and she tasted the fiery but smooth whiskey. 'Good choice.'

A ping on Simon's phone alerted them to the taxi outside. 'That's our cue.' He offered his arm to Lizzie. 'Are you ready?'

'As ready as I'll ever be, my lord,' Lizzie teased. 'And you?'

Simon gave a grin that was a little more strained than it should have been. 'Let's get this over with, shall we?'

Heading out to the taxi, Lizzie felt her own flutter of nerves, in sympathy with Simon. She knew how difficult this was going to be for him, and she hoped that having her by his side would help a little. In some strange way she felt as though she was finally returning the favour from twenty years ago.

41

As the taxi drew up to the front entrance to Cross Dean, Simon tried to force down the fear that had steadily been threatening to engulf him throughout the journey. He knew he should have driven them. Now there was no escape until the taxi came back for them at 11 p.m. Merely the sight of the wrought-iron gates, so often symbolic of the prison bars slamming shut upon his return at the beginning of a new term, made his palms clammy.

Lizzie, sitting beside him, seemed to sense this, and she took his right hand in her left one, squeezing it gently, as if to reassure him that it was all right, that she was here.

'Well, here we are.' The taxi driver stopped the engine and Simon was out of the car before he could have second thoughts. Dashing round to Lizzie's side, he opened the door for her, and helped her out.

'Here we go,' he said quietly. 'The entrance to hell itself.'

Lizzie stopped and looked at him. 'You don't have to do this, you know. You've come this far. You've seen the place. We could turn around and go back to the B & B now.'

Simon smiled and shook his head. 'Just one last time,' he said. 'And I'll never come back here again.'

'Well, if you're ready,' Lizzie said. She reached for his hand. 'Let's get this over with. And remember why you're here. It's not about laying ghosts; it's about seeing who might be able to be of use with RoseFest.'

'I'll try to remember that,' Simon replied. Somehow, the thought comforted him.

They ascended the stone steps to the large, curved oak door of the main school building, and Simon took a deep breath. The reunion was being held in the senior dining hall, a vast oak-panelled room where the older year groups jostled for hierarchy and took their meals. Simon was assailed immediately by the familiar scents of wood polish, stodgy food and the slightest undertone of teenage sweat, which must have been locked into the walls over so many years. He struggled to keep a foothold in the present as the past threatened to rise to the surface once again.

Lizzie must have noticed his reticence, as she gave his hand another squeeze. She leaned up and whispered in his ear. 'You're Simon Treloar, Tenth Lord of Roseford and founder of the inaugural literary and music festival in the village. You've earned the right to be here.'

Simon turned to her briefly. 'Thank you,' he said. They crossed the threshold, and immediately Simon spotted several familiar faces. He squared his shoulders and took a step forward.

'Well, there's no need to remind myself who *you* are.' A voice came from the table nearest the door. 'I'd have recognised you a mile away.' Behind the table, handing out name tags on metal pocket clips, was Mrs Etherington, who'd been the matron at the school in Simon's day. A tiny but forceful woman, she handed Simon his name tag without prompting, and then, double-checking with Lizzie, handed hers over too.

'It's good to see you, Matron.' Simon smiled down at the woman. 'I thought you'd have had your fill of this place by now.'

Matron twinkled at Simon, but he wasn't fooled; behind that gaze was a core of steel. Many a homesick boy had been put straight by Matron in his day, in a firm but compassionate way. He'd been among them. And when things had started to get intolerable, she'd seemed, somehow, to understand. That hadn't stopped her from sending him back into the fray, but she'd offered solace on many occasions.

'I could say the same for you, Simon,' Matron replied eventually. 'But it's good to see you all the same.'

Simon glanced down at the remaining name tags that had yet to be claimed. Some were familiar, some less so. But, he figured, many classes had gone before and after him.

'Let's get a drink,' he said. 'Then we can suss out the best places to hide if needs be.'

Lizzie grinned. 'We're here now. Let's make the most of it.'

After they availed themselves of a slightly indifferent glass of Prosecco each, Simon positioned himself near the bar, where he could keep an eye on the comings and goings.

'Simon Treloar? Is that you?' A familiar voice to one side of him made Simon turn. 'It's been bloody years, mate!'

Simon didn't need to look at the name tag attached to this friendly faced, rather plump man in front of him to recognise a once close friend. Slightly greyer and a little wider than the last time Simon had seen him, some ten years prior, he still had the same welcoming manner and game smile.

'Andy, how great to see you.' He turned to Lizzie. 'Lizzie Warner, I'd like you to meet Andy Watson. He pretty much saved my sanity at school.'

'It's nice to meet you, Lizzie,' Andy said, seizing her hand and giving it a good shake. 'My wife's here somewhere, but she just had a call from her mother so she's nipped out. Our youngest has got a bout of chicken pox, and is bad-tempered and very itchy, as you can imagine.' He grinned. 'Marina didn't want to leave her for the night, but I managed to talk her into it. First night we've had away together for ages.'

'And you chose to come back to this place?' Simon laughed. 'I thought I was a glutton for punishment!'

'Just had to see if it was still standing,' Andy replied. His face was suddenly serious. 'Didn't expect to see you here, though. Thought you'd had enough of Cross Dean to last you a lifetime.'

Simon smiled slightly grimly. 'I've a bit of an ulterior motive, as well as wanting to put a few ghosts to rest,' he said. 'I've got a new project on the go. Thought I'd see if anyone might be interested in backing it.'

'Ah, the old boys' network in action!' Andy replied. 'Well, if you can get anything out of a visit to this grisly joint, I say good luck to you. So, what's this venture, anyway?'

Simon took a deep breath, and before he could think better of it, he was off. Andy listened attentively, nodding in all the right places, until Simon had informally put his pitch.

'Sounds interesting,' Andy said, looking thoughtful. 'Look, I might be able to help. Marina's family is in publishing, so let me have a talk to her and I'll see what we can do. Put the word out in the right places, you know. Have you got a card or anything?'

Simon shook his head, wishing he'd been better prepared. 'It's all still in the early stages. I haven't even had approval from the BHF yet, but hopefully that'll come soon.' Simon pulled out his mobile. 'Let me give you my number though. It would be great to catch up, away from here, as well as just talking business.'

As they swapped numbers, Simon felt a rush of confidence. He could do this, he thought. He really could. Andy had been a great person to talk to about RoseFest, and he hoped that more opportunities would soon follow. As they finished swapping details, Andy's phone rang.

'Bugger. Sorry, mate. Marina's ringing me from the car park. I'll catch you later?'

'Sure,' Simon replied. 'I hope everything's all right with your youngest.'

'Thanks,' Andy called back over his shoulder. 'See you soon, Simon.'

Smiling broadly, Simon turned back to Lizzie. 'Well, that was encouraging.'

'Well done,' she said, smiling back at him. 'I told you you could do it.' Just as she was leaning forward to give him a hug, a much less pleasant voice cut into their celebrations.

'I thought it was you. Good to see you again so soon, *mate*.'

Simon's good mood evaporated instantly. There, in front of him, smiling insouciantly, was none other than Jago McAvoy.

42

'Jago.' Simon nodded coolly in his direction. 'I might have known I'd see you here.'

'Wouldn't miss a chance to get back to the old place for the night,' Jago replied. 'Especially since I'm thinking about sending my son here next year.'

'That figures,' Simon replied. 'Got to breed the next generation of twats and bullies somewhere, I suppose.'

Lizzie stiffened. The rudeness was so unlike the Simon she knew, who, though often mildly flustered, never seemed capable of outright bitchiness. She placed a hand on his arm. 'Shall we get another drink?' she said softly, hoping to defuse the situation.

'Not yet,' Simon replied.

Jago regarded them both, a look of smug amusement on his face. 'Now, now, Lord Treloar. No need to be like that.' His gaze lingered on Lizzie for a long moment. 'Nice to see the two of you finally found each other. You looked pretty cosy at the wedding. Is floristry going to be your new venture, Lord Treloar? Or are you just partial to dating the hired hands?'

There was no escaping Jago's tone, dripping with sarcasm, and Lizzie felt her own prickle of irritation at the carefully worded insults. His flat, bitchy tone reminded her of all those girls who'd made her own life miserable at school, and she could see clearly how someone like Jago would have made Simon's life hellish, too.

'What did you say?' Simon's voice was low, and dangerous, and Lizzie felt the hand that was holding hers clenching tightly.

'Only a joke, mate.' Jago gave an insouciant grin. 'We're all good friends here, aren't we? After all, I still haven't signed off on future weddings at that chapel of yours yet.'

'If you think you can hold that over me, you've got another think coming.' Simon had raised his voice and was pale with anger. 'After everything you put Sarah and me through when we were kids, you owe us your signature on that report.' He took a step towards Jago, and Lizzie got the very real sense that if she didn't step in soon, fists were going to fly.

'Come on, Simon,' she said firmly. 'There are plenty of people here to talk to. Let's not waste any more time here.'

As she said it, she was distracted by a woman coming up to join them. She was immaculately dressed in a simple, well-cut black shift, her blonde hair piled up on top of her head and the kind of make-up that looked subtle but actually took a long time to achieve. Her long neck was graced by a pearl pendant, and she was greyhound slim. She looked elegant, but awfully high maintenance, Lizzie thought.

'Sorry, darling, there was a queue for the ladies', as ever,' the woman said as she took the glass of fizz that Jago handed to her and sipped. 'Won't you introduce me to your friends?'

'We were just going to the bar,' Simon said quickly, the arrival of the woman causing him instinctively to back down. He glanced at Jago, the question in his eyes obvious.

The woman smiled up at Simon. 'Any friend of my husband's, and all that,' she said lightly. 'Oh, look, Jay Jay, there's Sukey and Marcus. Let's go and catch up.'

Lizzie was sure she didn't imagine the spreading colour in Simon's cheeks as the woman spoke. As reality dawned. 'Come on, Simon,' she said quickly. 'Shall we get that drink?'

'Yes, Jago,' Simon said, finally, and his voice sounded dangerously quiet. 'I'd do what your wife says, if I were you.'

If Jago was unsettled by the juxtaposition of his wife and the brother of the woman he'd spent the night with at the wedding, he didn't show it. He gave Simon a broad smile. 'They always know best, don't they?' he said. 'Some other time, then, Lord Treloar.'

Jago and his wife moved away from them, and Lizzie tried to wriggle her hand out of Simon's, but it was clenched so tightly she had to settle for pulling him away towards the bar. 'Come on,' she said firmly. 'Let's get that drink.' She was relieved when he followed her.

They grabbed a couple more glasses of Prosecco, and then Lizzie turned to Simon. 'Do you want to tell me about it?'

Simon shook his head. 'Not here. Not right now.' He took a gulp of his wine. 'But let's just say if murder was legal, Jago McAvoy wouldn't be left standing.'

Lizzie's brow furrowed. 'I know he was a twat to you, but is it really that bad?'

Simon looked down at her, and for a second his demeanour was so alien to the amiable man she felt she was getting to know that Lizzie felt a shard of unease worrying at her heart. How much did she *really* know about him, after all?

'I'm sorry,' Simon said, and in that moment he looked like himself again. 'I'll explain it all, I promise, but I kind of need to get through this evening first.' They walked over to the side of the hall, where there was a display of old photographs on fabric-lined portable boards. Lizzie, who was always fascinated by such things, couldn't help but be drawn to them. They ranged from copies of photographs from the turn of the last century, up to the most recent crop of Cross Dean graduates, and as Lizzie's eyes scanned them, she began to catch sight of a few familiar names.

'Is that your dad?' she asked Simon as he stood by her side. The display seemed to distract his attention, and Lizzie relaxed a little when she saw him smile.

'Yup,' Simon replied as they both spent a long moment staring at the figure in the back of one photograph. It was a shot of a group of older students, dressed in Combined Cadet Force uniforms, looking solemnly into the camera. 'Thank god they'd mostly phased out the CCF training by the time I left so no one else had to go through it.'

'Oh, I don't know,' Lizzie teased as they followed the timeline to the period when Simon had been at the school 'I think the military uniform kind of suits you!' Much like the photograph of Simon's father and his contemporaries, this one was a shot of another group of young men, around seventeen years old, dressed in stiff army attire and staring into the camera. Lizzie had no trouble in finding Simon in the picture. Despite the time lapse of twenty-one years, he was instantly recognisable.

'I can't say the training suited me,' Simon said quietly. 'But thankfully that's all in the past now.'

Eager to trace further back into Simon's history, knowing that a fair few generations of Treloars had attended Cross Dean, Lizzie followed the time-line backwards. There, in the turn of the last century's intake, was a picture of someone who made her catch her breath.

'That's Edmund Treloar, your great-great-uncle, isn't it?' she asked. The serious-looking boy in the photograph stared back at her.

Simon nodded. 'Yes. He rather took to the uniform, and enlisted into the Somerset Fusiliers straight out of school. As you know, he was killed on the Western Front a couple of years afterwards, along with most of that cohort.'

Lizzie was struck, once again, by the long line that Simon came from. It was one thing to see it at Roseford Hall, but another to see how those kinds of networks operated in the outside world. No wonder he was having worries about how he fitted into that history.

Noticing that Simon still seemed on guard and out of sorts, Lizzie suggested they get some air. 'Why don't you show me around while it's quiet? I'd love to see a bit more of it.'

Simon smiled down at her and then popped his glass on a nearby table. 'Why not? I'm hoping I'll never have to come back here again, so I might as well take one last look.' She had the almost tangible sense that he was pulling himself together as he said it, in order to paper over the cracks that the encounter with Jago had created, and, to a great extent, the fissures that being here had reawakened.

They headed outside into the humid summer night. All around them were the outlines of buildings fronting onto the central quad of the school. They reared up like implacable watchmen, timeless, stoic and full of history and experience, not just Simon's, but those of the generations of students who had come before and after him.

'It's really rather beautiful when you put aside the hideous memories,' Simon said quietly. Lizzie wanted to hear a light note in his voice, but couldn't quite find it.

'Was it that bad?' Lizzie asked.

Simon gave a hollow laugh. 'Some of the time I was asleep.'

And it was then that Lizzie understood exactly why Simon had been so gentle and careful with her that night he'd unknowingly rescued her from that awful stunt at that party. He'd seen, in her, something he recognised in himself. It hadn't merely been an act of kindness; it had been an acknowledgement of a shared experience.

'So, unlike you-know-who, you won't be sending your children here, then?'

Simon, who had been gazing up at the spire of the school's chapel, which formed the fourth side of the quad, turned back to her. His eyes were glistening in the moonlight, and he shook his head. 'Never,' he said quietly. 'I wouldn't put any child of mine through what I went through here.' He tried to turn away from her, clearly embarrassed about showing so much vulnerability, but she caught his arm.

'It's all right, Simon,' Lizzie said gently. 'You saved me once. Let me do the same for you now.' She drew him into her arms, holding him close for a long moment. She could feel him trembling, and she knew he was trying to get himself back under control, struggling not to break down in the face of so many memories.

Eventually, they broke apart, and to her surprise, Simon was smiling.

'Thank you,' he said softly. 'Thank you for coming here, and for holding my hand. It means a lot to me.'

Lizzie smiled back at him. 'Any time.'

They turned away from the chapel, arms still around each other. 'Shall we go?' Simon asked. 'I'm not sure I can cope with an evening of any more reminiscences.'

'If you're ready, then let's get out of here,' Lizzie replied. She looked down at her feet. 'I'm not sure I'm in the right shoes to walk back, though. Can we reschedule the taxi?'

Simon smiled. 'Of course.' He pulled out his phone, and in a few moments he'd cancelled the cab and arranged for one to come immediately. As he ended the call, he heard Andy Watson's voice from across the car park, where they were heading.

'Leaving so soon?' He was standing by a reassuringly normal-looking Audi estate, a few years old and with a child seat in the back. 'Had enough of the nobs?'

Simon grinned. 'Something like that. I was in two minds about coming, anyway.'

'Me too.' Andy grinned. 'Some things are better left in the past, I think.'

'Why do we put ourselves through this stuff?' Simon raised his eyes to the sky. 'Surely, if we'd wanted to keep in touch with people, we'd have done it.'

'Thanks,' Andy replied dryly. 'I was about to say how nice it was to catch up with you.'

'Well, perhaps there are exceptions,' Simon replied. 'It was good to see you again.' He paused. 'I thought you were heading off to check on your youngest?'

Andy shook his head. 'My wife managed to sort it all out over the phone, thank goodness. Aoife suffers from pretty heavy separation anxiety, and the chicken pox doesn't really help. This is the first night we've had away on our own since she was born. She's three now, and starting to come out of it, but it's been a long road.'

'I can imagine,' Simon said.

'My sister was the same,' Lizzie interjected. 'She did eventually grow out of it, but it took a lot of patience from Mum and Dad.' She smiled sympathetically. 'Thankfully, she got there in the end.'

'Before she was old enough to leave home?' Andy quipped.

Lizzie laughed. 'Just about.' She found she liked Andy, a lot, and hoped that Simon really would keep in touch with him, and it wasn't just an idle promise.

'Well, we'd better go and wait for the taxi,' Simon said, in the ensuing pause.

'Where are you staying?' Andy asked. 'I can give you a lift if you like.'

'We're at the Silverton House B & B in the next village,' Simon replied.

'That's where we are, too!' Andy said. 'Look, Marina's just popped to the loo, but we're pretty much fed up with this grisly evening. Why don't we all head back and have a proper drink? Catch up away from the rest of them?'

'I'd like that,' Simon said. Then, turning to Lizzie, 'Are you all right with that? I could vouch for Andy when he was sixteen, and he doesn't look like the type who'll abduct us.'

Lizzie laughed. 'I trust you. And yes, let's get out of here.'

Lizzie watched Andy's face soften as he caught sight of a smallish woman hurrying back to the car park. He introduced his wife to Simon and Lizzie, and then they all got into the car. The back of the Audi, and the child's car seat, meant that Simon and Lizzie were a little cramped, but it was only a short drive back to the B & B, and Lizzie was more than happy to be pressed up against Simon. He called the taxi firm back, apologising for the cancellation, while they were en route.

When they'd reached the B & B and clambered out of the car, Simon turned to Lizzie.

'Thanks for tonight,' he said softly, before Marina and Andy joined them again. 'It meant a lot to me, having you there to hold my hand.'

'You're welcome,' Lizzie replied. She leaned up and kissed him quickly. 'Now let's have a drink and hopefully Andy will be able to tell me what you were *really* like at school!'

43

A few hours later, a slightly less than sober Lizzie and Simon finally made it back to their room. They'd spent a long but enjoyable evening talking to Andy and Marina, and Simon wished that he'd jumped onto Facebook years ago and reconnected with his friend. It had been so easy to write off his school days as terrible after he'd left that he'd forgotten just how good a friend Andy had been to him; how they'd supported each other through some dark times, but also found moments to have a laugh.

And among the laughter tonight was the rather more serious notion of setting up the inaugural weekend of RoseFest. Andy and Marina had seemed genuinely interested and excited by the prospect of getting on board to help create the festival, and Simon was optimistic that, should he get the go-ahead from the British Heritage Fund, this could be achieved in the next year or so. As he and Lizzie retired to bed, he took her hand. 'Thank you for convincing me to do this,' he said. 'I never would have had the balls to, if you hadn't pushed me out of my comfort zone.'

Lizzie smiled back at him in the half-light. 'I've really enjoyed spending time with you.' She dropped her gaze, embarrassed. 'I really, really like you, Simon. And there's a part of me that just wants to stay in Roseford for good. I never thought, when I came back, that I'd be feeling like that.'

'I'm glad you did come back,' Simon said softly. He raised a hand and lifted Lizzie's chin so that he could see her eyes again. They looked wide open, and vulnerable, and he was seized, yet again, with the desire to protect her, to love her, not just right then, but for always. 'I don't want you to go home, either.'

Lizzie shook her head. 'I'm not quite sure where home is, these days. But it feels more and more like it's wherever you are.' She paused, embarrassed again. 'Sorry. That must be the booze talking.'

'Then let it talk,' Simon replied. He was simultaneously excited and reassured by her admission, and he knew that he was beginning to feel exactly the same way. The vision he'd had earlier about having children and sharing his life with someone had crystallised and he realised, with a jolt, that it was Lizzie he'd been hoping to share this with.

He took a deep breath. 'While the booze is doing the talking,' he began, 'then I might as well go for it.' He ran a gentle hand over Lizzie's cheek. 'I'm in love with you, Lizzie. And if I'm being honest, I've been in love with you for a little while. I don't want you to go back to your old life, and your old job, because the thought of being without you is filling me with emotions that your average teenage boy would be ashamed to admit, let alone a grown man. If and when you decide what happens in the next phase of your life, I want to be there to share it, if you'll have me.'

The relief that Simon felt as Lizzie wrapped her arms around him was so great that he only clocked how hard he was hugging her back when she yelped.

'Sorry,' he said, releasing her. 'I completely forgot about your collarbone.'

Lizzie looked back up at him. 'It's all right,' she said. 'I'll forgive you this once if you promise to kiss it better. Very, very slowly...'

'With pleasure,' Simon murmured. He dipped his head and began to kiss her neck, enjoying the scent of her skin and the remnants of the rose perfume she'd applied earlier. He gently made his way to her shoulder, and then kissed her across her collarbone, feeling a growing ache of desire as she sighed with pleasure.

'We'd better get to bed,' he murmured between kisses. 'Even if it is only for a few hours.'

'With pleasure,' Lizzie breathed.

They closed the bedroom curtains and in a few minutes had shed their clothing and were under the duvet.

'I meant to say,' Lizzie whispered as their hands began to roam, 'I love you too.'

Simon couldn't help the smile that spread over his face as he heard that. 'Is that just because I'm kissing you better?' he teased.

Lizzie pulled back so that he could see into her eyes. 'No,' she replied. 'I mean it, Simon. And believe me when I say I haven't said that to many people in my life.'

As the darkness began to fade into a soon-approaching dawn, despite being miles away from Roseford Hall, Simon felt as if he was coming home.

44

The next morning, Lizzie and Simon awoke to a knock at their bedroom door. Groggily, Simon grabbed a fluffy white towel from the rail in the en suite and wrapped it around his waist before he opened the door.

On the other side were Andy and Marina, grinning from ear to ear.

'Thought we'd give you a quick knock before we went down to breakfast,' Andy said. 'It finishes in twenty minutes, and we assumed you hadn't been down yet.'

'Thanks,' Simon said, unable to suppress a yawn. He and Lizzie hadn't slept for more than a couple of hours, in the end. 'We'll see you down there.'

Andy gave him a long look. 'I'd keep hold of Lizzie, if you can,' he said. 'She obviously suits you.'

Simon smiled. 'Yes. I think she does.' He closed the door and walked back to the bed, where Lizzie was sitting up, the white sheet wrapped around her as she reached for the glass of water on the bedside table.

'Andy's just given us our breakfast call,' Simon said, settling down beside her and giving her a kiss. 'We've got about twenty minutes if you want to grab something.'

Lizzie nodded. Her brow was furrowed and Simon noticed that her phone was open to WhatsApp where it lay on the bedside table.

'Everything all right?' he asked.

Lizzie glanced briefly at the phone again before she responded. 'Sure,' she replied. 'Just catching up on a couple of messages.'

'Anything urgent?'

The way she shook her head so quickly in response to the question made the back of Simon's neck prickle with unease. But he didn't want to push her. Perhaps he'd try to broach it with her on the way home. For the moment, as his stomach gave an almighty rumble, he needed something to eat.

They showered quickly and dressed, and then headed downstairs to the dining room, where Marina and Andy were sitting at a table by the window. Simon raised a hand and they all greeted each other. Andy beckoned them over to join them and they were soon tucking into full English breakfasts, with cups of strong tea to wash it all down.

Simon noticed that Lizzie, while adding little bits to the easily flowing conversation, seemed quiet. He began to wonder if she was having second thoughts about telling him she loved him the night before. They had drunk a fair amount, and perhaps in the cold light of day she was regretting being so frank with him. He became even more determined to talk things through with her on the drive home, although it might be awkward if she had had a change of heart, on a three-hour journey.

'So we'll touch base in about three weeks' time,' Andy was saying as they finished up. 'And hopefully, by then, you'll have heard from the BHF and we can get this show on the road.'

'I hope so,' Simon replied. 'I'll chase them when I get back, so with a bit of luck we can start the ball rolling.'

The couples waved their goodbyes after breakfast, and as Simon and Lizzie checked out, he couldn't help sharing his excitement with her. 'I can't believe RoseFest looks like it finally might be happening.' He gave her a grin. 'And if it hadn't been for you convincing me to come to this blasted reunion, I'd probably still be thinking about it, and staring at those notes.'

Lizzie gave a smile, but it definitely seemed to Simon that it was forced. He lifted her suitcase into the back of his car and then, when they were both in the front, he turned to her.

'Are you sure you're all right? You seem a little down this morning.'

Lizzie nodded her head. 'I'm just really tired.' She was rubbing at her collarbone again, and Simon wished they didn't have a long drive in front of them when she was clearly uncomfortable. He knew he should give her space; that if she wanted to she would confide in him, but he was desperate to understand, and to try to lift her mood. If she was upset about something, he wanted, he *needed* to help her.

* * *

Lizzie sat back against the comfortable leather seats of Simon's Range Rover, and tried to put everything out of her mind but the journey home. She appreciated Simon's concern, and he did really look worried about her, but she couldn't confide in him yet. In truth, she wasn't sure what she should say.

If only she'd ignored her phone! She should have just allowed that wonderful bubble, the one that she and Simon had been alone inside, to last a little longer. They'd had such a great night together, and then she'd had to look at her phone and the bubble had burst.

She knew she shouldn't let it bother her – a throwaway comment from her sister was something she'd become accustomed to ignoring over the years – but this, combined with Simon's enthusiasm for his new project, had ignited a fresh turmoil, and built on insecurities that she'd thought she'd conquered long ago. Georgina knew just how to get to her, and Lizzie couldn't stop thinking about what she'd written on the WhatsApp message.

They stopped briefly outside Oxford for a coffee and a rest break, and Lizzie, while quiet, managed to keep herself on an even keel. She needed time to think, and she was relieved when Simon drew up outside Bee's cottage later that afternoon.

'Thank you again for a lovely night,' Simon said as he cut the engine and turned to face her. 'Will I see you later?'

Lizzie gave a tired smile. 'Do you mind if we don't? My collarbone's really sore and I could do with an early night.'

Simon just about managed to disguise his disappointment. 'Of course. Call me when you're feeling better.' He leaned forward and gave her a kiss, and Lizzie had to fight every instinct she had not to collapse into his arms. She desperately wanted to level but now wasn't the time. She needed to think. And, much as she hated to admit it, she needed to talk to her sister.

45

'Lizzie? Thanks for calling me back.'

Georgina's voice came down the phone in its usual, slightly breathy way. Lizzie tried not to wince.

'I didn't have a lot of choice, really,' Lizzie replied.

'Well, I'm glad you're going to hear me out, at least.'

The words of the message that Georgina had dashed off to her last night flashed through Lizzie's mind once again.

Be careful, Lizzie. Simon might not be all he seems. Can we talk?

'Can you make it quick, George? I'm shattered.' Lizzie slumped back onto the single bed in her room, leaning against the padded headboard for comfort. The long drive and late night were starting to catch up with her.

'Sure,' Georgina replied. 'Look, you can tell me that this is none of my business, but I've heard through the grapevine that Simon's thinking of setting up some event in Roseford and that he's looking for backers.'

Lizzie shook her head. Could nothing be kept under wraps these days? She wondered how an idea that Simon had, until recently, only been toying with, had got out to the wider world so swiftly.

'Where did you hear that?' Lizzie asked. 'He's only just started seriously thinking about it. It's still in the development stages.'

'Well, that's as may be, and it's not really important who I heard it from. The person I'm worried about in all this is you.'

'Me?' Lizzie choked on the gulp of tea she'd taken while Georgina had been talking. 'Why are you worried about me?'

'Because I don't want you getting suckered in to backing a project just because you've got the hots for the lord of the manor.'

'What?' Lizzie's voice rose several notches. 'And why would you think I would do that?'

Georgina gave a sigh. 'Come on, Lizzie. Simon's gorgeous, and charismatic, and clearly has an excellent vision for what he wants to do to make his mark on Roseford Hall. But he's also broke. Why do you think he had to hand over the house and the grounds in the first place? It might not look like it, but he's barely got two pennies to rub together. And there you come along with a healthy bank balance from selling your company and suddenly he's all over you. Don't you think that's more than a little bit suspect?'

Lizzie's throat constricted and she had to swallow hard before she could continue. 'So, let me get this right. You're saying that the only reason, the only possible reason, that Simon Treloar would want to spend time with me is to fleece me for my money? Have you any idea how awful that sounds?'

Georgina paused a long time before she responded again, and Lizzie angrily imagined her composing her features into that oh-so-caring expression that she'd cultivated over the years for situations like this. 'Of course not, Lizzie,' she said eventually. 'I'm sure he's a lovely guy, and he's clearly very fond of you, but I'm asking you to look deeper, to see if there's more to it than that. I don't want to see you getting hurt.'

'You don't want to see me getting hurt?' Lizzie echoed incredulously. 'That's bloody rich. Where were you when Paul and I broke up? When I sold the company I'd spent my professional life building? When Dad basically came here and told me to go to that job interview? I didn't see you worrying then.'

'I'm sorry, Lizzie, I really am, but please, promise me you'll have a think about what I've said. Isn't this all rather... convenient?'

'And what the hell would you know about Simon anyway?' The fire was in Lizzie's blood now, and the temper that she tried so hard to keep under wraps normally was rising to the surface, prickling under her skin.

'I know you, Lizzie, and I know that you have a bit of a blind spot for giving away your heart when you shouldn't.'

'You don't know me at all!' Lizzie was shouting now. 'And don't pretend, after all these years, that you really care, either. Simon was there for me when I needed him, not just recently but back when you were too caught up with being popular and shagging that week's boy of your dreams to care what I was going through. So don't presume to lecture me on my so-called blind spots, Georgina.'

Her sister's silence on the other end of the phone spoke more than any words ever could. Eventually, she spoke again, and her voice was much quieter.

'I'm sorry, Lizzie, if I wasn't there for you. I'm sorry I wasn't a better sister. But please, please, think about what I've said. I just don't want to see you getting hurt, after everything you've been through this year.'

Lizzie shook her head. Once again, the prevalence of the word 'I' in Georgina's speech undermined every apparent good intention she had.

'I appreciate the thought, Georgina, but I think I'm able to make up my own mind.' Not giving her sister time to reply, she pressed the red button and ended the call.

Sinking back further onto the bed, Lizzie let out a long sigh, and battled with the urge to chuck her phone across the room. Georgina always had that effect on her. Lizzie had wished, for so many years, that the two of them could be closer, but she'd realised a long time ago that it wasn't going to happen. They were two different people, *too* different people. The best she could hope for was a kind of civility, and she was beginning to realise that even that might be out of the question.

But how the hell had she got wind of Simon's business venture? She kicked herself for not pressing Georgina for a name, and briefly considered calling her back. She was knackered, though, and for the moment she just needed to get her head down. The old doubts were creeping in, too, as they had started to when Georgina had sent her the text. What if Georgina was right, and Simon was only after her for her investment potential? What if he was playing her, and when he'd got what he wanted he was going to end up relegating her to the role of silent partner? Why, if he was such a great guy, hadn't he been snapped up by some gorgeous girl years ago? As she fought to clear her mind, and reassure herself, she couldn't stop sleep from overwhelming her, and she finally crashed out, more confused than ever. The last thing she remembered before she dropped off was the sound of Simon's voice, telling her he loved her. But now even that felt tainted.

46

The next morning, drained from the emotions of the weekend, Lizzie woke late, and feeling groggy. She glanced at the wind-up alarm clock on her bedside table and realised it had stopped in the night, so grabbed her phone instead. She was stunned to see it had gone 9 a.m. Sitting up abruptly in bed, she battled twin emotions of pleasure and doubt when she saw that Simon had sent her a text at ten o'clock last night, wishing her sweet dreams. But she couldn't shake the worries that the conversation with Georgina had provoked. She knew she needed to see Simon, to try to talk things through with him, but she wasn't sure where to start. Somehow, 'Hey, I know you've told me you love me but are you just using me for my money?' seemed like too crass a question to contemplate.

She knew she should ignore Georgina – she was hardly a reliable source – but Lizzie's insecurities were playing havoc with her judgement. Sighing, she dragged herself out of bed, and mooched through to the kitchen to make a coffee. Bee had left her a note, saying that she'd be late back from work as she had a big order for another wedding to fulfil, and not to wait for her for dinner. Lizzie thought she might go down to Rose-ford Blooms and help – she'd found working with the flowers so thera-peutic in the early days of her stay, and she wanted to be of use to her aunt.

Then she had another idea. She'd been turning things over in her head for the website for the flower shop ever since Bee had given her the go-ahead to design one, but she hadn't actually done anything about it yet. Why didn't she try to put something together to show Bee? It would take her mind off Simon, and she could take her laptop down to the shop later when she went in to help. Despite her worries, she felt a tingle of excitement. Lizzie poured a cup of strong coffee and went to find her laptop.

An hour and a half later, she leaned back in the kitchen chair and looked at mock-up of the logo and the website she'd created to advertise Roseford Blooms. Although Bee had made it clear that the flowers-by-post model wasn't something she wanted to explore, Lizzie wanted to claim an online space for Roseford Blooms to give it the recognition she felt her aunt deserved. She thought carefully about the colours of the shop itself: Bee already had some pretty distinctive branding, and she wanted to keep things consistent. She realised she'd need to take some photographs of the shop, the flowers and possibly Bee herself if she was going to make a good job of it, and so she resolved to do that when she popped down to Roseford Blooms later. In the meantime, she browsed as many websites as she could created by florists, those who had an online delivery model and those who focused on the shopfront, and began a virtual mood board of themes and ideas.

After another hour, fired up with enthusiasm and another cup of coffee, Lizzie decided to head down to Roseford Blooms and show Bee her handiwork. She realised to her amazement that getting stuck back into work had really lifted her mood, and taken her mind off things, and she was definitely feeling more optimistic as she walked down the hill to the village centre.

Once she'd arrived at Roseford Blooms, she could barely see Bee for the arrangements of flowers that were positioned all over the counter. The scents of white roses, freesias, myrtle and rosemary sprigs all mingled in the air, and Lizzie sniffed appreciatively.

'Hi, Aunt Bee,' she said as she closed the shop door behind her.

'Oh, hello, darling,' Bee called back.

Lizzie could hear the stress in her aunt's voice. She immediately put the laptop down on a patch of the counter that wasn't covered in flowers, and headed behind it.

'Can I help?' she said as Bee hurriedly placed another long-stemmed white rose into the bouquet she was working on.

'Oh, could you?' Bee replied. 'Do you remember how to do button-holes? The delivery was late and I'm up against it if these are going to be ready by the time I close.'

'Of course,' Lizzie replied. She pulled the tray of rose heads towards her. Bee had already cut the stems to about an inch and a half long, and they'd been in water overnight to condition them ready for making the button-holes. Carefully, she peeled off the weather petals, as Bee had taught her, making sure to remove any that had signs of damage or discolouration. Then, she carefully pinned the sepals, the small leaves between the base of the flower and the stem, with tiny hairpins of wire. Next, she carefully slid a piece of wire up the stem, and bound the stem with the fine silver rose wire to keep it in place.

Bee had chosen ivory wax flowers to go alongside the beautiful ivory-coloured roses, so the next step was to wire up that, and some delicate mimosa. The final piece of foliage was large leaf eucalyptus, which gave a wonderful contrast to the spriggy texture of the mimosa. Then came the taping. Lizzie had struggled a bit with taping the different flowers for Montana and Serena's wedding, so she went slowly, and checked in with Bee frequently. Eventually, following the example that Bee had already made, she taped the components together, snipped the wires and then rounded off the bottom with more tape.

She held up her first attempt for Bee's approval.

'Not bad,' Bee said. 'Try to keep a flat edge on one side so that they sit nicely against a jacket lapel, if you can.'

'Will do,' Lizzie replied, diving into making the next one.

They worked alongside each other in companionable silence, Lizzie uttering the odd expletive under her breath when she pricked her fingers with the sharp ends of the rose wire, but gradually she got into a rhythm and had made a dent in the huge pile of buttonholes that needed to be assembled by the end of the day.

'Thanks, love,' Bee said as she looked approvingly over at Lizzie's handi-work. 'I always said you had an eye for this.'

'I wish I had tougher hands!' Lizzie laughed. Her fingertips felt sore from manipulating the rose wire and catching herself on the ends, but she felt huge satisfaction when she looked at what she'd managed to achieve. That pride in seeing something tangible in front of her that she'd created washed over her again, just as it had before Montana and Serena's wedding.

'Let's stop for a cuppa, shall we?' Bee said as she finished carefully tying the bridesmaids' posies. 'The bride's bouquet will have to be done as late as possible, anyway, so I'll be back in here early tomorrow morning tackling that one.'

Lizzie headed to the small kitchen space behind the shop floor to put the kettle on, and soon she and Bee were taking relieved sips of Lady Grey and surveying their handiwork.

'You really need to take on an apprentice,' Lizzie observed. 'I bet you got here way too early this morning to tackle this lot, didn't you?'

Bee nodded. 'It was a rather early start, yes.' She put her mug down on the counter and sighed. 'And you're right, of course. But what happens then? I won't be able to do this forever, and then I'd have to sell the business and put someone out of a job.'

'Not necessarily,' Lizzie replied. 'Often, staff can be retained when the business changes hands.' She couldn't help thinking that Bee had been working in her own flower-decorated bubble for too long; she seemed to have lost track of what might make commercial sense. Along with her refusal to take Roseford Blooms online, she had a worrying tendency to stick her head in the sand about the future.

'Well, that's a decision for the owner after me,' Bee said firmly. 'I've got a year or two, at most, before I'd like to hang up my pruning shears and relax. Plenty of time for a new owner to decide what they want to do with a place like this.' Pausing, she looked at Lizzie shrewdly. 'It needs someone who can understand the business, but also someone who can take it to new levels. Hopefully there might be someone out there who can do both.'

Lizzie laughed nervously, sensing she knew what Bee was getting at. 'It's a big commitment, though, and you'd want someone who was trained properly. No point someone taking the business on who's not qualified.'

'Oh, there's a decent course at the local college,' Bee replied. 'And it's only about five miles from here. Easy enough, if someone had both the means and the motivation. I've had students here in the past, helping out as part of their placement. But I'm far too long in the tooth to train someone on a more permanent basis.' She paused. 'Unless I really wanted to, of course.'

Bee's hints were getting less subtle by the second.

Lizzie laughed, to break the speculative tension. 'Anyone would think you wanted me to take the business on!'

'Well, that's not a bad idea,' Bee replied, suddenly serious. She placed the rose wire she'd been twining around the several buttonholes she'd managed to complete during their conversation back on the counter. 'If it was something you thought you could manage, of course. And you wanted to.'

Lizzie put her scissors down. 'I'm flattered, Aunt Bee, that you'd consider me. But I know nothing about being a florist. I've been able to do a few passable buttonholes because you taught me so well, but learning all this?' She gestured at the serried ranks of flower stems on the stepped shelves around the shop, and those that were taking up most of the counter. 'I don't know if I'd ever be able to do it justice.'

'Being a florist is a mixture of art and pragmatism,' Bee replied. 'You make the most wonderful things you can with the things you have available. And with the move now towards more sustainable plants and flowers, the profession is changing. You have so much you could learn, Lizzie, and so much you could give to a business like this. New ideas that I wouldn't even have dreamed of.' She picked up the rose wire again to secure another set of sprigs to the rose head she'd been working on. 'But it has to be your decision, my love. I'm going to sell in a year or two, no matter what. If you were to train at the college you'd need that time, and then, if you wanted to, you could buy me out. You could even stay at the cottage if you wanted to. There's plenty of space, and I'd like the company.'

Lizzie couldn't deny that the offer was an exciting one. She'd felt rootless since selling Warner-Basset, and she had the funds to do the course, and then, if it worked out, she had enough to put down a substantial deposit for a mortgage on the business, she was sure. It would be a risk, but then what wasn't, these days? If there was one thing that this past year had taught her, things could be pulled out from under you at any moment. Wasn't it better to try to take control?

'Aunt Bee, that's a wonderful idea,' Lizzie said eventually. 'And thank you.' She leaned over and gave Bee a hug. 'Can I have some time to think about it?'

'Of course, love,' Bee said, smiling. 'I'm not going anywhere just yet, and you'd need to look into courses anyway. And obviously you'd need to think about whether staying in Roseford is what you really want. It's a sleepy old place compared to where you were before, and although you've had a decent time while you've been recuperating, you'd have to decide whether you'd want to be here permanently.'

'I could always get a place nearby,' Lizzie said. Then she stopped herself. She couldn't afford to jump in, feet first, and make a decision she'd regret.

'There's lots to think about,' Bee said. 'So take your time. Don't let your heart overrule your head, just because it's me who's suggested it. Try to treat it as you would any other business decision.'

Lizzie smiled, but it was tempered, yet again, with a little worry. Since speaking to Georgina, she'd been worrying that her judgement had been clouded as far as Simon was concerned, and she still needed to work out how she felt about that situation. And now Bee was offering her an exciting, totally new opportunity: a leap into the unknown. She had a lot to think about, and suddenly her relaxing summer in Roseford, getting better and sorting out her life felt a whole lot more complicated.

47

Simon had had a long and frustrating morning. Since his discussion with Andy and Marina at the weekend, he'd been trying to get hold of the contact at the British Heritage Fund he'd been given to see if he could move any further forward with his plans for RoseFest. Without their approval, there was no way he could start trying to get the capital, through sponsorship, that he needed to run the inaugural event. If it was going to take place in a year's time, he needed to get things moving.

Simon wasn't daft. He might have been raised in a country house that was falling down around his ears, but he was a quick learner and he knew that, without backing, RoseFest wouldn't happen. Handing over Roseford Hall to the British Heritage Fund had taught him a lot about red tape, property law and procedure, and, after realising his deficiencies in this area, he'd recently studied their business plan for the hall, hoping to get some guidance for the new venture. It was just the painfully slow process of waiting for the other parties involved to come back to him that he found frustrating. Since his night at Cross Dean, he was fired up with enthusiasm, and he couldn't wait to get started.

He huffed in frustration as his email registered no new messages. This wasn't doing anyone any good. He had plenty of other stuff to be getting on with: the BHF wanted a summary of any superficial repairs that needed doing inside the main areas of thoroughfare in the house, and although he knew a number of the staff had reported several issues, he'd been asked to confirm them and then fill out the online forms to get those repairs booked in. It was the kind of admin-driven, mind-numbingly dull exercise that his days were made up of, as family liaison. He'd be lying if he said he didn't find work like that irritating, but, he supposed, he was the one who lived here full-time now, in the grace and favour apartment at the back of the house that the BHF had renovated for him.

Shutting the lid of his laptop in irritation, he picked up his phone from where it had virtually disappeared under a pile of paperwork. Still no message from Lizzie. He felt his heart speed up a little with unease. She hadn't contacted him since they'd returned home yesterday afternoon, not even to acknowledge the text he'd sent wishing her sweet dreams. He knew he shouldn't read anything into it; she was probably just preoccupied, and catching up with Bee, who had another wedding on tomorrow, but he felt a little off-kilter. Sending her a quick *hello, thinking of you* via WhatsApp, he stared at the screen, willing the ticks to turn blue, to show she'd read the message. After a minute, they still hadn't, so he put the phone down again and tried to concentrate on the tasks in front of him.

Alas, the state of the plasterwork in the Queen Anne suite couldn't really hold his attention, so he decided to take a tour of the house and see if he could add any more issues to report. There was a part of him that was glad he and his family no longer had to foot the bill for the near-constant repairs, even though it meant the house wasn't theirs to do with as they wished.

Locking the door to his office, Simon descended the back stairs that led to a corner of the main hallway, and smiled at a few visitors, guide sheets in hand, who were taking in the sights of the ground floor. John Handley, a kindly older man with a frame like a polar bear and a silver-grey pelt to match, was standing in the corner of the Great Hall, holding forth in strident tones to a small group, obviously on a guided tour, and filling them in on the scandalous doings of one of Simon's ancestors. The Treloar family had its own share of rogues and rascals, and John Handley probably knew more about them than Simon himself. The irony of being surrounded by all of this history, Simon thought, was that it was difficult to retain it in your own head when you were living it.

But history was being taken care of by the BHF now. It was the future that mattered. *His* future. Simon smiled back at John as he raised a hand in greeting, but he didn't stop. He didn't want to get cornered by tourists. Usually, he didn't mind, but today he had other things to think about. He pulled his phone out of his back pocket again as he moved from the Great Hall towards the library, and glanced to see if Lizzie had read his message yet. Nope. She must be caught up with something. He tried to shake off his concern again. She'd definitely been a bit off when they'd parted yesterday afternoon, but he racked his brains trying to think of anything he might have done. As far as he was aware, they'd ended up having a great night.

The library, shrouded in dim light because of the blinds that were pulled down to stop the sun from damaging the rows and rows of books, hadn't had any issues reported. It was still his favourite place in the interior of the house, and although he didn't read nearly as much as he should these days, he liked to come and spend time here. He glanced along the shelves to see if he could find that first edition of *Alice in Wonderland* that he'd mentioned to Lizzie on the night of the Summer Fayre. He wasn't sure he'd be allowed to take it off the shelf, but it would be nice to know it was there.

He looked around the library, making sure there wasn't any damage that the volunteers had missed. Satisfied, he made to leave and continue his checks. If nothing else, keeping busy would stop him worrying for a little while longer. All the same, he willed his phone to ping with a message.

48

Later that afternoon, fired up with enthusiasm for Bee's proposition, Lizzie completely forgot to show her the mood boards she'd been working on. Instead, after helping Bee out with a few more of the displays for the wedding, she made another cup of tea and sat down in the tiny office space off the kitchen and started researching floristry courses.

Bee had been spot on when she'd referred to a course at the local college. The first step was a fifteen-week course, starting in September, which would give her a Level 2 qualification in floristry. It was only one day a week, but would certainly be enough to give Lizzie a clear idea as to whether she wanted to make a new career at Roseford Blooms. The rest of the week she'd be free to help Bee, and learn from her, and, hopefully, put together a solid business plan to take Roseford Blooms to the next level.

Lizzie nearly leaped up out of her chair with excitement. This could be it! This could be the thing that gave her the direction she wanted so badly. She was so enthused that she didn't hear the door to the office opening behind her, and when there was a discreet cough, she really did jump.

'Hi,' Simon said softly as she spun around in the chair and nearly went sprawling onto the floor. 'I, um, skipped lunch and thought you might fancy sharing a late sandwich at Lucy's café?'

Lizzie looked at him for a long moment. Georgina's words came flooding back to her, and she battled to ignore them, but it was difficult. To buy some time, she turned back to her laptop and shut it down. 'Hang on,' she said. 'I won't be a sec.'

Knowing Simon was still waiting for an answer, she closed the lid of the laptop and then stood up from the chair. 'Look, Simon, can we talk?'

Simon looked wary. 'That sounds serious. Like more than a quick sandwich at the café serious.'

Lizzie gave a quick smile. 'Doesn't have to be. But there is something I, er, need to sort out with you, if you've got time.'

Simon nodded. 'Of course. Do you want to grab a takeaway and we can have a wander while we talk?'

'Let's do the talking first,' Lizzie replied. Her heart started to gallop when she saw how concerned Simon looked, and she had to hold back the urge to rush and put her arms around him. She needed to get things straight first, and hopefully there would still be space for a hug afterwards.

'Fair enough.' Simon walked back out into the shop area, and Lizzie followed.

'I'll be back a bit later, Aunt Bee,' Lizzie said.

'Oh, don't rush,' Bee replied. 'I think we've got most of what we can do today sorted now. You two get out and enjoy the sunshine.'

Lizzie gave Bee what she hoped was a reassuring smile. 'See you in a bit.'

She and Simon walked along the high street and then veered off onto one of the public footpaths that bordered Roseford Hall's perimeter. It ran across the land that Simon still owned, Lizzie noticed, the site where he intended to stage RoseFest. She wondered if that was deliberate. They stopped at a bench under a huge, ancient oak tree, and Simon gestured to it. 'Shall we?'

Lizzie nodded and took a seat, and a deep breath.

'Is everything all right, Lizzie?' Simon asked, before she could speak. 'I know it's only been twenty-four hours, but you seem a little distant.' His eyes radiated concern, and Lizzie desperately wanted to believe that it was genuine.

'I need to ask you something, Simon,' she said quietly. She turned to face him, and her resolve nearly faltered again when she saw the look on his face.

'Of course,' he said gently. 'You can ask me anything.'

Lizzie paused, and the internal battle started raging again. How could she raise Georgina's doubts with Simon without turning it into an argument? At worst, she'd be proven right, and at best he'd be so offended that he'd never speak to her again. But she *had* to know.

'When we met, you knew I'd recently sold my business, didn't you?'

Simon looked confused. 'Yes. I think Bee might have mentioned it, or you did. I honestly can't remember. Why?'

Lizzie, unable to look him in the eye, glanced down at her hands. 'Did you look up anything about me, when you knew that?'

Simon shook his head vehemently. 'Of course not! Why would I do that?'

Lizzie, aware that he was getting upset, wanted this over with. 'Maybe because you had an idea for a new venture, and you were looking for a backer? Someone to put in the money to finance RoseFest? And then I came along?'

The words hung in the air between them, and the look of shock on Simon's face made Lizzie want to snatch them straight back.

'You think I've been spending time with you because I'm after your money?' Simon's voice was low and he sounded desperately hurt. 'Is that what this is all about?'

Lizzie shook her head. 'I don't know, Simon. My sister, Georgina, she said that you were pretty strapped for cash, and getting to know you has been so wonderful... I began to wonder if it was all a little bit too easy, you know? That you're looking for more than just my, er, friendship.'

Simon jumped up from the bench. 'If that was the case, then why would I have wanted you by my side at what could have been one of the worst nights of my life?' he snapped. 'And why would I have spent all that time talking to Andy and Marina about investing in RoseFest? It doesn't make any sense, Lizzie!' He ran a hand through his hair impatiently. 'I've been spending time with you because I wanted to. Because initially I really liked you, and then I found that I was falling in love with you. Christ, I even started thinking about how wonderful it would be if we made this a longer-term thing... I was clearly barking up the wrong tree there, if all you think is that I was in it to fleece you out of your bank balance!'

As if to echo Simon's sentiment, the throaty cackle of a pair of magpies taking off from the branches above their heads startled them both.

Lizzie stood up as well, and she could feel her throat constricting as she saw how upset Simon was. 'I'm sorry, Simon, really I am. I just needed to hear it from you.'

'Instead of the sister who, by your own admission, has done very little to make your life easier over the years.' Simon's anger made his speech short, and harsh. 'How could you believe that of me?'

Lizzie shook her head. 'I suppose it's a lot for me to imagine that someone like you could feel that way for someone like me.' She gave brittle laugh. 'I was the one they all made fun of, remember?'

'And I was the one who helped you, back then,' Simon said quietly. 'Try to remember that, Lizzie, please.' He glanced across the meadow, and then back to her. 'Believe it or not, I might not be rich, but the title of Lord Treloar is still enough to call in a few backers if and when I need them. I don't need to sleep with someone to get hold of their money.'

He raised a hand, as if he was going to put it on her forearm, but seemed to think better of it at the last minute. 'I suppose this is why you decided to talk first and eat later,' he said softly. 'Well, I think I've lost my appetite.' He looked into her eyes for one last, long moment, and gave a sad smile. 'Take care, Lizzie. And good luck with what you do decide to do with that capital of yours. I hope it brings you joy.' With that, he turned away from her, and hurried down the footpath.

Watching his receding back, Lizzie mentally kicked and kicked herself. How could she accuse him of using her for her money? Georgina, as usual, had played on her insecurities, as she always did. She'd made her feel small, and foolish, and unworthy. And that had happened too many times in Lizzie's life for her to just accept it, yet again. It had to stop. As if the conversation with her family hadn't been enough to make her realise she needed to take control of her own life, the error she'd made with Simon brought everything into razor-sharp focus. As she watched Simon's retreating back, she knew she'd made a huge mistake in doubting him, and she hoped against hope she could put it right.

49

Simon strode back to Roseford Hall, and this time he didn't stop to smile at any of the tourists or BHF staff who smiled at him as he passed. He was angry, angrier than he'd ever been before, and he needed to get some perspective.

How could Lizzie think that of him? He'd given her absolutely no reason to think he was after her money, that he saw her only as a potential investor. He cursed her bloody sister and that family of hers, who obviously knew exactly what to say to sow the seeds of doubt. He knew all too well the insecurities that could fester for a lifetime if developed early on, and it was only because he understood that that he wasn't livid with her, just the situation. He had to convince her, somehow, that he could be trusted. But how could he do it?

Getting RoseFest up and running would be a good start, he supposed. But now he felt conscious about even talking about it to her, let alone asking any advice. He didn't want her to think he was after something he wasn't. The truth was, he just wanted to be with her, to spend time with her. He'd grown to be passionate about this project, but he knew he was in love with Lizzie. But were those two things compatible?

Without realising it, he'd walked almost to the back entrance of Sarah's cottage. She was working from home today, and he could see her sitting at her computer in the small study off the living room as he made his way up the garden path. He cursed under his breath when he realised, too late, that she'd spotted him. He needed to have a conversation with her about what he'd seen at the reunion, but he was in no frame of mind to do that now, after his confrontation with Lizzie. And, he thought, was it really his place? Maybe she already knew that Jago was married and it simply hadn't bothered her?

Shit. She was waving at him. He'd better go and say hello. Before he could push open the bottom half of the stable door, a pair of syrup-coloured paws and an amiable face, tongue lolling out of the dog's mouth because of the heat, appeared over the top of it.

'Hey, Holmes,' Simon said, ruffling the dog's head and scratching him behind his ears. 'Bet you're feeling a bit warm today.' He walked into the house and smiled briefly as Holmes scampered excitedly around him, clearly expecting a walk.

'Grab a coffee if you want one,' Sarah called from the study. 'I'll be with you in a sec.'

Simon did as he was told. After all, he figured, today couldn't get much worse, so he might as well lean into the misery. Taking down a couple of mugs from the cupboard above the coffee machine, he filled them both, splashed in a bit of milk and a teaspoon of sugar for Sarah. Just as he was stirring in the sugar, she appeared in the kitchen.

'Thanks,' she said, taking the mug from him. 'I've got some flapjacks in the tin that Fleur made if you want one?'

Simon accepted and his stomach gave an almighty rumble as he bit into one of the flapjacks.

'To what do I owe the pleasure?' Sarah asked. 'I assume you're not just here to over-excite my dog?'

Holmes, who was now lying at Simon's feet, looked up expectantly.

'Not exactly.' Simon took another bite of the flapjack before he answered. 'There's been something I've been meaning to talk to you about.'

Sarah sighed. 'Let me guess.' She took a sip of her coffee. 'Jago, right?'

Simon started. 'Got it in one.'

Sarah's face flushed. 'Well, you don't have to bother. I know.' She bit defiantly into the flapjack she'd taken from the tin. 'If it helps, I didn't know he was married when I spent the night with him after the wedding, but after I sent him a Facebook friend request, and he stupidly allowed me access to his full profile, it became pretty obvious I'd been had.' She shook her head. 'I should have known, really, that he was only in it for the sex. But I was so overwhelmed when I saw him... I guess my judgement went out of the window.'

'What are you going to do about it?' Simon asked. He was relieved that he didn't, at least, have to break the news to Sarah, but he knew exactly how devastated she'd been in her teens when Jago had broken up with her.

'I'm not going to do anything.' Sarah gave a short, slightly shaky laugh. 'Why would I? What's done is done, and it was a one-night stand. It was a massive error of judgement on my part, but I have no intention of ever seeing him again. To be honest, even if he hadn't turned out to be married, I wouldn't really fancy a repeat performance. He didn't exactly set my world on fire.'

'That's not what you said the other day.'

Sarah blushed. 'I was on the defensive, and I didn't want to look like a complete idiot in front of you. I knew how pissed off you were that it had happened in the first place.'

Simon smiled. 'I'd have understood... eventually.'

'Sorry.' Sarah took a sip of her coffee. 'I should have realised... once a shit, always a shit, right? You'd think I'd have learned by now.'

'Everyone makes mistakes,' Simon said. The irony of that wasn't lost on him, given his confrontation with Lizzie. 'It's what you learn from them that counts.'

'Very profound,' Sarah teased. 'And I definitely learned that you can't go back. The past is something that's best left there. Jago and I might have been in love once, but that was a very long time ago. And his wife has to deal with him now, not me.'

'I hope she walks out on him someday,' Simon said. 'And really gives him what he deserves.'

'Time, and karma, will tell,' Sarah replied. 'But he's not my problem, thank god. I feel guilty for falling for his charm, but you live and learn, I guess.'

They drank their coffee in contemplative silence, until Sarah spoke again.

'So, how goes it with you, big brother?'

Simon sighed. 'Until about an hour ago, fine. Now, I'm not so sure.'

'What's happened?'

Briefly, Simon recounted his conversation with Lizzie. As he did so, he felt his gut tensing again, and he swallowed hard, trying to dislodge the horrible, heavy sensations that thinking about it caused.

'I'm surprised she'd believe what Georgina told her,' Sarah said, outraged. 'I mean, doesn't she know you at all? You wouldn't have the bloody wherewithal to scam someone for their money, even if you had thought of it.'

'Thanks,' Simon said dryly.

'Oh, you know what I mean.' Sarah looked at him. 'Did you want me to speak to her?'

'I don't think that's a great idea,' Simon replied. 'Even though you two have cleared the air, it might not be totally believable, coming from you.' He sighed. 'No. This is something I need to sort out for myself. I'm just not sure where to start.'

'You never were that good at emotions, were you?' Sarah said. 'I remember whenever I broke up with a boyfriend, you left the room every time it looked as though I was going to start crying, in case you were required to say something comforting. I'm amazed you're actually confiding in me now, to be honest!'

'Maybe there's hope for me after all.' Simon surprised himself by laughing. Then, suddenly serious, 'Being so far away at that school didn't help. I felt as though we barely knew each other when we were teenagers. I'm sorry I didn't make more of an effort back then, Sarah.'

'Oh, don't go all mushy on me,' Sarah shot back, but her expression was gentle. 'We had a lot of blessings, when you think about it. And at least we get to spend time together now. It could have been worse. It sounds like poor Lizzie's still working through her family relationships. Georgina was my friend back then, but she wasn't the most loyal of people. Sounds like she still isn't, if she's trying to come between you and Lizzie, even if there is no reason for it.'

'Sometimes people don't have clear-cut motivations like they do in the movies,' Simon replied. 'Sometimes, they act out of spite, or insecurity, or because they can't stand to see other people happy. Maybe there isn't a reason.'

'Maybe,' Sarah mused. 'But whatever the score, I know you can fix it. Lizzie's hurt, and I know you are, too, but try to remember that what she said came from a place of deep uncertainty. She's spent her whole life comparing herself to her sister. You need to show her that it's her you want.'

'How very wise you are, sis!' Simon laughed, but he knew that Sarah was right. 'The question is, how and when do I do that?'

'You'll work it out,' Sarah replied. A ping from her computer made them both jump. 'That's my next work call. I'd better get back to it.'

'Thank you,' Simon said as he got up. He grabbed Holmes's lead from the hook by the back door and attached it to the dog's collar. 'I'll get this chap out of your way for a bit, shall I?'

'You're a star!' Sarah called over her shoulder as she retreated to her study once more.

Holmes was overjoyed to be out and about, and Simon tried to focus on the positives. He and Sarah had cleared the air – now he just had to sort things out with Lizzie. He had the feeling that it might be easier said than done.

50

Stupid, stupid, stupid! The thought repeated itself with every pace Lizzie took back to Roseford Blooms. She'd never forget the look of hurt in Simon's eyes as the reality of her accusation had dawned on him. Yet again, her own insecurities had led her into a poor choice. And this time, it had probably cost her a relationship that she knew was incredibly special. Even though it had only been weeks since they'd met, her feelings for Simon had blossomed, and she knew that if she'd trusted her instincts instead of her sister, she'd be getting ready to spend another blissful evening with him.

'Everything all right, love?' Bee, who was sitting on the stool behind the shop counter, called out as Lizzie came through the door.

'Fine,' Lizzie replied quickly. She didn't want to burden Bee with her troubles. Looking over at her aunt, she noticed how tired she looked.

'You need a break,' Lizzie said firmly. 'Let me take over the rest of the buttonholes for a while, and you can put your feet up and have a cuppa and a sandwich. I'll go and grab you one from Roseford Café if you like.'

'Thank you, Lizzie dear,' Bee said. She stretched out her back, and Lizzie was suddenly aware of what a physically demanding job her aunt had. 'That would be lovely. But I've brought a sandwich with me. I'll go and put the kettle on and sit down for a bit in the office, if you don't mind getting back to work on the buttonholes.'

'Of course.' Lizzie smiled at her aunt. It was exactly the kind of repetitive task she hoped would help her to take her mind off the immediate problems with Simon.

Lizzie set to work, and, sure enough, the buttonholes were a great distraction. While Bee ate her sandwich and took a well-earned break, Lizzie finished them. And, to her admittedly untrained eyes, they didn't look half bad. Even though her fingers were still sore from poking, twisting and threading the wire that bound them together, she felt a whole lot calmer than she had when she'd re-entered Roseford Blooms.

'Nice lunch with Simon?' Bee asked as she emerged from the back office with a cup of tea for Lizzie, which she placed on the counter.

Lizzie paused, unsure whether to tell Bee what had happened. But the pause itself seemed to be a giveaway.

'What is it, love? Did you fall out?'

'Something like that.' Lizzie slumped back on Bee's stool. 'I accused him of something totally ridiculous, and he, quite rightly, has taken offence.'

'And what would that totally ridiculous thing be?' Bee asked. 'Bearing in mind that I've heard some mad things in my time, of course.'

'I accused him of being after my investment for his RoseFest project.' Lizzie sighed. 'And he didn't take it well.'

Bee shook her head. 'I bet he didn't.' She looked curiously at Lizzie. 'And where exactly did this idea come from? Did it just land in your head, out of the blue, or did someone else put it there?'

Unsure whether or not to disclose her conversation with Georgina, and unwilling to tarnish her sister's relationship with Bee into the bargain, Lizzie paused again.

'Was it your father?'

Lizzie shook her head. 'Nope. Although I wonder, now, if he might have had a part in it. He wants so badly to get me back where he can keep an eye on me. He was pretty put out when I refused to jump to his tune and go to that interview at Howard Harper's company.'

'Let me guess,' Bee said softly. 'Georgina, in her own careful and subtle way, suggested that Simon might not be all he seems?'

Lizzie nodded. 'Yup.'

Bee took a sip of her tea. 'Well, I wish I could say I was surprised, but she's always been terribly jealous of you.'

Lizzie nearly spat out her mouthful of tea over the box of newly made buttonholes. 'Georgina! Jealous? Of me? I don't think so! I mean, what on earth would she have to be jealous of?'

'Oh, Lizzie.' Bee sighed. 'You've always been the successful one. You got the best grades, you built a career and a business from the ground up, and you sold it for a tidy profit. Georgina, while arguably the more socially successful of the two of you, settled. Settled for a man she knew would provide for her, a life she thought was easy and a future of nothing but carefully curated boredom. She's always been a bit of a stirrer, because she's too fed up to do anything else. Now it looks as though you're going to make a future with a man who's not only genuinely very fond of you, but also a lord of the manor, no less, the Jane Austen heroine in Georgina is consumed with disappointment and jealousy. So she played another little game, knowing that, with your insecurities about her, you'd bite. And now she can swoop in, with your mother and father, and pick up the pieces.'

Lizzie shook her head. 'No, Aunt Bee. It's not like that. Is it?' She thought back to the conversation she'd had with Georgina: the careful way in which she'd laid out her suppositions as facts. Beautifully curated facts, as light as gossamer wings, which were actually a tissue of half-formed opinions, manufactured to amplify Lizzie's own fears: the fear of being used, the fear of being rejected, and the fear of just not being good enough. And she'd allowed herself to become trapped in it all.

'I have to talk to Simon!' Lizzie exclaimed. She clanked down her cup of tea on the counter, narrowly missing the stems of the last bouquet that Bee was going to tackle today, and made for the door.

'Calmly, if you can,' Bee advised as Lizzie grabbed the door handle. 'Simon's not great with unpredictable emotions, as you probably know by now, and, despite it all, he has pride. You need to be clear, but careful with him. And honest.'

'I will,' Lizzie said. Suddenly, it all made sense. And the person she needed to see was Simon. She fervently hoped he'd still have the desire to listen to her.

51

Oh, to be as carefree as Holmes the retriever, thought Simon as he watched the dog gambolling up and down the vast green meadow behind the curated gardens of Roseford Hall. To be able to take such pleasure in the simple sights, sounds and scents of the summer afternoon. Holmes might be a pest, and neutering him had done little to curb his escapologist's tendencies, but he knew what his priorities were, and he wasn't afraid to chase them.

Right now, Holmes was intent on chasing the white, fluffy tail of a rapidly departing wild rabbit who, catching the scent of the retriever, had made an ill-advised run for it towards the dry-stone wall that bordered the field on three sides. At the bottom of the field lay a patch of woodland, and safety, but the rabbit wasn't quite there yet.

Simon knew Holmes didn't stand a chance of actually catching the rabbit, but he kept a close eye on the dog, ready to call him back if it looked as though he was gaining too much ground. In his pocket was a packet of mini biscuit bones, which were Holmes's favourite treat, and he'd tempt him back with a few in a moment or two. Holmes's antics were a good distraction, and almost took his mind off the argument with Lizzie. Almost.

He'd be lying to himself if he said he hadn't been angry and hurt by her accusations. He was only human, after all. He prided himself on his honesty, and, he thought, given the amount of rogues in his ancestry, his integrity. But, he had to admit, perhaps if the roles had been reversed he might have been wary, too. He had no clue how wealthy Lizzie was, but he knew she could afford to invest in his project, if she chose to. He wanted her by his side but as a loving partner, not an investor. He wanted to have her in his future, but not financing it.

He was about to call Holmes to heel when the dog veered off in a different direction, seemingly having forgotten the rabbit. In the distance, Simon caught sight of a figure by the kissing gate that led into the meadow. A familiar figure. A figure with dark hair and, as she drew closer, he could see she had a nervous smile. Lizzie bent down to give Holmes a scratch behind the ears and the dog responded voluptuously to her touch, rubbing his face into her knees and calming instantly.

'He's such a tart,' Simon said nervously as the two of them drew closer. 'He can't resist showing off.'

Holmes gave him a disdainful look as Lizzie straightened up again. Sniffing around the ground by her feet, he trotted back to Simon when he saw Simon taking a biscuit bone from the pocket of his jeans.

'I, er, went to Sarah's first,' Lizzie said as she moved through the gate and it closed behind her with a clang. 'She told me you'd taken Holmes out. I hoped this was where you'd be.'

'Poor old boy doesn't get walked nearly as much as he should,' Simon said as Holmes, having gobbled up his snack, bounded away from them both again, chasing flies and running in a wide arc as a gust of wind ruffled his rump.

'But at least you get to hand him back at the end of the walk,' Lizzie observed. 'The best way of having a dog, I think.'

Simon regarded her, and he couldn't help playing back the way they'd left things earlier that day. 'I don't think you came here to make small talk about my borrowed dog, though, did you?'

Lizzie, apparently surprised by his directness, shook her head. 'No. I didn't. I wanted to apologise.'

Simon took a step closer to her. Lizzie was touching her collarbone again, and seemed so nervous. He fought the impulse to gather her up in his arms and forgive her there and then, but something, possibly the hurt pride he was feeling, stopped him. If she needed to apologise, to explain, then he'd let her.

'I'm listening,' he said softly. Glancing at Holmes, to make sure he was within shouting distance, he turned his full attention back to Lizzie.

'I should never have doubted you,' Lizzie began. 'But, as you know, I have a habit of second-guessing pretty much everyone in my life. And my sister, Georgina, has always known how to exploit that. But when it comes to you, I wasn't second-guessing at all, and that frightened the life out of me as well as being exciting, and wonderful.' She shook her head, as if she was impatient with herself for taking so long to explain. 'I suppose, once Georgina had put the idea into my head, I found it so difficult to believe that you might want me for anything other than my money. Even though my heart told me otherwise, my head kicked in and I put up my defences again. And I'm sorry about that, Simon, I really am. I love you, and I want to believe that you love me too. Not for what I could offer you, but for who I am. Is that still right?'

Simon's heart raced and he took a minute to draw a steadying breath. He knew what he wanted to say, but he somehow felt the words being trapped on the tip of his tongue. Eventually, he spoke.

'I'm not going to pretend that the thought didn't cross my mind that I wanted you involved with RoseFest,' he began. 'It's a huge project, and one I don't think I could tackle on my own. And when I discovered you were a marketing whizz, with a proven track record, I did hope you might be able to help me.' He paused, trying to gauge her reaction. She was concentrating on every word he said, as if she was still anticipating that unpalatable truth, that moment that she'd be right for doubting him.

'But I never expected you to invest anything other than your expertise, Lizzie, and only then as a paid adviser. I might not have the financial resources to get this festival off the ground myself, but that doesn't mean I was looking for a meal ticket from someone I was...' He paused, knowing he was putting himself on the line again. 'Someone I *have* fallen in love with.'

This time, he saw Lizzie's face flush, and, further encouraged by the slight smile that lifted her features in response to his words, he continued. 'If you... if you choose to believe me, then I would love to seek your advice about how best to launch RoseFest. You're the kind of expert I want on board, to take this project forward. But, Lizzie, much more importantly than that, I want you in my life. If you decide that you want nothing to do with this project, then I'm absolutely fine with that. What I wouldn't be fine with is you walking away from here, from me, under the misapprehension that I want anything else from you other than your love, your friendship, and to make those the basis of what, I hope, will be a partnership of a different kind.'

The pause between them yawned like Cheddar Gorge, and for a long moment Simon felt as if he'd abseiled off the top without a rope. He could see that Lizzie was considering his words, see the internal battle raging in her eyes as she took in what he'd told her. He knew she was dealing with trust issues that would make anyone wary, but, when they were layered with her complex history concerning Roseford, he was unsure what her response to his honesty was going to be.

Eventually, she spoke. 'When I first came back here, I was in such a bad state, Simon. If it hadn't been for Aunt Bee offering me a place away from the rest of my family, I don't think I'd ever have returned to Roseford. But now, being able to face what happened to me all those years ago has given me a better perspective. Not just on that, but on everything.' She paused and leaned down to give Holmes a little ruffle. Bored of exploring, he was now standing like a big, furry buffer between the two of them.

'My gut instinct was to mistrust you. I was so badly burned by Paul and having to sell my half of the firm that I couldn't see why anyone would be interested in me for anything other than my money. And my sister has always liked to stir things up. Bee reckons it's jealousy, among other things.'

'I can see why that would have been confusing,' Simon began, but Lizzie held up a hand to interrupt.

'I need to say this, Simon.' Being careful not to step on Holmes's paws, she took a pace towards him, and he could see the sunlight reflected in her eyes, making them shine even more brightly. 'I love you. And even if I didn't, I'd love to help launch RoseFest. You have a marketing adviser whether you want one or not!' She laughed nervously. 'And, also, whether you want me or not, you have me by your side. Now, will you kiss me so that we can get back to where we were before this lunchtime happened?'

Simon gave a wide smile. 'Well, when you ask so nicely...'

As their lips touched, Lizzie wrapped her arms around Simon, and pulled him closer to her. All was well, for a long, wonderful moment until Holmes pushed a wet nose up between them, requesting a treat from Simon's pocket.

'Bloody dog has no sense of occasion,' Simon murmured, somehow managing to retrieve a biscuit bone without breaking the kiss.

EPILOGUE
THE FOLLOWING SUMMER

From the wings of the stage that had been set up in the meadow, Lizzie squeezed Simon's hand. They looked out to the audience, and saw, with a combination of relief and delight, that there was barely any green between the picnic blankets and chairs that had been set up. This musical end to the inaugural Roseford Literary and Music Festival, RoseFest for short, would be the crowning achievement of all the hard work that had taken nearly a year.

'I still can't quite believe Montana's going to do this,' Lizzie whispered. 'I mean, are we insured if she goes into labour onstage?'

Simon grinned. 'She's got six weeks to go, and her midwife gave her the once-over this morning, so I don't think we need to worry.'

'I hope you're right,' Lizzie replied. 'Perhaps we should be more worried about Finn falling asleep, given their new addition isn't sleeping through the night yet.' Lucy and Finn had become proud parents to a baby boy, a few months back, but the broken nights were a trial.

The two-day festival, which had comprised a plethora of smaller events, including readings from authors of all genres, workshops in Roseford Hall itself led by former Writer in Residence Stella Simpson, and smaller scale musical events, including an afternoon of folk music in the village square, was now drawing to a close in the meadow. Finn Sanderson and Montana de Santo's much-anticipated gig, set against the backdrop of the fading sunlight, was guaranteed to be a magical experience. Finn, who was more of a director than a film star these days, had agreed to come out of retirement for one night only, for free, to help his friend Simon bring RoseFest to a spectacular close, and Montana, who still loved to act and perform, despite her ever-growing bump, had been delighted to team up with her friend again. As they took to the stage, which had been decked out with beautiful flower arrangements at the front from Roseford Blooms, Lizzie felt a surge of pride.

At the end of last year, Lizzie had taken the Level 2 Floristry course at Cannington College, and, so fired up by learning a new skill, she'd enrolled in the Level 3 course immediately she'd finished. On the other four working days, she'd been alongside Bee, who'd taught her the valuable skills that running a bricks-and-mortar business involved, and then, shortly before Easter, Bee had officially begun the process of handing over the business to Lizzie. Now, three months later, the contracts had been signed, the website was ready to go, and Lizzie felt ready to call Roseford Blooms her own.

She looked back from the stage to Simon. True to his word, he'd paid her as his marketing adviser, and between the two of them, with a lot of assistance from Marina and Andy, who were sitting on a picnic blanket near the front of the stage, they'd made RoseFest happen. This was the first event, but they'd put in enough future-proofing that, barring a disaster, it wouldn't be the last. The process had been a huge learning curve, but one they'd both enjoyed. Lizzie also felt confident enough that Simon, based on what she'd taught him over the past year, would be able to manage Rose-Fest into the next few years, while she focused on building Roseford Blooms.

It was amazing, she thought as she heard the swell of cheers and applause over the opening notes of one of Finn and Montana's past smash-hit songs, that so much had changed for her this year. Spending time with Aunt Bee in Roseford Blooms had given her a new career she'd never dreamed of, but found that she adored, and taking on the business would secure her own financial future. She'd cleared out her flat, and, after staying with Bee for a little while longer, had eventually put down a deposit on a little house on the other side of Roseford. Moving into her own place had been wonderful, and liberating, and although Simon was keen for her to move in with him, she was happy, for the moment, to have her own space.

Falling in love with Simon had been a wonderful but at times scary experience, but they'd navigated their ups and downs and grown all the stronger for it, and now, watching the climax of their first joint endeavour, Lizzie felt incredible optimism for the future.

Just as she was about to head off the stage with Simon to take a spot on the picnic blanket next to Marina, her phone buzzed in her back pocket. Pulling it out, she frowned, and then, without hesitation, she ended the call.

'Anything important?' Simon glanced down at her, his eyes showing concern.

'Nope,' Lizzie said firmly. 'I'll talk to her some other time.'

Trust Georgina, with her unerring sense of timing, to call right at that moment. Taking Simon's hand, she smiled up at him. 'Let's enjoy the show, shall we?'

ABOUT THE AUTHOR

Fay Keenan is the author of the bestselling *Little Somerby* series of novels. She has led writing workshops with Bristol University and has been a visiting speaker in schools. She is a full-time teacher and lives in Somerset.

Visit Fay's website: https://faykeenan.com/

Follow Fay on social media:

 facebook.com/faykeenanauthor

 twitter.com/faykeenan

 instagram.com/faykeenanauthor

 bookbub.com/authors/fay-keenan

Boldwood

Boldwood Books is an award-winning fiction publishing company seeking out the best stories from around the world.

Find out more at www.boldwoodbooks.com

Join our reader community for brilliant books, competitions and offers!

Follow us
@BoldwoodBooks
@BookandTonic

Sign up to our weekly deals newsletter

https://bit.ly/BoldwoodBNewsletter

Ingram Content Group UK Ltd.
Milton Keynes UK
UKHW040746090323
418173UK00002B/6